The 9ᵗʰ District.

The 9th District.

GILLIAN LONG © 2024
All rights reserved.

First Published, 2024

ISBN: 978-0-9945598-6-9
Cover Photo John Russell
Millaa House Publishing
PO Box 89
Millaa Millaa,
Queensland 4886

The 9th District.

Out of the ashes comes hope.

GILLIAN LONG

Millaa House Publishing
2024

Contents

Author's Note

The 9th District is based on real events in 1930s Far North Queensland cane fields. This was a period, when the Communist Party of Australia (CPA) made significant inroads into Queensland communities, especially after a charismatic cane cutter by the name of Jack (John Clyde) Henry became leader of the 9th District.

In the 1930s, when Weil's disease claimed hundreds of victims, the Australian Workers Union was accused of refusing to help defend their members against the disease. The CPA stepped in to support the workers in a battle to have infected cane burnt before it was cut, thereby lessening the chance of contracting the disease.

The novel shows the role the renegade unionists and communists, many of whom were immigrants, played in the industrial activism in the sugar industry. They then threw their support into helping the Spanish Republic during the 1930s Spanish civil war, sending several of their members from the region to fight with the International Brigades. These citizens exited Australia illegally in defiance of the ban on Australians fighting in this foreign war.

You can't have capitalism without racism.

(Malcolm X)

1934.

1. Weil's Disease

To hate is a self-righteous act and Mark Anders was trying hard not to indulge, but it was becoming increasingly difficult. The disease had so far killed six men since the 1934 cane harvest had started four weeks ago. The real number was probably treble that, and there were at least 120 men ill with it. The hospitals were full, with staff working around the clock. They'd commandeered private homes because the wards were overflowing.

He could scarcely bring himself to believe the growers and the company weren't keen to act. There was little wonder the men turned to the communists for a solution. He sympathised with their cause although he couldn't yet bring himself to join the Party despite Jack's efforts. The power of the individual to improve his lot in life through hard work was just too beguiling a belief, although recently he was beginning to question if even that was possible.

The Airdome Theatre, the only dedicated picture house in Innisfail, was filled with sugar workers from the mills closest to the North Queensland regional centre. The meeting was supposed to relay what was being done about the workers dying from something called Weil's disease, but he knew they would learn nothing new. Naming something doesn't explain what it is, its cause or how to cure it, but they all knew how to prevent getting it, except it didn't seem anyone in authority was listening.

He scowled down at the scarred, cane-cutter hands clenched on his knees—knuckles white with tension—and raged inwardly. Any ordinary person presented with the compelling evidence of so many recent deaths in the industry couldn't fail to act, but it seemed no one had explained this simple philosophy to the company or the Cane Growers' Association. Yet, from what the speaker on the stage was saying, they seemed to think the problem was one the men must fix individually.

As if that was an option. Individual responsibility in the face of rampant disease, what a crock that was! Power of that sort, a man could only dream about, but he wished someone would stand up to them. Anyone! But who? The union behaved as if they were as powerless as their members, fearful of threats that any industrial action might interfere with the ratification of the national sugar contract. Had they forgotten who they were supposed to represent? The band of anger tightened around his head, but he composed his features and forced his hands to unfurl and relax. Showing rage would get him nowhere.

He glanced up to the cinema's ceiling and walls. They were usually hidden in dim shadows, but in the heat from incandescent globes spiderwebs glistened on rough-hewn battens. Moths and beetles crashed-tackled the naked lights. Bats on the hunt, flickered in and out of the spiralling trails of tobacco smoke as they escaped and returned through gaps in the roof and wall.

Mark was sitting three rows from the front with the rest of his cane-cutting gang. All of them were scrubbed carbolic-clean and wearing their town going best, although Mark noticed his trousers had a worn spot above the knee. He ran his palm ruefully over the thinning patch of moleskin wondering how long before they wore through completely.

He blinked his smoke-sore eyes and shifted his gaze back to the speaker—a balding man with a paunch—clearly not one of them. None of the cane cutters had any excess flesh, not with the gruelling hours they put in each day in the tropical heat. Like most of the men, Mark was all sinew and ropy muscle.

The speaker's voice rose breaking into his reverie. "You men must take your own precautions. Wear sturdy boots. Wash your hands. Look after your personal cleanliness." With each pronouncement his finger jabbed the air in hard emphasis.

The speaker was a Council health officer, and he was standing on the stage in front of red velveteen drapes, which were hooked back to expose a large white movie screen. At that moment, a cane rat ran along a batten above the screen. It stopped halfway and looked out across the hall as if surprised by what it saw. Then it scampered off, disappearing through a gap behind the screen. Some of the men pointed and jeered as though it were an evil character in a pantomime.

The health officer turned around just as the rat disappeared through a gap. He laughed and said, "The blighters are everywhere."

A voice from the front row shouted, "What's the council doing about it?"

At last! Mark craned to see who had spoken.

The health officer shot back. "Everything within our power, but in the end, it's up to you men to protect yourselves. I'm just here to tell you cleanliness is the key. The company and the Cane Growers' Association agree..."

The statement propelled Mark from his seat, anger overcoming discretion. "Bullshit! Men are dying." He pushed his way into the aisle. "Doc Coffey says it's the rats causing it, just like in the Somme trenches, and you blokes are ignoring the perils."

The health officer glanced across at the union organiser, but the organiser looked down at his feet. The Council had asked for this meeting, and Mark guessed the organiser wasn't going to put himself in the middle. He didn't blame him. Neither had he wanted to put himself forward, believing that rational men would come to see the real problems and act without a need for any theatrical posturing. Yet here he was, and deep down he knew he would regret it.

He moderated his voice. "You know and I know, the only way to get rid of the problem is to burn the cane before harvest." He turned to appeal to the men. "Up north, Mossman cutters fire the cane, and they don't have the disease. Are they better men; are their wages different?" His gaze travelled across worried faces.

All he'd ever wanted was to learn the industry, save his money so that one day he could become a cane grower with his own crop, but standing up in public like this made that impossible. His actions were a declaration, and he felt a target growing on his chest in the same way as photographic film, dipped in the right chemicals, brought out an image.

He'd seen that done once and was captivated by the craft although unlike a photograph he didn't want or seek to become publicly visible. With his ethnic background that would invite trouble. Nevertheless, it was done. May as well take it all the way.

He drew a breath. "I tell you, it's company greed. Their foremost thought is profit. They care nothing for workers' health."

He paused again, giving himself time to take in the men's expressions. How many would support him? This was class warfare, and they all knew it, but it didn't hurt to remind them.

"While those bastards swill French champagne and cognac—bought with our sweat and blood mind you—our mates sicken and die, wallowing in this rat-infested swamp, and those in charge do nothing, just blame us for not washing properly."

Murmuring came from the rows and men shuffled their feet.

Mark narrowed his eyes. "Not just one man—but one hundred men—and more!" He breathed deeply to force the drumming in his head to slow down. "These are our mates." He gazed around the expectant faces. "These are men like us, in hospitals across the region hanging on to life right this minute. How many must die?" He pointed at a man in front of him. "You?"

The man shrugged.

With a curt nod, Mark formed two fingers into the barrel of a revolver and said, "That's right mate, the next one could be you!" His breath exploded from behind pursed lips. "Dead!" he said as his fingers jerked upwards with the imagined recoil.

The man was visibly shaken. "Not me, mate."

Mark walked away. "We all think that it will never happen to me—until it does."

The men nearest him shifted in their seats, eyes following him.

He wasn't used to performing for crowds, but he found speaking his mind like this strangely cathartic, although he knew he was coming across as a radical rather than the voice of reason, which was what he preferred.

In a more moderate tone, he asked, "Does the union act in our interest by leaving a man to die because of the work we do?" He turned to the union organiser. "What are you going to do about it?"

All the men's eyes swivelled to the organiser, who shrugged, 'We're doing all we can. You know that Anders.'

"Bullshit! You lot are too bloody frightened of missing out on the National Sugar Agreement, so you ignore this peril." Mark swung back to the men, his fist thumping into his hand. "We must demand the company recognise this thing as an industrial disease, pay compensation to those affected and protect us by burning the cane."

Murmuring rose to a loud hum and then the man in the front row, who'd spoken up before, took up the challenge. "Burn the cane!"

Others took up the chorus.

Mark stood back relieved and grateful he was no longer the centre of attention. Then the foot stomping started, and he pressed his lips together. The noise was more to voice their fears than real anger, but perhaps that would come.

At first, he had thought the bosses just didn't understand how fearful it was to go to work every day, knowing this threat was out there. Then he realised they knew but just didn't care. Frightened workers were more compliant, focussed on surviving rather than increasing wages.

This was not a hygiene issue but an industrial disease. They couldn't just blame the workers. The company had the power to do something and if they refused, then the union must act to force them. If the union wouldn't, then the militants in the rank-and-file would. He just hoped one of Jack's comrades would take up the banner, but the swell of noise abated as the organiser moved his hands down in a silencing gesture.

Mark vaulted onto the stage. Once more the men's faces lifted towards him as his voice rang across the smoke-filled hall. "We pay our dues, 25 bob for the union to look after our interests. Now we demand they act, or we'll take this into our own hands."

The men's restraint ruptured, but Mark didn't wait for the verdict. He had lit the fire, now Jack and his members needed to take it forward. The fight required a Britisher to lead. Anyone else would be crushed by the industry.

He walked through the shouted arguments, and out the main doors into the crystal air of a tropical winter's evening. Then squaring his shoulders, he stepped from the foyer of the Airdome theatre and onto the pavement. Let the pennies fall however they might. What did he care anyway. He was never going to achieve his goal, not in this system where everything was stacked against him.

2. A Company Man.

The Townsville to Cairns steam train rattled and swayed north belching soot as it wound through cane fields. Beatrice Langham laid her novel in her lap and stared out the window, knowing it had been a mistake to come here. She shivered and crossed her arms against the vast primordial landscape.

Her father had seen all this before. He was seated opposite her in the first-class compartment reading a newspaper, his jaw appearing as if set in unrelenting resolve. Arthur Langham was an imposing figure of authority. Above average in height. in his late forties, immaculately tailored and manicured—a city gentleman with sharp-features, and blond hair silvering at the temples.

As far back as she could remember he had been the unbending oak in the tempest of her life, schooling her to hold her tongue whenever she voiced an opinion about anything other than fashion.

Yet even then, he didn't listen.

It was he who had suggested this trip to visit his sister Emily, while his wife was away visiting her father in Britian. Beatrice suspected his motives were more to do with his work at the company, rather than any thought for her wellbeing.

She turned her gaze back to the cane fields, stretching away towards the western mountain range where clouds brooded in shades of bruise-purple and gunmetal-blue. Although the late afternoon sun still baked the carriage causing her hat, an Elsa Schiaparelli madcap, to stick to her scalp.

She took it off and fluffed up her limp hair, wishing her colouring was more like her father's. Her mother said she took after her grandfather, who had hair the colour of hazelnuts, a classic English colouring, or so she claimed. But nowadays blondes were so much more fashionable. She replaced the hat at what she imagined was a rakish angle,

The dress she wore was a green and grey striped silk, cut on the bias as fashion dictated, and although it was supposed to cling to her curves, it was not expected to resemble a sodden leaf. Her father had brought it back from one of his many trips abroad, saying the green was the same colour as her eyes and would make such a good impression on her aunt and uncle.

Not only was her father's colour comparison hyperbolic, but he knew nothing about proper attire for women in this tropical wilderness. She was tired of men thinking they always knew best. In her experience, they usually made a mess of things.

She longed for a bath and steady ground under her feet. The journey from Sydney, first by steamer and then by train had seemed endless. Soot marked her gloved fingers, made her eyes gritty and left smudges on her cheek. She sighed and looked out toward the flickering lightning above the Great Dividing Range,

A swampy plain outside the train harboured a couple of Brolga cranes who bowed and swayed in a time revered ritual as they danced next to a shallow pan of water. She imagined their cries echoing across ancient mantles stripped of jungle, sculpted into this manufactured coat of sugar.

Acres upon acres of sentinel cane stalks stretched towards the mountain range on one side, and the sea on the other. The only interruption to the endless plain was occasional remanent rainforest nestled in gullies and alongside rivers.

In the distance, the eternal massive of Bartle Frère, the highest mountain in Queensland, came into view, rising up only to disappear into dense cloud. In its shadow, two mighty Johnstone Rivers meandered indifferently across a land split asunder 10 million years ago, in a cataclysm only the earth remembered.

Finally, two and a half miles inland from the coast, the township of Innisfail came into view. It squatted, in the tropical winter heat, beneath billowing white clouds of steam from the company's mills, at a junction where the North and South Johnstone Rivers merged.

The train rattled across a bridge and wheezed to a stop at Innisfail station. She clutched her father's hand as she alighted from the carriage, her senses assailed by the cacophony of Babel. People and voices from every corner of the earth called to each other, shouted commands, chattered, and laughed. Sun-mahoganied men unloaded supplies and pushed trolleys piled high with wooden crates and sacks, stamped in large black letters: flour, rice, tea, salt, cloth, boots, knives, and cement. Others loaded postal sacks and produce onto the train, vegetables, bananas, dried fish, and a pallet of dried koala pelts.

A boy, not more than 10 years old, with white-blond hair and pale lashes, tugged at her father's attaché case. "Carry your bag, sir."

"Be off with you!" Her father lashed out with an elaborately carved walking stick; an affectation he employed without useful effect.

Beatrice made a moue of disapproval and gestured to the boy as she stared defiantly at her father. She pressed a shilling into the child's hand. Her father glowered, but at that moment he was distracted by the ringing bell of a passing ambulance.

Men stopped what they were doing and removed their hats.

Beside her, the boy said, "Another one for the morgue."

Beatrice gasped and stared at the child.

He looked up at her solemnly and said, "Sure as rats live in the cane fields, if he ain't dead now he will be in a day or two, and that will make five this week."

The station master strode towards them with a porter to carry their luggage. He shooed the child away.

Beatrice stared at the roadway where the ambulance had passed. The tropical light, brilliant with discord, caused her to narrow her eyes against its glare. She shrugged. The boy had probably exaggerated although that thought wasn't very reassuring.

A vague sensation of impending doom lingered, and the riotous and unfamiliar surroundings didn't help. Begonias dropped colours from hanging baskets, and beyond the station fencing, crimson Bougainvillea competed with splashy Ixora in a riot of red, yellow, pink, and orange. The scent of mock orange blossom hung in the air like a Catholic benediction mingling with seamier fragrances from a nearby creek.

Rocket-fuelled parakeets shot along the length of the platform, disturbing a flock of cockatoos browsing in the trees at the far end. They rose in an indignant white cloud squawking in protest, and she had an intense urge to scramble back into the stale safety of the train compartment.

But already familiar figures were hurrying toward them. So, Beatrice smoothed her skirt, straightened her shoulders, lifted her chin, and picked her way decisively through the raucous throng to greet her aunt and uncle.

3. A British View

Alfred Denton walked with the stride of a younger man to his office on Broadway in the City of Westminster. He was sixty years of age but carried himself easily with the unassuming air of a moderately successful man on his way to a steady but unexciting job, perhaps in a bank or insurance company, perhaps in sales somewhere. To complete the image, he wore a bowler hat, not his preferred style, and carried an umbrella although it seemed doubtful that he would need it.

The late spring weather was glorious and, like him, the other people on the street walked with lilting strides and lifted faces. Yet the dry days were not all good news for it had been a worryingly arid year for British agriculture, but then 1934 was turning into a trying year all-round. He was just grateful Britain didn't have the problems America was experiencing, where it seemed that the whole continent was losing its topsoil to dust storms.

Nevertheless, Britain had its own difficulties, what with hunger marches descending on Trafalgar Square, and Mosley's Blackshirts creating mayhem in the streets. It wasn't looking any better in Europe either, with rioting in Paris, lawless stormtroopers in Germany, general strikes in Spain, an emergency in Holland, and civil unrest in Austria.

Despite the sunshine, Denton felt trouble brewing like it was the blood pumping through his arteries. The problems weren't just in America and Europe. In their desperate search for raw materials to feed growing industrialisation, Japan had designs on China. Denton made a mental note: a decision was needed about the status of the British legation in Peking and whether an embassy was warranted.

Political strife was everywhere, and to some extent Denton blamed the economic depression. If people couldn't trust their governments to provide a decent standard of living they would turn to populist strongmen like Benito Mussolini, who promised Italy a return to imperial glory, to a time sanitised by nationalism and nostalgia. Britain must avoid that at all costs. Yet, the British national unity government, formed to manage the financial crisis, had not learned any lessons. Constant bickering frayed the edges of accord with the latest quarrel over welfare policy. He sighed, resigned to the increasing political manoeuvring.

While global conflict percolated in the back of his mind, Denton automatically checked in the shop windows for reflections. Not that he was worried, but it was an old habit that he found hard to shake. If anyone were shadowing him they would be severely disappointed for he did this walk most days from his home in Pimlico to the office.

Strictly speaking he should have taken the car, but this was the only exercise he managed to get most days and he guarded it jealously, ignoring suggestions that it was below his station to walk to work like a commoner. He sneezed, drew a handkerchief from his pocket, and stepped into a narrow alleyway to blow his nose.

As if all the diplomatic problems both at home and abroad weren't enough, his daughter had taken it into her head to visit from Australia, ostensibly to look after him because he'd come down with the flu. But by the time her ship had arrived, he was already back at his desk. In reality, he suspected she was here to restock her wardrobe and create domestic chaos before she departed again. Either that or she and her husband had quarrelled.

He loved his daughter, but she did demand her dues. It was exhausting, particularly her nagging they should take possession of the Surrey house, which was rented to some American family. She had a crazy notion of turning the place into a charitable hospital for Great War veterans. It was a bit late for that. He'd told her time and again it was not his decision, and she should speak to her daughter, Beatrice. That made her sullen, and she would fly into a rage of organising his household, saying that he could not possibly be expected to manage with just a valet and a housekeeper.

Today she was busy scouting around for a maid, and a chauffeur to drive her on errands because she couldn't tolerate Denton's valet, Symonds. It was probably to do with Symonds's attitude, which was admittedly faintly disdainful towards women. He sighed. Domestic life was exhausting, but perhaps he'd gone back to the Ministry before he had quite recovered.

He turned into his building and walked up the stairs. His secretary greeted him warmly, taking his hat, overcoat and umbrella and asking if he wanted a cup of tea. He shook his head and walked into his office.

On his desk was a new report. He sat down and hooked his round wire-framed spectacles around his ears before he picked it up, noting his name at the top of the shortlist of people cleared to read the file's contents. It appeared that some Russian official in Berlin was making secret overtures to Hitler, all the while negotiating a pact of mutual assistance against Germany with both France and Czechoslovakia. What was Joseph Stalin playing at? Hedging his bets, no doubt.

Denton rested his chin on a long thin hand and gazed out the window. He'd been a tall and dashingly handsome man in his youth, clear-eyed and certain, which had suited his role as a naval commander, but with age, he'd grown to see that not everything was certain; not everything was as he saw it.

He turned away from his reverie and took a file from his drawer. It was a report on Australian deportations of immigrants back to Italy. While he received diplomatic reports from around the world, he had a special interest in Australia. Not only was it where his daughter usually resided with his granddaughter, but he'd been instrumental in establishing the Australian section of the colonies' intelligence service when he was over there before the Great War, outwardly advising on the setup of the Royal Australian Navy.

The file on his desk contained a report about some Italian immigrants who had established a criminal gang in North Queensland. Their activities included prostitution, abductions, extortion, revenge killings, and bombings. Normally this kind of report would never reach Denton, but he was interested because of a public gun battle that took place earlier in the year, on the main street of Innisfail.

Innisfail was where Denton's granddaughter Beatrice was heading with her father. He'd ordered further information and the new report sat in his in-tray. He cast his eye across it and was reassured that the shooting was not a regular occurrence, and his granddaughter was not in any real danger.

All the same, he would ask to be kept informed of any further trouble in the North Queensland region. The last thing he needed was to have to worry about his family's safety as Europe ratcheted up the prospect of another war.

He picked up the draft brief he was writing for the Prime Minister. Stanley Baldwin was desperate to establish Britian's diplomatic policy of appeasement. Of late, Hitler had been clamouring for a treaty with Britain to allow Germany to build a small navy and the British Navy were in all favour of this violation of Part V of the Versailles Treaty. It was a badly kept secret that the Germans had been building U-boat's since the cessation of the Great War and Baldwin was in favour of allowing their clandestine operations to become official, and observable.

Appeasement wasn't a case of complete capitulation. Current conventions promoted a diplomacy of realism, which recognised that the national interest and the struggle for power resided within the nation-state, and without which, it was thought, anarchy would prevail. Baldwin's appetite for an Appeasement Policy focussed on how differences might be settled by negotiation and compromise.

Was this a better model than Bismarck's realpolitik, based on pragmatism, or even its opposite, the internationalist notion of idealism? It was the question Denton had been trying to answer objectively, while his default prejudice sneered that Baldwin's appeasement was less realism and more idealism.

Idealism lay behind Internationalism of the kind expounded by the Soviet Comintern. Idealism demanded that legislators refrain from immoral or illegal actions in world affairs, and practice what they preached at home and abroad. Then there was the real world where people harboured all sorts of desires, goals, and vices.

Without stating that connection aloud, he would argue that appeasement was a kind of idealism because there was no way of enforcing it. It might be possible if all parties remained rational and wanted peace. But what of corruption and a desire for unfettered power? Look at Joseph Stalin, supposedly an idealist, but so paranoid he thought everyone was out to unseat him and was determined to maintain power at any cost.

There was an American and Canadian school of thought that advocated a government run by technocrats or specialist experts rather than elected politicians but where in that system could accountability be a certainty. Diplomacy needed expertise, rules, conventions, and accountability, but in a liberal democracy, it also needed to tolerate differences.

Baldwin favoured tolerance as did the British public. Yet tolerance also had its downside. How much should be tolerated, and where must the line be drawn? Perhaps an agreed international law was the only answer—leave it to Lady Justitia. Women were much better at compromising for the good of humanity. Certainly, it could not be left to the League of Nations. Compromise would not win the day.

Diplomacy needed something more substantial, something to curtail Hitler and Mussolini's designs on expansionism and to dampen Stalin's paranoia. But what: who might run it, and most importantly, who would enforce it? Totalitarian advocates listened to no one. Rational arguments to benefit humanity bounced off any would-be-dictator's grandiose noggin although he was beginning to think that also applied to some British politicians.

He sighed. He couldn't say any of that in a brief although a wise politician might draw on an eclectic selection of all types of diplomacy, depending on the circumstance. Of one thing he was certain, the type of laissez-faire diplomacy that Baldwin called his *Appeasement Policy* would not sort out the mess Europe was in at the moment.

Denton had a horrible hunch that Winston Churchill was right, and the world was teetering on a precipice. Only early and decisive action could avert a new war. What was the Roman saying? *Qui desiderat pacem, praeparet bellum.* Let him who desires peace, prepare for war.

4. The Campaign Launch

Mark waited under a sodium streetlight outside the Queen's hotel for Bert Manzoni to join him. They were to head on down to where Jack Henry was holding his election campaign launch.

The launch meant Mark had to turn down an invitation to the Ambulance fund raiser at the Regent Theatre. Mark's cousin's friend had asked him to go. Both the cousin and the friend were nurses at the hospital and Mark would have like to have gone. The local establishment all supported the Ambulance fund, and it was his chance to meet some of them. He shrugged off a twinge of regret. His promise to attend Jack's launch was given before the invitation arrived, and keeping his word was important to him.

Still, Mark hadn't come to Innisfail to get involved in industrial politics. He had come to make enough money to fulfil a lifelong dream of owning his own farm. In these lean times sugar was the country's salvation, and he counted himself lucky to have a job in the industry. Over the past few years, a lot went without, men with haunted eyes and hollow bellies crisscrossing the country in search of work or starving on the Government's parsimonious Susso.

Yet, despite his intentions, he had become involved in politics the moment he'd met Jack Henry, the leader of the Australian Communist Party's 9th District. The man was nothing if not persuasive although Mark was a Labor man to the core. Yet he had to admit Jack was right. The state Labor premier was showing signs of becoming an authoritarian fascist.

A car crested the hill, its headlights illuminating the Catholic cathedral, bathing the building in a golden glow before swooping along the road, growling effortlessly towards where he stood. Chrome flashed in the streetlight, wheel arches flared into running boards that dipped and swooped along the length of the car.

The 1930 Bentley 8 litre came abreast and someone behind him whistled. A face stared out from the rear window of the vehicle The pale oval, indistinct in the yellow light, seemed to fix on him, swivelling as the car purred past.

Conflicting emotions coursed through him. What would it be like—that kind of life? Despite everything, he couldn't help but hanker after it. Becoming a grower with his own farm would give him entry to that echelon of society. That kind of status would give him a say in conditions, able to argue for a better deal for the men.

Jack was trying to do that through politics, but Mark didn't hold with revolutionary talk. It would never work no matter what Russia had achieved. Australia wasn't Russia and no matter what Jack said, Stalin was just another authoritarian thug, who had twisted Karl Marx's treatise to suit his own agenda. Jack might argue otherwise but Mark was a staunch believer in liberal democracy and the rights of the individual. A level of state socialism was necessary, redistributing wealth to help those on the bottom rung, but Stalinism was not the answer.

Mark had already decided he would tackle the issue of inequality by convincing the power players within the social elite that there was a better way, where everyone could be a winner. Although with his recent actions, and his subsequent election as the rank and file delegate he'd probably wrecked his chances.

The Bentley slowed towards the junction at Edith Street, turned right and disappeared around the corner. Just then a hand on his shoulder startled Mark from his reverie, and he looked around into Bert's wise black eyes.

The two men walked towards the intersection taking the same direction as the Bentley had taken. As they approached the junction an evening breeze danced up from the Johnston River, bringing the smell of salted fish and bananas from the wharf, stirring eddies of dust in the gutters, and ruffling Mark's hair.

They drew abreast of Regent Theatre and strains of music floated out from the brightly lit doorway. Mark glanced across the road to where a man in a tailcoat held out his arm to his companion. He hadn't realised the ambulance fund raiser was such a formal event. It was just as well he hadn't accepted that invitation.

They crossed the next intersection to How Kee's corner, where a crowd had already gathered. Maybe sixty people. A fresh breeze tugged the women's skirts and billowed the men's shirts. Laughter greeted him, and for a brief moment Mark forgot his regret, forgot his anger at the company, forgot his sacrifices to his ambition, and buoyed by their mirth, he slipped into the crowd.

Beatrice lost sight of the crowd on the street outside the hotel as the car turned the corner and slowed to a crawl. Ahead was a large building with raised ornate plaster letters proclaiming *Regent Theatre*. A white banner hung below with *The Ambulance Ball* embroidered in red. A red carpet ran across the pavement and in through two large open wooden doors. Festive lights spilled out across Edith Street illuminating cars lined bumper to bumper along the pavement.

The driver pulled into the entrance gap at the edge of the carpet and stopped the car. While Beatrice waited for him to open her door she glanced towards another crowd gathering at the junction, but it was obscured by the vehicles lining the road. Her uncle had muttered something about a Bolshevik meeting. Such a strange place: a society ball held half a street block from a radical street gathering.

She fidgeted with her reticule, wondering if she could slip away just for a quick peek. She would never have another opportunity like it, and how grand to be able to boast of such things when she returned home to her set in Sydney. Lawrence would call her brave, although he always said that. In his eyes, she could do no wrong and that in itself was rather annoying.

Beatrice followed her aunt and uncle into the theatre foyer, from which a wide archway opened into the ballroom. Green bamboo canes crisscrossed alcoves casting colossal shadows across the dance floor. Gilded mirrors along the walls reflected glittering orbs of light, and red and gold streamers fluttered across the ceiling. On a raised dais across the room, the Rah-Rah Boys swung out a spirited

Tiger Rag.

Beatrice caught her breath.

Her uncle nodded at the hall's décor. "Colours of the Ambulance Brigade." He bent over her hand slightly and said, "Your aunt will make the introductions."

He strode off towards a group of men on the other side of the ballroom. They were similarly dressed in the standard evening dress of white tie and tails.

She followed her aunt across the ballroom floor, casting a glance at her reflection in the mirrors they passed. The backless oyster satin had been a good choice, paired as it was with the iris mink stole. She was relieved to see all the other women wore similar evening wear although possibly not of the same quality as her or her aunt's gowns. But then they didn't have their advantages or the availability of European fashion houses.

Her aunt looked a little livelier this evening, patting her neat hair as her faded gaze flittered about the room. The pale blue and white silk dress she wore suited her blondeness She pulled up the ruching of her white lace gloves and took Beatrice's arm. "Come, my dear. I will introduce you to the good ladies from the hospital committee who have organised all this." Her hand gave a small all-encompassing sweep of the room.

As they passed the group of men with whom her uncle conversed, Beatrice heard him say, "Another war's a certainty. You mark my words. It's just a matter of time, and Chancellor Hitler, now that he's sure to take the presidency, will sort out those Russian Bolsheviks once and for all. Time we did the same thing here."

A man broke away from the group and walked towards them, leather heels clicking against the wooden floor. He was of medium height and build, dressed in the obligatory white tie and tails, and had very short dark hair and a pencil-thin moustache.

He stopped before her aunt, blocking their way, and said, "Good evening Mrs West. May I beg an introduction?"

Before her aunt could respond he was speaking again, but this time addressing her. "Miss Langham, it's a pleasure to meet you. Howard Rainer, at your service." He grinned, placed his hand on his left breast and bowed his head.

His obliviousness to protocol caused Beatrice some amusement as she saw her aunt's frown, but she also noted his fingernails needed a manicure.

"I wanted to be the first to claim a spot on your dance card. I've heard so much about you. Well, I should say the whole town has been looking forward to meeting you. You are the closest thing to royalty we've ever had visiting our town."

Beatrice felt her face growing red. How awful that they all knew. It was a social peculiarity with which Beatrice was very familiar, and once people knew they treated her differently. It was all very fashionable to claim a relationship with British gentry, but not actually be one of them. That immediately put you beyond what amounted to an antipodean pale, with unsubstantiated accusations of putting on airs and graces.

She shrugged. "You're mistaken, Mr Rainer. It is my English grandfather to whom you refer. I am no one, not even close to anything, let alone royalty." She modified her tone, and said, "Really, I'm just a city girl out of my depth in all this glorious tropical wilderness."

Fred Paterson, the 9th District's barrister, stood on a box as he spoke to the people who had gathered for Jack's election campaign launch. Mark admired Fred's commitment to the Communist Party, but he pitied his wife, who rumour had it, often put up with pumpkins as a pay packet in lieu of money.

He'd met Fred once or twice, but he really counted Jack Henry as his friend and in many ways his mentor. He was his aunt's neighbour and had helped Mark get the cane cutting job when he'd first arrived.

Mark figured he owed him, but it was more than that. Jack was a man among men, someone to trust and look up to. He cared about people and knew stuff about how systems worked, particularly politics and how the elite-maintained power.

Mark had become a keen student although he wasn't yet committed enough to relinquish his ambitions. Working class solidarity was all very well, but who didn't want to control their own destiny, have nice things, provide for their families. In other words, who didn't want to move from working class deprivations into the comfort and security of the middle class.

To a certain extent, even Jack had achieved that although he refused to admit it. He'd come from farming roots in Grafton in New South Wales. On leaving school he had travelled north to Queensland arriving in the cane fields when the Tully Mill opened in '25. Now, he was the leader of the Communist Party's 9th District, a sub district created specifically for him. He was respected among workers from Noosa to the Torres Strait Islands but loathed by the establishment.

Everyone still thought of Jack as a gun cutter and expert timber getter, and despite his elevation to Party leadership, he claimed his working-class roots like a badge of honour. That surprised Mark who had always tried to ape the British establishment.

Yet, while Jack dismissed Mark's bourgeois aspirations, he worked tirelessly to ensure those who had less might have opportunities to improve their lot, or at least have a respectable life with a job that paid a liveable wage. Of course, that attitude set him against the sugar industry and consequently the State and Federal governments. For not only was the industry trying to reduce wages to compete with countries who exploited cheap labour, they were also ignoring the perils of the job. And they had government backing to do so.

Increasingly, disillusioned men turned to Jack for answers and Mark gave him good odds in the election this year. Maybe he wouldn't steal the seat of Herbert from Labor, but his popularity would show the growing commitment of the sugar workers to the working-class cause.

Labor had lost its way under Forgan-Smith and his AWU cronies, but everyone admired Jack. He was fair-minded—a straight talker, held his liquor, and looked after his mates. You couldn't ask more. Besides, he'd got it right when he said the only thing the bosses cared about was reducing wages to increase profit. So, while Mark wasn't a member, he supported Jack's election ambitions and held some sympathy for the communist's point of view.

A streak of light blazed across the tropical night sky and a pang of nostalgia took Mark by surprise. He remembered wishing on shooting stars, closing his eight-year-old eyes, and refusing to speak in case his voice broke the magic. Now here he was, not through enchantment but serious graft, and it wouldn't be long before he'd have his own farm, master of his own destiny. That's if he didn't die of Weil's disease first.

The farm was all he'd ever wanted, although his father called it a fool's dream, and blamed his mother for creating the desire in the first place. His dad's Norwegian stoicism and brand of socialism, based on the British Fabian model, remained unimpressed by land ownership. He was actually his stepfather but to Mark, he'd always been, just dad.

His mum was the opposite and had always enthused over Mark's ambition, painting pictures of the rolling green hills of Italy's mulberry estates where her Nonno once laboured to produce silk on land owned by a noble family. His dad scoffed at that, dismissing Italian nobility as the ultimate exploiters, although his mother defended them saying not all of them were like that.

Mark didn't care about landowners or workers in Italy. He was concerned about the here and now. Neither did he care about growing mulberry trees for silkworms. Sugar! That was the future, and he was convinced it could be fairer for everyone, not just the rich growers.

He glanced around at the people in the crowd, nodding to a few acquaintances. The headlights of a vehicle, pulling up outside the Regent Theatre, lit up the crowd around him, and once again he felt relief he hadn't attended the fundraiser. The place was crawling with rich cockies. If he'd accepted the invitation, he'd have made a fool of himself for certain.

A movement from across the street caught his attention. A woman in evening dress hesitated, glancing behind her before stepping onto the road. She looked like a ghost sheathed in mercury drifting across the void, sidestepping horse dung and puddles.

Her form filled Mark's vision as the breeze fluttered her dress, the silk rippling across her body, showing the long curve of her waist and the sleek length of leg beneath its fluid cling. Soft nut-brown hair, fluttering about her face, lifted to expose a pale neck. Her skin looked almost translucent, but it was just a trick of the headlights that backlit her form.

"Merda!" Bert's exclamation jerked Mark from his fantasy and his chin lifted towards the woman. "She shouldn't be here."

Mark's eyebrows rose in surprise. "Do you know her?"

"No," Bert shrugged. "Ah, maybe a little. I met her last week in the library. She let me have the newspaper she was reading, and we had a brief conversation."

Just at that moment, Fred introduced Jack to the crowd. It was a formality. They all knew Jack.

The woman stepped onto the pavement. The throng of people parted and swirled around the exotic intruder, wary of the potential threat in their midst. Bert moved behind her gesturing to Mark to join him as he tried to keep her from being jostled.

A fur wrap hugged her shoulders but beneath, Mark glimpsed a smooth and naked back, the exposed band of flesh merely an arm's length away. He stared transfixed at the curve of her cheek. What the hell was she doing out here? She looked as out of place as a cane knife in a banqueting hall.

A long slim hand slid up to cup the back of her neck as if she could sense his gaze hot on her skin. Was she a supporter? There was no doubt Jack was popular with women. They loved him. Some of the men called him a womaniser but he treated them as equals, listened to their opinions, and would not allow the other men in the Party to interfere with their organising endeavours. But this woman was dressed for a ball so why was she out here, unless she knew

Jack?

He tried to imagine what she saw as Jack took off his hat and jacket and rolled up his sleeves, then stepped up to shake Fred's hand. Jack's serious dark gaze swept the crowd. His silent authority drew everyone's attention until talking stopped, and only the shuffle of feet remained.

The silvery woman inhaled, placing her palm at the base of her throat. What Mark would give to have such an effect on her. For a brief moment he imagined his hands running across that pale skin and down her naked back. He shook the crazy image from his head, folded his arms, feeling the calloused skin of his hands between thumb and forefingers, and turned his attention back to the launch.

Jack's voice carried across the crowd. "Shall we strengthen a fascist Lyons government?"

Mark grinned as the mob shouted, "No!"

Jack asked again. "Shall we endanger the labour movement and impoverish small farmers and the workers?"

Again, they shouted back, "No!"

The crowd pushed forward, and Mark held out a hand to keep them away from her.

"Shall we allow our wages to continue being reduced and lower the living standard further in Queensland?" Jack demanded.

The roar became louder as Jack worked his magic on the crowd. But the unruly mob seemed to upset the woman, and she looked around, her darting gaze seeming to seek a way out.

Mark wished he had the presence of mind to do something, but he was too late.

Bert stepped towards her, lifting his hat, and saying, "Miss Beatrice, it's a pleasure to see you once more."

She flinched, and Bert said, "I did not wish to startle you. You were engrossed, no?"

She sounded uncertain as she said, "Doctor?"

Bert filled in the rest. "Manzoni. You remember? We met last week at the library."

Mark could see the heightened colour in her cheeks even in the sallow glow from the streetlamps. Jack's voice faded and became meaningless as he watched Bert take the woman's elbow and escort her away from the crowd. He found himself following as if drawn on by irresistible magnetism.

Behind him, Jack's voice rose. "Shall we defend the Italians, the Aborigines, the Chinese, Spanish and all other workers who toil on this land?"

The woman stopped and looked back, her gaze brushing past Mark to fix on Jack.

Men folded their arms, their faces grim. Murmuring rippled out from the crowd. For a minute Mark feared it would turn ugly. It wasn't unknown for the industry, or even the police, to plant saboteurs at Party gatherings and sometimes that resulted in a street brawl. He'd had Jack's back in quite a few.

Jack's chin thrust forward as he glared at those with folded arms. Pointedly he asked, "Will we fight chauvinism, Fascism and victimisation?"

Mark was ready, willing, and keen to fight the first man who dared show disdain for any one of the multitudes of ethnicities in the cane fields. It was a fight they'd both had many times for different reasons. For Mark it was personal, often directed at him, for Jack it was a principle. Another reason why Mark admired the bloke.

He readied himself, but the men shifted under Jack's glare, and then some wag broke the tension.

"What about the women Jack, can we defend them against your charms?"

Laughter and cheers and the standoff was over.

Jack smiled. "The women must join our cause for they can fight alongside us just as well as the men."

Someone shouted, "You haven't met my missus, Jack."

"Better he doesn't, chum," a man in a singlet called out.

More laughter broke out, and two men wrestled briefly.

The silvery woman took a step back towards the crowd as if she would leave Bert standing in the street.

Bert followed. "You should not be out here alone, Miss Beatrice. I shall escort you to your destination. Which way are you heading?"

She shook her head. "It's all right." She was still casting rapid glances back at Jack. "I just stepped out for some air. It's just a little way to the side door of the ballroom." She caught Mark staring at her and dropped her gaze. "Perhaps I should get back, but I can manage myself, thank you."

Mark watched her walk down the road towards the Regent Theatre before he turned back to Bert. "Why didn't you introduce me?"

"Ha! Chi non vede il fondo, non passi l'acqua," Bert said and walked back to listen to Jack.

"*Don't cross the water unless you see the bottom.*" Mark translated. "What the hell does that even mean?" He frowned at Bert's retreating form and then turned back toward the Regent Theatre, but she had gone.

He sighed and followed Bert back to the crowd. If only he'd

accepted that invitation to the Ambulance Ball, he might have wrangled an introduction. Although it was more likely he would have made an utter fool of himself.

5. Sunrise Sugar Estate

Beatrice decided the tropics were dull. Not even the pioneers, who sixty years ago had seized the region for the Crown, had any imagination. Both the big rivers converging at Innisfail, distinguished only by their geographical designation north or south, were named after the Native Police Inspector Robert Johnstone.

Johnstone had stumbled across their confluence when searching the jungle wilderness for the shipwrecked survivors of the brig Maria. Beatrice didn't know why he should be so honoured when really, he sounded like an opportunistic thug.

The North Johnstone River cradled Beatrice's Uncle George's farm, Sunrise Sugar Estate. Flowering trees from the far corners of the Empire flanked the gracious old plantation homestead, casting shade and crimson petals across the gardens, protecting the house walls from the blistering sun.

The house was situated on a sprawling swell of land, surrounded by undulating fields of sugar cane, paddocks for beef and dairy cattle, horse yards and outbuildings. It was less than 50 years since Uncle George's father had cleared the jungle here, at a time when the town was still called Geraldton.

The old stories sounded horrendous, at least judging by what she had overheard her uncle telling her father about the dispersal raids that his father and the Inspector had engaged in. When she asked why they needed to disperse the local inhabitants, her father told her the natives weren't local. He said they didn't settle but ambled across the land in a kind of migration, hunting along the way. They were a menace to any landowner. He'd explained that the problem was domestic animals which were too tempting an opportunity. Easy prey, d'you know, he'd added.

Beatrice asked, with some scepticism, why if they didn't settle did they need dispersing? Her father expressed his usual exasperation at her curiosity about unsuitable subjects, saying it was the law of nature where civilised races must inevitably subsume the natural world through modern progress.

So now, she only ever heard snippets when she eavesdropped. Not that she approved of snooping. It was undignified although often unavoidable. And no matter what evil deeds he'd done, the man had given his name to the North Johnstone River that now bordered her uncle's farm.

Before the British, only the first people knew this place, paddling the rivers in canoes and living off fish, a lifestyle that sounded so romantic. Then her uncle had said, rather disparagingly, that the natives hadn't bothered to clear the forest and grow crops. As if hard physical work and the destruction of nature were the only things worth doing in life.

But now the natives were dispersed and there was not a black skin in sight. That was, aside from the Melanesian servants. Although her Aunt Emily told her there was most probably a good deal of native blood in the servants' veins, but best not to mention it.

Despite those in his employ, her uncle complained of too many foreign blacks, who he said should go back from where they came. To her great puzzlement, he referred to the Greeks and Italians and other foreigners of whom there were a great many in the town.

Her father had to explain that Uncle George referred to a special Queensland Royal Commission that had categorised Italian and Greek immigrants as non-European, which seemed decidedly odd. Didn't they come from Europe and if they were living here now, could they be classified as foreigners?

If that was the case was she herself a foreigner? After all, she had been born in England, and her mother was English, although Beatrice really knew very little about Britain other than from romantic novels and the occasional visit to her grandfather. Nevertheless, she had never felt any different from her father, born of a long line of British settlers who had taken up land grants on Liberty Plains, now part of Sydney, and which was still her home, at least in Australia.

The family's ancestral seat, which Beatrice would inherit when she married or turned twenty-five, was in Britian. It was where her mother grew up. Where she was born and had spent her early years. It was where her grandfather and his ancestors had always lived, although he now lived in London for convenience.

When her father had enticed her to accompany him to

Queensland's tropical north, she had imagined Creole islands with cool breezes, waving coconut palms, inviting turquoise seas, but it wasn't like that at all. It was hot and sticky with only taciturn jungle or whispering sugar stalks for endless miles. To make matters worse her cousin Charles wasn't even coming home from England so she would have no one to keep her company.

She hadn't seen Charles since he stayed with them in Sydney before he left by ship to go to university. At the time she'd become sick with envy for she had always wanted to study the classics. Now Charles had completed his course, or as the English said, he'd come down from Cambridge University.

He had been booked to sail home, but a letter arrived last week saying he would not be coming as he had received an offer from the British Broadcaster. It wasn't fair. She had always longed to go to university, find a paying job and become completely independent of her father. Why couldn't she have such an opportunity?

Her Aunt Beryl, her father's cousin, was the first woman in her family to go to university and now she was a columnist with the *Women's Weekly* Magazine. Beatrice admired Beryl more than anyone and tried to emulate her, and Beryl had told her not to let her father dissuade her. She said no amount of longing would give him back the days before suffrage, no matter how much he might wish it.

Her father was adamant that girls didn't need an education to marry. He accused Beryl of being a bad influence with her brazenly modern ways. But Beatrice didn't want to get married. She wanted to travel and find adventures and be of use to the world.

The last thing she needed was to settle down with sweet little

Lawrence Anderson and his persistent desire to marry her. He was so keen that in terror of succumbing to his gentle but unrelenting pressure, she had seized on her father's offer to accompany him to the north, just to get away from Lawrence for a while.

Her father approved of Lawrence because his family were as rich as the mythical Croesus, from some alchemy to do with the manufacture of beer and spirits. Not even the Depression had made much of a dent in his family's profits, although they needed her father's sugar.

Beatrice had complained to her mother that she was the pawn in a pact to cement a business relationship. Her mother had told her she was lucky someone cared enough to want to marry her and that was the end of the discussion.

As soon as she inherited the money from her grandmother's legacy, she planned to travel to Europe. Father couldn't deny her that although he would remain a trustee until she married. She supposed marriage was inevitable although it seemed like a career in pursuit of slavery. Rather she would prefer to carve out a career where she might earn her own money and escape her father's dominance once and for all. She would do it too, come hellfire or flood. She glanced about guiltily as if her blasphemous thoughts might be overheard, but she was alone.

She would go to back to the School of Arts library in Innisfail, find an angle about the place to write about and try to get a story published. Luckily there was more than one pathway into paid work. She was an organised person and loved the library. Researching and writing stories about events and places came to her naturally. Now she just needed to be imaginative and use her time wisely. Although sometimes she wished she'd gone with her mother to London or remained at home with the housekeeper.

She missed her Sydney set to the point where she even thought of Lawrence with nostalgia. Worst of all she was lonely. The only people who ever seemed to visit were old military men, public officials, and businesspeople from the town. All after her Uncle George's money, her father had complained.

That's all anyone cared about these days was money. Beatrice thought people were far more important. Money was merely a means to an end. Although she had once voiced that opinion to one of her teachers. The teacher had retaliated that was because she had never gone without. She wanted to argue but remained silent as manners demanded. Money wasn't real, merely a fabrication of a sovereign state.

The same teacher had told her class a story about the British colonisation of West Africa, which proved Beatrice's point. When the colonisers wanted to establish the value of British currency, they demanded the West Africans pay tax in that same currency, and when they didn't, they burned down their huts as a penalty. The irony was that the British currency was only available if the Africans worked for the British.

Why the Africans hadn't revolted she didn't know. She would have if someone had burned down her house. How angry would they have been? Surely the villagers outnumbered the British coffee planters.

She had asked her father about that slice of history. He'd demanded to know where she had gained such a notion before he denied it. When she returned to school the teacher, who had challenged her had vanished, and Beatrice never had a chance to interrogate her further.

Still, she understood money was a necessary evil. It was one the old Scotsman Adam Smith, who her father was fond of quoting, said organised the way the world operated. Although frankly, it wasn't doing a very good job of it at the moment because it seemed there wasn't enough to go around. She didn't understand why the Government couldn't create more for a bigger pie giving jobs to all, given it was theirs to make and theirs to take.

Really the whole Depression situation had ruined conversations at the dinner table. Now it was all about balancing accounts, balancing debt, balancing payments: it drove her to distraction. She secretly believed money was the Mammon of her father's existence although, of course, she could never say that out loud. In fact, there wasn't much she could say aloud in polite company. Perhaps, after all, tradition and manners would have prevented her revolt even if her house had been set on fire. She had never mustered the courage to flout protocol, although she fantasized about doing so radically and frequently.

She put her thoughts aside as she strolled through the rambling house looking for someone to talk to. Anyone! But it seemed she was alone in this mausoleum. She imagined despondency oozing in through its large bright windows, seeping from its harsh white walls, sliding across the high shadowy ceilings, and stooping through the tall, white-painted doorways. She saw it meandering through the clutter of European oak furniture, upon which squatted artefacts and reminders of global British triumph and spotted it hiding behind brightly coloured cushions. She stopped in the drawing-room.

On one wall a painting of her uncle's father, William Archibald West, stared out with forbidding expression and rigid self-righteousness. Cruelty was creased into the bracketed lines around the mouth, and an air of indifference to humanity was etched deep in his leaden eyes.

There were no portraits of her uncle's mother. The dead woman remained unremembered, except for the whitewashed headstone in the family cemetery. She had died when George was only a boy. Yet her presence could be felt everywhere in this house. Beatrice imagined her ghost drifting through these rooms, which seemed stale as if imbued with the private despair of history.

Aunt Beryl, when she went through her spiritualism stage, had said, the dead don't know they are dead, but drift among the living in ignorance. It would certainly explain why her relatives chose to ignore her even though she was a guest in their house. Perhaps they were all dead, which would clarify an awful lot because that would mean she had come on this trip not as she had thought of her own volition, but because death gives one little choice. She stopped. Why on earth would the dead come to this godforsaken place? She shook her head. The dead could not be expected to know everything.

Even so, she quite liked the notion that she might be no longer mortal flesh for it would explain why, when she came upon Aunt Emily, she usually didn't react. Beatrice found clearing her throat occasionally worked. At least Emily offered a flicker of recognition through her habitual Bayer's induced heroin fog.

She would turn towards Beatrice, a radiant but inane smile plastered across her face. Yet, the acknowledgement seemed to contain less energy than the shiver one might feel in response to clammy ectoplasm, an attention so vague it might snuff out as easily as extinguishing a Tilley lantern flame, like the one carried by the maid Ida as she made her way home at the end of her day.

Beatrice's roll of fantasy stopped abruptly, and she tilted her head at the painting, having no idea where Ida lived or any of the servants for that matter. She turned away and continued her journey through the house, whiling away the minutes until Howard Rainer arrived to collect her.

She had danced with Howard several times at the Ambulance Ball, and she quite liked him. His manner was confident and authoritative, fitting for an officer in the Commonwealth Investigation Branch. He'd told her his role was to keep watch on foreign criminal gangs, a vitally important job in the defence of Australia. So important he said, even the British security services wanted to be kept informed.

Beatrice remembered the newspaper headlines she had seen in Uncle George's office shortly after they had arrived. The article talked about terrorists in Innisfail. But her uncle had assured her that was all over now. Howard had patted her hand and told her that it was nothing for her to worry about. A sudden desire to stamp on his toes swamped her. It was just the sort of thing her father would say, but instead, she had averted her eyes to hide her irritation.

He'd missed none of her expression. That was the trouble with policemen, they saw too much, but he did explain that the criminals who called themselves the Black Hand had been mostly deported or were in gaol.

Innisfail was so full of people from across the world that Beatrice sometimes felt as if she'd wandered into a foreign country. Not that immigrants in Sydney were scarce, but here they were more obvious, occupying the streets as if they owned the place, talking loudly in funny languages that Beatrice couldn't understand. Besides, it was so hot and sticky all the time, so full of strange creatures and manners...

Why, only last week she had no option but to talk with the man who sat down next to her in the library. He'd asked if he might read the newspaper once she'd finished with it. Meeting Doctor Manzoni had quite distracted her from her sugar industry research mission. Not that she had minded the distraction. The sugar industry was quite boring, refusing all humanity in favour of plant strains and biological agents.

Thinking of Doctor Manzoni brought a reminding flash of the political candidate speaking on the street the night of the Ambulance Ball. Mr Henry had said the most amazing things. Regretfully, she had allowed Doctor Manzoni to lead her away from the crowd despite wanting to stay and listen, but just as she collected her wits to protest, she saw Doctor Manzoni's companion staring at her, very boldly. It had quite taken her breath away and she experienced an urgent need to flee back to the safety of the ball.

She wandered out of the drawing-room, trailing her fingers along the walls, curious as to the whereabouts of her aunt and uncle. Her father, as usual, was away on a business trip. The first she knew about his plans, was when he'd come out of the house at the beginning of the week, holding a suitcase in his hand, his air forbidding, his posture upright and his suit as sharply tailored as ever, even as her dress hung off her like a limp rag.

He'd stooped to bestow a kiss somewhere in the air above Beatrice's head, leaving behind a waft of Blenheim Bouquet and cigars as he told her he was off to Ingham and would be away for a few days.

Beatrice had tried to look cheerful, but she was ready to scream. All she did was read, write letters, or fill up her journal. Occasionally she dabbled with embroidery, but she wasn't much good at sewing and preferred anything, even a constitutional walk, to the constraint of tidy stitches.

She resolved to make inquiries about volunteering for the Ambulance Brigade or the hospital just to get out of the house. It was why, when Howard had asked if she would like to attend the rowing regatta today, her gratitude had been almost pathetic.

The doorbell jangled but Beatrice refused to appear eager and continued her amble along the corridor, waiting for Ida to find her. At the hall mirror, she stopped and pinned on a straw hat.

A little way along the corridor, her uncle's study door was ajar, and she pushed it open to peek inside. The room was empty, so she walked across to look out the window to see what kind of vehicle Howard drove. Of course, it was dull, black, and official as one might expect of a policeman's car. Nothing like the red and gold-trimmed Cabriolet that Lawrence drove. She sighed. The roof creaked with her as if in sympathy.

Her hand slid down the brocade curtain, as she absently admired its quality. The house had been added to over the decades and was now a warren of architectural styles in deference to Empire, with wide verandas accommodating the tropical weather, and a new wing added after the 1918 cyclone.

A voice from behind her said, "Miss Beatrice?"

Beatrice jumped and swung around. Ida stood in the doorway, a small dark figure dressed in white, with a white cap pinned to her head. She bobbed, a jerk that acted Beatrice assumed, as a curtsy.

"There's a gentleman, Mr Howard, asking for you. He's waiting in the morning room." She bobbed again.

Beatrice tried to gain control of her thumping heart, and said,

"Thank you, Ida."

She checked herself in the mirror once more, pinching her cheeks to gain some colour and then made her way towards the morning room at the front of the house.

In the motor car on the short drive to town, she quizzed Howard. "I saw a man speaking on the street corner the other night. A candidate for the seat of Herbert, a Mr Henry I think."

"The communist leader?" He glanced across at her, his brow furrowed. "You shouldn't wander the streets by yourself at night. It's not safe."

She ignored his concern. "He called the Prime Minister a fascist."

She waited for Howard's reaction. She knew Mr Lyons and several of his Cabinet including Mr Menzies. They had been to the house to visit on occasion, and it wasn't the first time she'd heard the word, fascist. Her father had much admiration for Mr Mussolini's Fascist Italy and said it was exactly what Australia needed to recover from the Depression. But why the candidate had looked so angry was a mystery.

Howard said, "You needn't worry about fascists. They're mostly the stalwarts of the community, many of them are doctors or returned soldiers, and farmers, even some of the lawyers in town are fascist sympathisers. No, it's the Eyetalians, the Black Hand, and the Bolsheviks we need to worry about. In my opinion, they're the ones likely to cause trouble. But it's the Bolsheviks who are the real terrorists and they're a growing menace in this town. All they want is a revolution, too lazy to work, and it's much easier to overthrow hard-working businesses and landowners and steal their profits." He glanced across at her. "It's my job to make sure they don't get their way, and Jack Henry is the red devil behind much of it."

Beatrice glanced at Howard's beaked profile, noting the clenched jaw beneath the thin moustache. She admired men who did not bend to fashion, but she suspected Howard's moustache had nothing to do with the changing times and everything to do with inflexibility.

His knuckles on the steering wheel showed white-edged strength as he turned out the driveway and onto the road leading into the town. Fine black hairs like sparse wire coils coated the backs of his hands and disappeared up his wrists into his jacket sleeves. The hair made her think of an animal pelt, although nothing about him looked soft.

She turned away to gaze out the car's window. Beyond the garden's tree-lined borders, an impenetrable wall of cane undulated prettily across the alluvial valleys. But she knew that up close the segmented stalks holding the silken flower heads looked blood-streaked and creaked menacingly when the wind blew.

On occasion she watched from her bedroom window as passing clouds cast moving shadows across the cane and imagined a monstrous beast slithering through the stalks to its secret lair. She shivered, envisaging becoming lost, forever condemned to wander alone in a maze of sugar. It was of such density, surely only insects, rats, and snakes could prosper.

She had imagined the tropics would be so romantic, but they weren't at all. They were too lush like overripe fruit, and perspiration coated her skin as if at any moment she might turn into some fetid marsh creature.

"Howard, how far away is the seaside?"

"As the crow flies about two and a half miles I'd say, but there's no direct road. The only way without travelling for miles is to go to Flying Fish Point by river ferry."

"Oh." She waited, hoping he might suggest they go.

He glanced at her. "I would take you to the beach, but I have to go down to Ingham tomorrow, there's some civil unrest. These Bolsheviks again, I'm afraid. Perhaps when I come back."

"My father's in Ingham." She clutched her gloved hands tightly, raising them to her chin.

"Yes. I know," he said. "But you needn't fear, he'll be fine. I'll be there to protect him." He grinned at her, and the smile changed his face, softening its hawkishness and making him appear more endearing. Then he ruined it by saying, "It's nothing for you to worry over. Seriously, your father will be fine. They're just some disgruntled anarchists demanding better wages or some such nonsense."

Why did men always assume they could tell her how she should feel and behave? She stared out the window as they drove into the outskirts of the town. It was a bad start to the day, and she had a feeling it wasn't going to get any better.

6. The Encounter

As far as the eye could see sugarcane flowered across the land, acre upon undulating acre topped by feathery fronds that glinted in the dawn light, all ready for harvest. Its beauty gave Mark a moment's pause, before he grabbed a canvas water bag, hooked his knife to his belt, picked up his file then followed the gang down the barrack steps, heading for the day's section for harvesting.

A soft drizzle wet his face, and mist lay like smoke puddles in the shallow valleys, but Bartle Frère was free of its perennial shroud. That usually meant wind from the west. So, despite the morning mist, the day might still turn out fine.

When he arrived at the paddock, the sight of cane covered in a tangle of thorny weeds made his shoulders sag.

Finn sidled up. "What d'you reckon? Chuck a match in."

Mark tilted his head sideways and glowered through slit eyes at his younger brother. Finn had that eager look he'd worn as a boy trying to persuade Mark to join him in some mischief. "Don't even think of it."

Finn pulled a sour face and turned away and grumbled something to his friend Billy.

Mark bent to run his knife-edge against the file, while he stared out across the field.

Danny walked up and asked, "How're your hands Mark?"

Danny, the ganger, seemed like a giant of a man, although his impressive stance owed more to his broad flat cheeks above a jutting square jaw than to his actual stature, for he was the same height as Mark. He was a good leader, gruff but fair, and he held the men's respect.

"Good now. Thanks..." Mark scrutinised his scarred hands, knowing Danny worried about infections. The gang couldn't afford to lose another man at this stage of the season, especially after the last bloke, Johno who had succumbed to the rats' disease.

Mark had never met Johno, but Finn had said they'd found him running down the street naked and shouting that demons were chasing him. No one had wanted to touch him in case whatever he had was contagious. It was Danny who pinned him down and ordered the blokes to help, using threats of a flogging if they refused. They had delivered Johno to the hospital but were too late, and he'd died a little while later.

Keith Bannerman joined them, wiping mist from his face. He was a small wiry man who walked with the rolling gait so often seen in cane cutters. He unhooked his cane knife from behind his back and said, "Delicate hands, dear."

"Piss off Keith."

When Mark had first started in the cane, tiny pearl-like blisters spread across the criss-crosses of his palms. By the end of the second day, the blisters had grown into great pulpy envelopes. The next day they burst leaving his hands like raw meat. Danny had told him to piss on them, but he hadn't thought that was a good idea.

His cousin had painted his hands blue with Gentian Violet so he could continue working. It had helped and the skin eventually scabbed over, growing hard with calluses. He knew Danny had worried he wouldn't make it, but Mark was not going to quit.

He had never regretted following his younger brother to the cane fields, although he had been concerned about leaving his dad to work the tin dredge by himself. But since the financial crash there just wasn't the money in tin for three grown men.

Yet leaving home and coming here hadn't been the wrench he'd expected. He hadn't really minded the almost exclusive company of hard-eyed men or the decay of humid, mist-filled valleys at the base of these jungle-clad mountains. Not even the nostalgic memories of the spicy Iron Bark trees shivering off dust in the bone-bleaching winds, called him home. Because at £5 a week this was the best paying job around. A bit of pain wasn't going to make him quit.

Finn's best mate, Billy Hewitt lifted one leg letting rip.

Danny said, "Point your arse at the cane and shoot one of your Goding's fireflies at that Badilla bastard."

Mark walked away. The Great Fire of Tully, two years earlier, had come about for the same reason Finn wanted to chuck a match into this field. Burnt cane was dirty, but easier to harvest and less hazardous to health. The industry, for some reason known only to themselves, wouldn't countenance it. Goding, a cane cutter in Tully, had developed a method of setting fire to cane fields without anyone knowing who had done it. A cyclist could chuck a burning wick in the field and be gone long before the flame took hold. Trouble was, the Great Fire spread too rapidly, threatening the town, and burning more than the men could harvest before the cane was spoilt.

Lance Mackay, late as usual, rode up and chucked his bike down as he blew a gob of spit to the ground. "The Tully fire got rid of the weeds, but." His face was a mass of dark freckles under an enormous straw hat that got knocked off regularly while he was cutting, slowing them all down.

Mark reckoned he was probably lucky his own skin just got darker in the sun. Even Finn suffered from sunburn.

Billy grinned. "It got rid of the rats and snakes too."

Finn joined in. "We should do it here."

Danny said dryly, "There'll be no fireflies under my watch. Goding's little lark got out of control. He was lucky he wasn't caught. The growers would have strung him up."

Of the eight man gang, Lance and Keith were both married and didn't live in the barracks. Bert did the shopping and cooking for the gang. Billy and Danny were veterans, harvesting cane the longest, and then there was Javier Cruz, a quiet American who kept to himself and who'd only been in the cane a little longer than Finn.

Mark had a lot of time for Javier, and for a moment the two men remained side by side in companionable silence as they surveyed the crop. Javier took a rollie from his breast pocket and lit it, his cupped hands sheltering the cigarette from the drizzle. His fingers were grimed with embedded red dirt and nicotine stains.

Then in his American drawl, he said, "Burning's better than getting the rats' disease. I heard more workers are down with it in Ingham. They are demanding a meeting with the union to do something, but the union say there's nothing they can do unless we find out what's causing it. Mark, you should go down to Ingham and talk to the guys. The least the union can do is hold a meeting and discuss what can be done."

Danny said, "The Ingham men are saying it's the rat poison that the council are using for bait that's causing the disease."

"Bejesus," Lance said. "Last year they said it was typhus, then they said coastal fever."

Javier ignored Lance. "They might be right; the baits stink enough."

Danny laughed and said, "You forget the rain, they always blame the effing rain. You'd wonder why we do this graft. Come on lads, finish your smokes. Time's a-wasting."

Mark suspected Danny made light of it to prevent the gang from getting panicky, but the company's reluctance to act was beyond him. He had written a letter requesting a meeting as the rank-and-file minority delegate, but a week had passed and still no response. He stabbed his copper file-tube into the ground and took his place at the head of a row of cane. "Maybe if we get up a petition."

"It's worth a try." Javier chucked his smoke into the dirt and ground it out beneath his heel. Then he took the row next to Mark.

The rest of the gang each lined up at the start of a row. On Danny's signal, they moved forward in synchronised battle. One step in. Arm around the plant to grab the cane low. Slash the stalks above the soil. Straighten your back. Top and tail leaves and roots. Chuck the clean stem behind to form windrows. Move on to the next plant.

It was critical to keep up with each other. Moving at a different pace risked serious injury, especially if you met a cutter coming back along the row next to yours. The slash from a cane knife could do a lot of damage. As it was, there were too many accidents.

The bone-crushing weariness Mark had felt in the first weeks of the season had abated, just as Danny had promised it would. At first, he doubted he'd make it. Even at night, he dreamed he was redoing the day's work. All night long, bend, grasp, slash, top, tail, twist, stack and on to the next plant, to do it again. On and on along the rows, plant by plant, tram by tram, hands stinging from a thousand tiny cuts, blisters popping and bleeding making the knife handle sticky.

As the new chum Mark had to work hard to keep up, and barely raised his gaze even when bees crawled up his arms vying for the oozing sugar juice. He switched off his mind, imagining he was a machine in perpetual motion, ignoring the smells of musty brown silt, sour rat's piss, acrid sweat, and the sharp herby smell of the weeds, but he remained alert for snakes, particularly the vipers that lay in ambush.

At the end of each day, once the sinking sun began to cast purple shadows across the plains, he would stand straight, stretching his back, ignoring his own stink, and sweat, and dirt and pain. The great expanse of cleared paddock left with only stubby stalks poking through the cane trash. The earth looked ravaged, but he knew that in a few months, new cane would sprout from the ratoons to cover old scars, just as new skin formed hard calluses on his palms. It was a protective shell for the soft underbelly that was once forest floor.

After cutting all day, Mark and Javier would lay out the tracks for the wagons to collect the cane from the piled windrows. The men would load them, stacking clean stalks in layers in a kind of cross-hatching that gave the whole thing balance.

When Mark first started, he was slow. He knew it and was mortified when the others jumped across to help him finish cutting his rows, or when his stacks on the wagon slid sideways sending the lot crashing to the ground. Javier had reassured him. The men forgave inexperience easily, but they didn't forgive slackers.

This was the hardest work he'd ever done, much harder graft than working on the tin dredge back home. At least now he no longer lagged behind the others, although he had a way to go before he could beat the pace of the experienced men, particularly Danny. He admired him most. This was a different game from tin mining, all right.

Saturday was now a half-day, so at knock-off time the men looked forward to a day and a half of the Union's hard won freedom. Back at the barrack, Bert had left a copper boiling on the fire for them, and Mark stripped off and threw his clothes into the sudsy water. Dressed only in a pair of frayed shorts, his feet bare in the dust, he used a wooden paddle to stir the boiling clothes. The strong smell of carbolic from the soap mingled with the scent of wood smoke, and the heat from the boiler sent sweat trickling along the contours of his chest.

Finn leaned on the barrack veranda rail, smoking, and intermittently making scornful comments, but Mark didn't want to get the rats' disease, not if he could prevent it. Anyhow, he had thrown in both sets of working clothes, so why Finn complained Mark had no idea. It wasn't like he was doing the washing himself.

At times, Mark thought he was cursed with having to look out for his reckless brother who seemed to believe he was invincible. The council's health officer at the meeting said cleanliness was the key, so that's what Mark would do until he could persuade the bosses it was in their interests to let the men burn the cane before harvest.

Burning did no real harm to the sugar content so long as it was harvested immediately, so he couldn't understand their reluctance, but a bit of extra effort to keep clean wasn't a tough ask either. Mark was just exasperated by his brother's attitude.

Billy came out of the room he shared with Javier.

Finn threw his cigarette away and said, "We're off. Meet us at the swimming enclosure. We can get something to eat at the pub later."

Mark nodded.

After hanging out the washing, he drove to the swimming enclosure in his battered 1924 Dodge truck. He parked and got out, his gaze sweeping the area for any sign of Finn or the gang.

A couple of dozen people sat on the grassy bank watching others swimming. Rowing skiffs, moored to posts, bobbed on the swirling waters outside the wired-off enclosure. Bikes and cars cluttered grassy verges lining the road. A horse stamped in its sulky's traces and dropped its head to nibble the grass growing beside a model-H Triumph motorcycle. People stood around in groups or sprawled on picnic blankets.

He waited, unwilling to barge in anywhere particularly when the place was full of Britishers, ashamed of the fraying shorts he wore under his trousers. All these people had proper bathing suits, and money to spare, their parents somebody in the town, well-off farmers, business owners, officials.

They could be as friendly as the next person one minute but turn on you for what seemed no reason at all. He'd seen it at Herberton station. They'd collared a man riding the rattler and almost strung him up. If Mark hadn't stepped in and taken him home for a feed, he didn't know what they'd have done to the poor bloke.

Their attitude had never worried Finn, but he was fair-skinned and light-haired like his dad and was often taken for one of them. Mark had inherited his family's colouring and cutting in the sun all day made his skin even darker.

When he'd first joined the gang, Billie had stared at him before asking Finn if he was sure Mark was his brother. For a while afterwards, jokes came thick and fast about his mother and some imagined milkmen. Mark ignored them but they stopped when Finn explained they had different fathers.

It wasn't the way Mark saw their dad, for he'd known no other. His mother always told him he had blue blood running in his veins, but Mark had long ago seen his mother's stories as pure fantasy. She had never told him anything more about his biological father and he figured she either didn't know or it was too painful for her to remember. In any case his dad had warned Mark not to go there.

Why she had chosen the Italian landed gentry for her tales baffled him. They had ruined life not only for his own mother's family but also the other Italian workers on their holdings and in their factories. Yet landed gentry in Italy were no different from their kind all over the world, ruining the health and prosperity for the workers just like they were currently doing here.

It didn't have to be like that.

According to his stepdad, his biological father had been *en drittsekk*. In other words, a shitbag. Again, Mark didn't care. He

56

loved the man he called dad and didn't wish to know that another man might have sired him.

He spotted Finn leaning against a tree, chatting to a curly-haired brunette. Maybe the rest of the gang had gone to the pub already. Mark pulled off his shirt and stripped down to his shorts. He left the pile of clothing under a tree far enough from the crowd to be inconspicuous, and walked down the sloping bank, slipping into the river, and swimming underwater across to the other side of the fenced enclosure. He surfaced and trod water looking back towards the riverbank.

It looked like Finn might make headway with the girl. She was giggling, her hand held in front of her mouth, while she looked around for her friends. Or maybe she was looking for an escape route. Mark grinned and rolled onto his back, his mind drifting as he gazed up at the sky: blue and cloudless. It was warming up. Another month and the heat in the cane would be a killer.

His stomach rumbled. He wondered what his Aunt Zarah was cooking for supper. It would be good to eat something decent for a change, although the food had improved markedly since Bert had arrived. The gang's previous cook seemed to know nothing more than salt beef, cabbage, and boiled potatoes.

A splash outside the wire caused him to roll over and swim to the bank. Even the chance of a crocodile in the vicinity wasn't one he was willing to take although they had been hunted almost to the point of extinction.

As he hauled himself from the water, he saw her. She was standing higher up the slope with that Federal john, Howard Rainer, who asked too many questions. Rainer had a dossier in his office on each of the Party members and their supporters. It was best to avoid him.

Mark walked up the bank and picked up the exercise book and pencil that he had carried with him always. Well, not the same book and pencil, but ones like it. He was a keen observer and recorder of what he saw, and piles of similar books filled with drawings, were still stacked in the bedroom of his childhood home.

More recently, he'd had quite a few of his political caricatures published in the local paper under a pseudonym. It wasn't something to brag about, for if it got out, the gang would never let him live it down. Recording humanity was his secret and he'd recently bought a Kodak 616 Junior to make that easier. He hankered for an ARKA, a new super speed camera with built-in flash that was used by pressmen, but they were out of reach financially, at least if he was going to have enough money to buy a farm, so the Kodak would do for now. Although it was not something to wield about in this company. Drawing was less intrusive.

His mother called him an artist, but he preferred to think of his work as that of a journeyman, capturing and reporting moments in time to show the world his view of humanity and its vulnerable frailty. He would have liked to have been a pressman, but his kind didn't aspire to such careers, not in northern Queensland at any rate. Besides he wanted, no needed, to own land. That desire took precedence, so he had to be content with the occasional publication of his drawings.

He sat with his back against a tree and sketched the scene in front of him. It gave him an excuse to watch her without being too obvious. That was the good thing about drawing. It didn't call attention the way a camera might.

After a while, Rainer went down to the water in his one-piece bathing suit. The woman was fully dressed and sat on the grass in the shade, her legs bent at the knees and folded neatly to her side. Mark was certain she was the same woman he'd seen the other night.

Miss Beatrice, Bert had called her. He couldn't forget that face. As he sketched, he became lost in concentration until she looked up and caught him staring. He nodded and gave a small smile, but she ignored him and looked away. Damn Bert for not introducing him. How could he contrive a meeting? He must remember to ask Jack if he knew her. Or why else had she been at his campaign launch?

She stood up and walked down to the river. Rainer was in the water talking to a man in a rowing skiff on the other side of the wire enclosure and didn't seem aware she was presumably waiting for him.

Eventually she turned and marched purposefully up the slope towards him. His pulse thudded as he stood up. Was she going to speak to him?

She did.

"Do I know you?" She crossed her arms and clutched her elbows, a gesture belying her boldness.

"Yes." It wasn't strictly true, and the day suddenly seemed airless. His free hand slid across his naked chest, and he bent to pick up his shirt to put it on.

"I don't remember where we met?" She squinted up at him, tilting her head to deflect the sunlight that lit-up her eyes so they seemed like translucent pools.

"At Jack and Patto's street meet a few weeks back."

A frown flittered and was gone. "Who?" Her nose wrinkled in apparent confusion.

He said, "You're Bert's friend."

"Who?" Blood rushed into her face. "I'm not sure who you mean. Perhaps you have mistaken me for someone else." She turned to walk away as if dismissing any social obligation to continue speaking to him.

"Please." He lifted his hand towards her as if he might prevent her from leaving, then dropped it quickly. "I remember you in your silver dress. You spoke to my friend Bert Manzoni."

She turned back. "Oh." She breathed out and placed her fingertips against her lips. "I do remember Doctor Manzoni."

"Yes, Bert–Roberto. He's my friend. I'm Mark Anders." He made a move as if to hold out his hand, hesitated and dropped it to his side.

For a moment she held his gaze and her lips parted, but a tram rattled past distracting her, and she glanced away towards the rail line. When she looked back the moment was gone.

She said, "Is it true that he's a doctor and a cook? He told me that when we talked at the library, but I wasn't sure if I believed him."

He smiled at her candour. "He was an academic at the Milan University in Italy before he came to Australia."

"But he said he's a cook now."

His smile faded at the incredulity in her tone. "A job's a job."

She glanced sideways at him. "What were you writing?" She pointed at the book in his hand.

"It's just a drawing." Was she always this blunt? He moved the book behind his thigh.

"May I see it? Please." Her cheeks became pink, as if recognising her behaviour was not that expected of such a brief acquaintance, and she looked down at her feet. He decided he liked her, more than just because she had a pretty face. He liked her because she was unaffected.

"Beatrice." Rainer's voice crashed across the grassy slope like the clatter of a cane knife on a concrete floor.

She clamped her mouth into what he imagined, or hoped, was a frustrated line, as she turned towards Rainer. Then she swivelled back. "I must go."

Mark didn't want to draw Rainer's attention either. The man wasn't liked or trusted among the cutters, so he lowered his voice. "Can I see you again—next Sunday, here, at noon?"

She didn't acknowledge his request. "It was nice to meet you again Mr Anders."

Before he could say more she strode back towards Rainer. Mark hadn't had the chance to ask if she knew Jack or why she was at the campaign launch. He bent to pick up his things and left the enclosure.

He'd catch up with Finn later. He got into his truck and drove to his Uncle Guido's guest house.

After dinner that evening, Mark left his aunt and uncle, planning to head back to the barracks. His truck was parked in the street outside the guest house. The driveway was full of other vehicles, some belonging to his relatives, some to the guests at his uncle's boarding house.

The moon had slipped behind a cloud and Mark paused to allow his eyes to adjust to the low light. Streetlights had not yet reached this far from the first-class district at the centre of town. Guido's

Guest House was closer to the tram line and railway station. A less salubrious part of the town where the roads were unpaved, and at this hour, usually deserted.

Mark took his keys from his pocket and had just opened his truck door when something hit him from behind. He fell to his knees, and a hard object pressed against his temple.

A muffled voice said, "Keep your eyes on the dirt Dago scum."

The moon came out and Mark stared at four sets of shoes on the ground around him. Four men and a pistol. Not the moment to be a hero. Remember the shoes.

Three pairs of Oxfords. Colour in the dim light was difficult to discern but two looked brown. One worn at the heel. One with a broken lace, knotted in repair. One black pair with broguing, those small, perforated holes currently in vogue. Expensive. One pair of boots. Police issue.

The voice again. Probably speaking through cotton. "Stick to your own kind, Dago."

He couldn't help himself. "What kind is that?"

"Your Dago kind, shit head."

"You must be mistaking me for a Spaniard."

"Fucking black Italian. Think you're clever do you?"

"If you say so." He shouldn't have opened his mouth.

A boot took him in the gut, making him heave. "The government says so, Dago scum."

Another voice, also muffled behind its face covering, said, "Enough chit chat."

Mark's head was yanked up by the hair and he almost let lose a yelp of pain.

"Stay away from white girls, or you're a dead man Anders."

"There's a vehicle coming." The voice sounded worried.

"Fuck! Shut your eyes Dago and sing the national anthem."

Mark turned his head to look up at the man. "Tell Rainer to go fuck himself." The boot in his face knocked him over, and the one in his stomach left him gasping for air.

Lights swooped down the street and his assailants scattered.

The vehicle screeched to a halt, truck doors opened, and footsteps thundered towards him.

"Are you all right mate?"

Jack helped Mark stand.

Bert chased after the men. He came back after a minute. "They took off in a Ford. One of those AA Stake trucks."

"What colour?" Jack asked.

"Hard to tell, dark, maybe blue."

"Won't be hard to find out who owns it."

Mark's breathing eased and he dusted the dirt off his clothes then fingered his eye. It was already swelling shut. "Bastards jumped me."

"Did you see who it was?"

Mark shook his head. "Pretty sure at least a couple were coppers."

"Did they say why?"

Mark shook his head again. If he told them he would have to tell them about Beatrice and he didn't want to talk about her. Besides, Bert would tell him he had asked for trouble, by speaking to her in Rainer's company.

She was way out of his orbit.

7. Queensland Cane Growers

Mark strode into the Ingham Cane Growers' building and confronted a man at a reception counter. The man ignored him until Mark thrust the letter under his nose. Reluctantly, he got up and led Mark down a corridor to a large conference room. Several men in three-piece suits and ties milled about talking and Mark took a moment to observe. He was probably under-dressed for the occasion, but these were his best, worn in deference to the status of the meeting.

The Cane Growers' Association were a powerful regional force with influential links into state and national decision-making, and while he didn't always agree with their policies, they had significant sway in how things were done. If he was ever going to make a difference, this was his chance.

He removed his hat and stepped into the room. "Good morning

gentlemen. I'm Mark Anders, from the minority group. You responded to my letters."

The men fell silent, staring as if something alien had washed up at their feet.

Eventually one man spoke. "Ah yes. The militant minority group I think you call yourselves." He emphasised the militant part and looked Mark up and down, stopping at the dark bruise blooming along his jawline and ending at his eye where the assailant's boot had connected with his face. Then he turned back to face the men around the table. "Pack of Bolsheviks!" he said under his breath.

The accusation was unjust. Many of the minority group weren't Communist Party members, and the militant part stood only for taking action, but it was a bad start. He'd have to persuade them he was no danger and just wanted to see justice and decency served. Surely, they wanted that too. It was a win for everyone.

The men took seats around a table in silence leaving Mark where he stood. It seemed unnecessarily rude, although perhaps it was procedure. What did he know of protocols in this place. It had taken a while to get an invite to this meeting and he'd only received a response to his correspondence after his fourth letter demanding someone speak to him about the Weil's disease problems. Rudeness or not, he would not let the opportunity go to waste.

He glanced around. The man from the reception had vanished. Mark leaned against the nearest wall clutching his hat and a pile of papers to his chest, the latter being the workers petition with almost two thousand signatures. It would show the growers the men were serious, and he wasn't acting alone.

Another man, obviously the President, called the meeting to order. Then he said, "We are honoured to have two special guests today. Dr Cilento, the director-general of health whom you all know. He nodded at a man with a sanctimoniously held mouth, and pin and bar through his shirt collar.

Mark knew Cilento also had Italian heritage, a paternal grandfather, and hoped he'd be sympathetic. Yet he feared the man's hooded eyes indicated he knew which side his bread was buttered on. So too the president, another Italian, but without an ounce of fellow countrymen simpatici on offer.

The president continued with the introductions, indicating an expensively dressed man at the head of the table. "You've all met Arthur. We are very privileged to have someone so distinguished from CSR visiting our humble neck of the woods."

The man called Arthur nodded. He was obviously high up in the company, and wore a morning suit, unusual in the north except for weddings and funerals. Gold cufflinks matched a gold tie pin with what looked like a diamond stud. A Homberg hat, driving gloves, and carved cane lay on the table in front of him. CSR must be worried to send such a high-ranking executive.

The two men on either side of Arthur also sported pins in their suit lapels although these ones signified not vanity, but affiliation with Mussolini's Fascists. Gold rods bound together with an axe head on top.

Mark frowned and looked down at his feet. He'd read a couple of years back in La Riscossa, before the newspaper was banned, that Frank and his mates had put paid to any designs for establishing a Fascista in Ingham. Yet it seems they had failed to eradicate all adherents.

The pins were bad, but the disease was an immediate problem, and he should focus on the issues at hand. These industry men and farmers were practical people, and fascist or not, the disease still killed you.

Before he'd arrived in Ingham, Mark hadn't realised how badly the disease was affecting the men here. Even when Jack had said they were afraid to go to work, it hadn't dawned on him how dire the situation was. They were all scared, but these blokes had greater cause. If the growers only knew the real dangers, they would see the need to do something.

Eventually, the president invited Mark to speak.

He stepped forward and respectfully but firmly put the men's petition on the table and explained its purpose. He spoke for about three minutes and then summed up. "Burning the cane before harvest is the best way of reducing the risk and it will save the industry having to pay out compensation."

One of the fascist badge-wearers interjected. "It's not a compensable industrial disease."

Mark opened his mouth to reply when the president showed an open hand toward Cilento. "What do you think, Doctor?"

Dr Cilento said, "The disease is almost certainly typhus fever. It is not an industrial disease."

Mark shook his head. "Dr Coffey from the Innisfail hospital said he was pretty sure they are all Weil's cases. He has a theory that it's caused by rats urinating on the cane. Burning will kill the bacteria causing it."

Cilento frowned and stared at the man across the table as if he could not be expected to countenance this man questioning his authority.

The secretary checked his watch. "Thank you, Dr Cilento. By your leave Mr President, we need to get on. Item three on the agenda is important." He looked up at Mark. "Thank you for your time, Mr Anders. You can find your way out?"

"Hang on." Mark wasn't finished and he wasn't going to be shoved out by this arrogant fool.

The president sighed. "What do you want from us Mr Anders?"

"I want you to take this seriously. Men are dying and you have a responsibility to them." He glanced at the CSR executive, who by this time was gazing out the window as if bored with proceedings.

The president said, "As you yourself pointed out, there is some dissent in the disease's source. Until we know what's causing the problem, there is little we can do."

Mark took a deep breath and the thumping in his chest slowed. "You can allow the cane to be burnt as a precaution before we harvest it. You can pay compensation to the men brought down by it."

The CSR executive was still gazing out the window, but he interjected. "If we did agree to burning there would have to be a penalty. Burnt cane has a reduced sugar content."

Mark hit back. "Not by much, so long as you harvest and mill it immediately. The Mossman cutters do it, and they don't pay a penalty."

The executive looked down at his manicured fingernails. "The Mossman cutters don't work for CSR mills. A penalty would have to be in the region of at least a shilling a ton. Go and ask your members if they will accept that."

Mark stared at him. So, it was true, CSR were trying to reduce their wages. Jack had said as much but Mark hadn't believed him.

"Good day Mr Anders," the secretary said. "Mr President, item three on the agenda."

Mark looked around at the men's faces but none of them returned his gaze. What could he do without making a complete fool of himself? He walked out before magma forced its way up from his stomach to spew from his throat. Words of anger would do nothing to change these men's minds. For that they needed to feel pain, and pain for these people could only be felt in their wallets.

Outside, the broad streets of Ingham baked in the tropical sun. He rolled his shoulders to release the tension and tried to control the rage. The whole thing had been a disaster, and he'd blown his one chance.

Doubt struck. Perhaps he hadn't been clear, hadn't emphasised the urgency of his case, or properly explained the men's concerns. Could he have approached the whole thing differently? Hell, he wasn't cut out for this! He needed a beer to wash the bitterness from his mouth. He set off towards the Italian Club.

When he arrived, he thumped up the steps to the clubhouse. Jack waited for him inside, along with Frank, Con and Luigi. Jack would have handled the situation better, but those men in fancy suits wouldn't talk to the likes of Jack. He was no longer an employee of the mills, but the enemy of the establishment.

Jack looked up as Mark came in, and Frank got up. "You look done in comrade."

"I don't think I did any good." Mark sat down and rubbed his temples.

Frank handed him a beer.

Mark took it gratefully and said, "They're talking about one shilling a ton penalty if the cutters burn the cane."

Jack scowled. "Cheap bastards. They've been hankering to reduce wages for years to compete with the international markets.

What they want is slave wages, and now they see their chance. It's a retreat to last century's labour tactics, but instead of shanghaied Kanakas, they'll enslave the working class. Well, they won't get away with it. Drink up, and you can tell us what happened when everyone's here."

Mark walked over to the door with his beer and stood on the top step.

Outside, men alone or in small groups, moved towards the old iron shed next door. The shed was euphemistically called the Embassy Palace and was mostly used for dances, weddings, and other social events but today it was a meeting hall.

More men rounded the corner and strolled along the pathway, greeting each other in various European dialects. They joined the groups waiting outside. Five women arrived and went into the hall.

A familiar car approached.

Mark turned back to Frank. "Did you invite the union?"

Frank jumped up and raced to the door. "No! He needn't think he's coming. He does nothing but undermine the cause."

Frank clattered down the steps to confront the organiser, followed closely by Con and Luigi. Jack and Mark stayed in the club watching from the doorway. Mark took a long swig of his beer.

Jack said, "This might be entertaining."

The organiser's Scottish brogue carried to where they stood at the top of the stairs. "Carmagnola," he shouted. "You cannae hold this meeting. It's not authorised."

Frank made a rude gesture. "Fuck off chum, this is a private meeting."

The organiser's tone changed to a wheedle. "Ach! Come along then Frankie. I'm your rep."

"You! I don't think so. We've been asking you blokes for a meeting for 18 bloody years, but you just ignore us. Anyway, you overcharge for membership and then cut off our voting rights, so we can't vote—what's the point? Now we organise and meet without you. No fees. Everyone votes, even the men's wives, but not you. You're not invited."

The organiser tried to push past Frank, to appeal to the others. "Come on now Lou, Con, see some sense. Just wait 'till tomorrow. I'll arrange a meeting at Halifax Mill, and we can discuss this properly."

Jack called out, "They don't understand your foreign accent, Harry. Try speaking Italian."

Mark laughed, but the union organiser's face turned red.

He shouted, "Away and boil your head, Jack Henry. You're a disgrace, calling yourself a white man." He turned and stomped back to his vehicle.

Jack grinned at Mark. "Should we join the meeting?"

Mark finished his beer and he and Jack went down the steps and across to the hall to join the others. When all the men and women were in the hall, Mark closed the doors and stood next to Jack.

Frank stepped onto a raised dais. The room fell silent, broken only by breathing and the odd scraping chair.

Then Frank thrust his clenched fist into the air. "Resistere!"

A forest of fists thrust towards the roof trusses, and with a roar, the crowd finished off the rest of Italy's anti-fascist slogan, "Rivoluzione!"

When the echo died away, Frank called on Mark to provide an update.

Mark made his way to the front of the hall. He didn't know many of the people in Ingham, so he began by introducing himself. First in English and then in Italian, explaining where his family were from and to whom he was related. This was important information for the men and women to trust him.

It took a while longer to explain what had happened at the Cane Growers' meeting, but he thought it was worth it because quite a few of the newer immigrants didn't understand English that well. It was better to take his time and make sure they all understood that the company was going to try and screw them to the wall.

By six o'clock that evening the Ingham mills had voted to strike along with their cutters, but Mark was apprehensive. Not all the men had been in the hall and the strike wasn't sanctioned by the union. If they didn't have everyone, then they may as well have no one, because those who didn't agree would just go to work tomorrow.

He voiced his concern to Jack and Frank.

Frank shrugged. "Easy, we'll pay them a visit. Con, you take the Macknade area, we'll take Victoria and Luigi, see if you can round up any outliers in town."

Mark and Frank squeezed into the front of Jack's truck and took off under Frank's direction. Two hours later, Frank said he thought they had reached out to all the men. Mark noticed some had needed a bit more persuasion than others, but all had agreed. They drove back and dropped Frank off at the Italian club. Then he and Jack set off back to Innisfail.

Mark yawned. It had been a long day and he'd eaten nothing since breakfast. His eyes drooped and he rested his head against the cab door and drifted into a torpor.

Jack's voice interrupted his lethargy. "Now, what do you think they're up to?"

Mark opened his eyes. "Who?"

"Them." Jack nodded at a truck that had turned off the main road and was racing towards Halifax. The tray was loaded with men.

Jack followed and Mark said, "Who are they? Come on, Jack, what's going on?"

"I don't know but I reckon, nothing good. That was a dark Ford AA Stake truck. Sound familiar?"

It sped ahead, leaving Mark and Jack behind in its dust. The road turned east hugging the Herbert River and on its far bank Mark could see the shape of the mill, dark against the deepening dusk. Cane trucks lined up outside like crouched river monsters, waiting for the mill to start in the morning. But the mills would lie idle tomorrow. The cane would sit for days, losing all its sugar content. It would be ruined.

They rounded a bend in the road and drove towards Halifax. A police car blocked the road ahead.

"Damn!" Jack slowed the vehicle to a stop.

One of the officers walked towards the truck.

"Where are you heading?" The officer stooped to peer into the interior of the cab.

"What's up?" Jack asked. "Hey, is that James Toohill?"

The officer pulled in his chin. "Don't be daft man, what would the Inspector be doing out here manning a roadblock?"

"Well, it's almost dark mate, but give Jim my best when you see him."

"Friend of yours, is he? What name shall I say?"

"Jack Henry."

"Ah, one of the Henry boys from Cardwell?"

Jack didn't disillusion him, just said, "We go back a long way."

The police officer relaxed. "We had word the Black Hand Gang are up to no good. Something's going down tonight. Who's your passenger?"

"Mark Anders from out Herberton way. Tin miner."

It was all prevarication. Jack wasn't related to the local Henry farming family or at least not within a generation or two. and while Mark had been in tin mining, he wasn't now, but the lies lulled the suspicion in the officer's face.

The officer said, "You're a long way from home."

Mark replied, "Just visiting."

"Staying in Halifax?"

Jack intervened. "Look mate, we're trying to catch up to a mob of blokes we saw driving a Ford truck. Did they come through here?"

"You're the first, and I've been here for an hour."

"I reckon that mob we were chasing could be your Black Hand culprits. They looked like they were up to no good. Maybe you should check some of the side roads But if you're on to it, we'll head on back to Ingham and leave it to you." Jack turned the truck around and headed back the way they'd come.

When they rounded the bend and came abreast of the mill they saw the fires. Men were running through the night with burning torches, setting fire to the loaded cane trucks. Flames leapt high, sparks shooting off like fireworks.

Jack pulled up and got out of the truck. Mark joined him. They stood staring across the river as the flames lit up the night.

Mark said, "Do you suppose it's Frank's blokes or is it really just criminals?"

Jack shook his head. "No idea, but Frank's people are all

Anarcho-syndicalists and don't take kindly to any form of authority. So, who knows? It could be them, or it could be the Black Hand as the police seem to think although that seems less likely. It might just as well be the fascists trying to discredit us. If that was the same Ford truck that your assailants were using, I've seen one similar parked outside the fascist club in Innisfail. They know the cane will not get crushed. Burning it and then blaming the strikers is good propaganda against the cause. Come on, that copper will be along any minute. We'd better get out of here before we're arrested. I hope the fires don't spread into the paddocks. That would have the growers frothing at the mouth."

It was almost dawn by the time Jack dropped Mark off at the barrack near Goondi. He trod the few steps up to the veranda as silently as he could so as not to awaken the others, and worn ragged, he flopped onto his bunk fully clothed.

Striking was the only thing to get their attention. He agreed with Frank that the mills didn't care if a few Italians died—so what! No one cared about the Italian-Australian workers. In fact, in the newspapers, they weren't even Australians. In the worst papers like Smith's Weekly, they were foreign dago scum. At best they were foreign workers but never Australians, even though some were born in the country, and some like Mark had become naturalised. Many who hadn't the papers or the English, lived in fear of deportation back to Fascist Italy. These were people like Bert and Frank, who'd fled Italy fearing imprisonment, torture and even death.

Mark had thought he could reason with the growers, but he was beginning to doubt it was possible. Yet he clung to hope, for no matter what their beliefs, you couldn't argue with the fact that men were dying. Even so, the Ingham men might have gone too far.

Frank was hot-headed, and if it was his men who'd overturned the cane trucks and set the fires, it would be bad publicity. The cane didn't matter. It was useless anyway or would be in a day or two, but the capitalists just wouldn't tolerate crime against private property, especially the property of a company like CSR. That would put them all in jail.

Yet, the men were fearful of the rats' disease and their powerlessness to do anything about it made them angry. Hell, he was angry. But while Frank craved revolution, and Jack planned it, they would need more men and greater resources to even contemplate it.

Far better to use persuasion and the ballot box to make change. If he could get to know the growers better, he was sure he could convince them that fairness and justice paid off.

Besides, a revolution wasn't what Mark wanted. It was just a dream, something people talked about to relieve their anger. If history showed anything, it showed revolutions were bloody and unhappy events where the poor and weak suffered most. It was better to try reasoning with the company. He was convinced they'd make more headway through negotiations. Striking was a bargaining chip but there was a long way to go before they could claim victory if any of them survived that long.

8. Suspicion

Sunday dawned with a fresh south westerly breeze bringing cool dry weather up from the southern regions. The cobalt sky arched, uninterrupted, from horizon to horizon. Mark bent his knees to see his face in the small round mirror tacked up on the wall outside the barrack bathroom. It was too dim inside to see properly and he needed this shave to be a close one.

He splashed water from an enamel basin over his face then dried it with a cotton hand towel, wincing as he ran the rough material over his tender jaw. The bruise had begun to yellow but the spot where the assailant's boot had collected him was still tender, particularly around the eye area.

What the hell was he thinking? She wouldn't be there. He was wasting his time, but he would still go to the swimming enclosure. Rainer wasn't going to dictate who he could speak to, no matter how many thugs he sent to do his dirty work. All the same, Mark was certain he was wasting his time. She hadn't said she would come. Why would she? But she hadn't said she wouldn't either.

He shrugged into his good linen shirt, buttoned it to the throat, tucked it into his trousers and pulled the braces over his shoulders. He remembered the thinning patch over the knee and checked to see how noticeable it was. Perhaps he should fork out for a new pair.

He walked along the veranda and into the room he shared with his brother.

Finn was lying on his bunk reading the Sunday paper. He looked up when Mark walked in. "Where the hell are you off to?"

"Swimming enclosure."

"What? All gussied up like a spiff."

"I'm meeting someone."

Finn sat up. "Who?"

"None of your business."

"Ho Ho intrigue."

Mark picked up his truck key and walked out.

Finn yelled after him. "Meet us later at the Crown."

"Maybe."

He climbed into his old Dodge and drove into town, parking on the grassy verge near the swimming enclosure.

She was sitting alone under a coconut palm, and his heart leaped up to form a wodge in his throat. He walked up behind her and saw she was writing something in a notebook. As he got closer he saw the words scrawled large, underlined, and punctuated with an exclamation mark.

Death in the Cane!

"You came."

She looked up and her cheeks flushed pink. "I nearly didn't."

"I'm glad you did. What are you writing about?"

"Nothing." She closed the notebook and laid it aside, her eyes lowered as if hiding something.

He smiled. "Who died in the cane?"

"You saw."

"Yes. Didn't mean to spy, but it sounds interesting. Tell me about it."

"Oh, it's nothing." She took a breath. "I was contemplating writing a piece for the local paper."

"Are you a reporter?"

She shook her head. "I wish, but no it was a silly idea really."

"Why?"

"No one will publish something I write."

He waited for more, but her mouth twisted in wry self-depreciation before she dropped her gaze and plucked at a blade of grass.

He prompted. "Why won't they publish what you write?"

She sighed. "I don't have a recognisable by-line. You can't just write something and expect to get it published, especially not if you are a girl. I would love to be a magazine columnist, but I don't suppose it will ever happen."

"There are lots of women journalists now. I can't see why being a woman would make a difference if the piece were good and interesting. You should give it a go. I'd buy a newspaper if it had your story in it."

She smiled and changed the subject. "What do you do Mr Anders."

"Mark please. I cut cane."

"That sounds like hard work."

He tilted his head. "Its good money."

"Oh." Her face flushed, and she looked away.

Had he said something wrong? "What about you? If you are not a reporter what do you do?"

She looked stricken as if he had criticised her. "I don't do anything, but I don't live here. We are just visiting."

A feeling of dread engulfed him. She couldn't be married, could she? "Who is we?" His voice was wary.

"I accompanied my father. He's on a business trip but we have relatives here, my father's sister and her husband. They have a son who was supposed to be here too, but he got a job offer so he didn't come home. It's all a bit dull with just my aunt and uncle. I don't really know anyone else."

"What about Rainer?"

"I didn't realise you knew Howard. I met him at the ambulance ball. My Uncle George knows him quite well, through the Lodge.

"Lodge?"

"Masons."

Mark raised his eyebrows. "I don't really know him, just who he is."

"What do you mean?"

"He's in the Commonwealth Investigation Unit so I guess everyone knows who he is."

"Do you know many police officers?"

Mark laughed. "No, why?"

"There is one walking over here."

Mark turned his head and saw the copper making a bee line towards them. He said, "Excuse me," and jumped up to intercept the constable before he came any closer.

When he returned he apologised to her. "I am really sorry. Something's come up and I have to go."

"I hope there's nothing wrong."

"No. It's fine, just need to clear some things up."

She hesitated. "Are you sure everything is all right?

"Yes, it's fine. Just a problem at work."

She seemed to relax as if this was a familiar excuse.

"I've really enjoyed talking to you. Can we do this again next weekend? We could go somewhere for lunch. Sunday, same time, and place." He held his breath hoping she'd say yes.

She hesitated, seeming unsure. He pressed her. "I am so sorry I have to leave now, but I really have no choice and I would like to continue our conversation, get to know you better..."

"All right. I'll try."

She smiled at him, and his stomach clenched but he had bigger problems to worry about now although he didn't want her knowing what they were. He turned and hurried away.

The police constable had given Mark a choice. Either go voluntarily to the station to answer questions or have a wagon come and pick him up. Mark played it cool and after leaving Beatrice, he followed the constable to the station.

As they drew closer his breathing became a little more erratic. It was just bad luck the bloke had been passing and recognised him, although Mark was relieved the copper had been a bit discrete. If it had been one of Rainer's thugs the situation would have been different.

Mark walked at his side and asked again what it was they wanted with him, but the constable wouldn't expand, except to say it was something to do with the Ingham strike and the fires at the mill.

When they arrived at the headquarters he took Mark into an interview room and left him there, saying an officer would be along shortly.

Mark sat at the table and forced his pulse rate to slow, but he had a bad feeling. How had the constable recognised him? Mark didn't know any coppers, at least not in Innisfail, and it wasn't as if he was a well-known person in town. The only reason he knew Rainer was because Jack had pointed him out and warned him to be wary of the man.

He waited in the room for what seemed like hours before anyone came near him again. He was just contemplating banging on the door to get some attention when Howard Rainer walked in, paused, and surveyed Mark as if he were the slime wiped off his boot.

Rainer sat down across the table and opened a notebook. He felt his jacket pocket and withdrew a fountain pen which he unscrewed slowly, almost as if it were a ritual.

It was a Parker, one of those flash American button fillers with a gold nib, and it seemed to Mark that Rainer was showing off. He glanced at Rainer's shoes under the table and drew in a breath.

Rainer said, "Mr Anders, are you a member of the so-called Cosa Nostra?"

"What?" Mark was still thinking about Rainer's shoes, smart black Oxford brogues, when the question penetrated his brain.

"I believe it is sometimes referred to as the 'Ndrangheta or Comora but known here by the name the Black Hand."

"I thought this was about the fires at the Macknade Mill."

"Yes. We know you started them, but we would like to know who your fellow conspirators are."

"Hang on. I didn't start any fires."

"We have an eyewitness that will put you at the scene of the crime."

Mark stared at Rainer in disbelief, but all he said was, "Nice shoes."

It was Rainer's turn to look surprised. He glanced down and then frowned as if puzzled by the reference, but the interlude had given Mark time to think. If Rainer knew Mark's whereabouts that night from the police officer at the roadblock, he would also know that Jack had been with him. Had Jack been interviewed? He remembered Jack saying, never speak to them if they ask anything. Demand that they call in your barrister then either call me or Fred. They have no right to detain you for no reason without a warrant.

Rainer wrote something on his pad then looked up. "We know your Uncle Guido de Luca is Sicilian and a member of the Communist Party. Your mother is also Italian, and you were born in Florence, so, what I want to know is, what is your role within the Black Hand?

Mark couldn't help himself. "My uncle's Calabrian."

"Same thing."

Mark shook his head. "The whole thing is ridiculous. The Black Hand are just a bunch of petty thugs. No self-respecting Italian would have a bar of them, and I am Australian. I have lived here since I was a year old." He paused, then asked, "What are you really after, Rainer?"

"You know my name."

"It's just as well, as you didn't bother to introduce yourself when you came in. You also seemed to know mine, but if you want us to keep talking, you'll need to wait until my barrister can get here. I think you've met Mr Paterson. Otherwise, unless you have any legal reason for detaining me, I'm going home."

Mark stood up and stared Rainer in the eye. He wasn't sure he'd got away with the bluster, but it seemed maybe he had because Rainer screwed the cap back on his pen.

Rainer leaned back, one arm on the back of his chair and examined Mark. "You seem to be confusing the issue. I am acting on behalf of CIB, the Commonwealth Investigation Branch, rather than the Queensland Police. I understood you came in voluntarily to share information. My concern is not with the crimes you may have committed at the Macknade Mill, but with your association with subversives. Foreign gangs and organised crime are one area of enquiry, but if Mr Paterson is your barrister perhaps the subversive activity relates to your membership of the Communist Party. Are you a member of the CPA Mr Anders?"

Shit. He'd given the bastard another opening. "Mr Paterson to my knowledge is a member of the Bar and has many clients from all parts of our society."

"But the night of Macknade Mill fire you were with a Mr Henry. I realise now that this would be the communist, Jack Henry, not a member of the upstanding Henry family, as the duty officer assumed. This is even more interesting Mr Anders. Were you instrumental in instigating the strike activity at the Ingham Mills? I must warn you that fomenting civil unrest is an offence for an alien, for which you may be deported."

"First, I am not an alien. I am naturalised and that makes me a

British subject."

"Nevertheless, since the 1926 Crimes Act if you were born outside of Australia and encourage a strike or are a member of an illegal association that attempts to do so, you may be deported, naturalised or not."

Mark swallowed. That bit of information, if true, was of significant concern. "I am a member of the Australian Workers Union. Last I heard, this was a legitimate union. I was merely visiting fellow union members and did not, and would not, have a say in whether the Ingham men strike. They make their own decisions and don't need outsiders to do it for them. You also assume that to take strike action is acting against the nation's interests. Furthermore, Jack Henry happens to be my aunt's next-door neighbour and is running for the forthcoming parliamentary elections. Hardly a subversive act. Neither he nor I are members of any illegal associations."

Rainer stood up. "Mr Anders you are here voluntarily."

"Not what I was told."

"Regardless. You are free to leave at any time. If you feel you do have information to share please call on me in my capacity as CIB agent. However, you will need to make yourself available for questioning further about the Macknade Mill fires, should I be called upon to investigate these in my capacity within the Queensland Police."

He walked out leaving Mark fuming but powerless. What a waste of time and just when he was getting to know Beatrice. Was that the point?

It wasn't until Mark was back at the barrack that Bert told him that the police had come looking for him. Billy had told the coppers he'd seen Mark's truck down at the swimming enclosure.

Mark would like to have pushed in the idiot's face for ruining his afternoon. His brother never did have any sense when it came to choosing his friends, but Billy was just a goose, and he couldn't really blame him.

Beatrice was out of his league anyway and he doubted she'd even turn up next Sunday, but Rainer was proving to be a problem and Mark suspected it had all come about because he'd been seen talking to her.

First the beating. He fingered his jaw. Now the deportation threat. Rainer obviously thought he had a stake and wasn't about to let competition interfere with his pursuit. Fuck him. She would make her own choices.

9. A Daring Moment

Beatrice sat on a sofa in the morning room, staring out of the window. Her nails played a tattoo on the sofa's linen-covered arm. The only other sounds came from the house as it creaked and cracked when the sun came out from behind a cloud.

Her uncle and aunt were attending mass at the Catholic cathedral in Innisfail. Her father, sitting on the sofa opposite her, was a good Protestant and had declined their invitation to attend. Thus, Beatrice felt she needn't go either, since she wasn't a Catholic—although neither was she a good Protestant. Although she wouldn't acknowledge that to her father, who took her piety for granted.

Should she go to the swimming enclosure? The image of him smiling at her made her stomach churn and all week she had obsessed over whether she should go and meet him again.

Last week he had left so suddenly, it would have seemed rude had it not been for the policeman, and the plausible explanation of pressing work commitments. At least, she suppose whatever called him away must have been important. She knew what that was like. Her father was always being called away to work.

Arthur shook out and then refolded the broadsheet. A headline caught Beatrice's attention. *Home Secretary outlines plans for a gigantic campaign.*

"What are you reading about Daddy?"

He lowered the paper and looked over the top of his glasses. "It's just business stuff, nothing for you to worry about my dear."

She ignored his warning, seeing that further down the page a line said, *Government Has Cabled for Special Serum from London.*

"Is that about the disease killing the men in Ingham?"

He sighed and put down the paper. "My word, Beatrice. This is not a suitable subject."

"But Daddy, I heard Uncle George saying Weil's disease has no cure."

"I am not yet convinced that it is Weil's, as they claim. Don't you have something else to do?"

Beatrice stood up. "Well actually, some of the girls I met at the Ambulance Ball asked me to go along to the cricket club and try my hand. They have a ladies' club here, apparently."

Arthur wiggled his eyebrows. "Ah, very good, you run along then."

"I won't be back for lunch." She held her breath. "And I might be a little late this afternoon." A pulse in her neck thudded at her deception, and she realised it was becoming a habit. But Arthur was already re-engrossed in the newspaper and merely made a noise that

Beatrice decided was an approval.

Half an hour later she arrived at the bathing enclosure. As she leaned her bicycle against a coconut palm Mark pulled up on the verge, got out of his truck and walked towards her.

"I'm glad you could make it." He picked up her bike and hefted it onto the tray.

"What are you doing?" Her heart hammered in her throat.

"Taking you to lunch. I said I would last week. Look, I am sorry about being called away. It couldn't be helped. I want to get out of here before someone else decides to interrupt." Mark gazed at her for what seemed like a full minute as if coming to some conclusion before he said, "that is if you still want to have lunch with me..."

"Yes, of course." Bravado pushed her forward, although she was in a bind, a double dilemma.

It was completely rash getting into a virtual strangers car to go off to who knew where, but she remained silent mostly because the fear of driving off with a stranger was nothing to the embarrassment of making a scene. She made mental excuses. *But Daddy you told me to always act with decorum even in the face of kidnapping and murder.*

She watched Mark's profile, which seemed to remain serene as he drove through the town to a part that Beatrice had never before seen. "I thought we were going to a café." She twisted her fingers as she looked out at the unfamiliar streets and houses.

He glanced across at her and said, "Somewhere much better. You won't get food this good in any café."

The road became rougher as they headed out of the centre along Edith Street, and Beatrice tapped her lips. Should she demand to be taken back. It was too late. They turned into a side road, and then into a driveway. A sign on the gate said *Guido's Guest House.*

Mark parked and got out to open her door. Music drifted on the breeze as she followed him around the two-storey building.

A long table was laid for lunch. It occupied the centre of the yard in the shade of passion-vine covered pergolas. People sat around the table in silence listening to a man playing the mandolin. Beatrice caught her breath at the poignant sound.

A woman wearing a headscarf waved and called out in a language that Beatrice didn't understand. The woman scurried around the table, clutching her apron, saying what sounded to Beatrice like, "Tesoro!" The woman flung her arms around Mark.

Mark hugged her and kissed both her cheeks. "Hello, Nonnina."

The man with the mandolin stopped playing and waved. The others turned and called greetings. A swarthy man, who seemed a little older than Mark, hoisted a child off his lap, handing the baby to the woman in a red sleeveless dress sitting next to him. Her alabaster arms slid around the little body as she turned in their direction. To Beatrice's astonishment, she saw the woman was Chinese.

The swarthy man picked up two chairs and placed them at the table. Then he strode towards them, hands held out towards Mark, but eyes on Beatrice. "Who's this you've brought to grace our table, young cousin?" He shook Mark's hand, all the while staring at Beatrice.

The old woman, whom Mark had called Nonnina scowled, drawing parallel lines between her eyes.

Mark's neck had mottled under his tan. "This is my friend Beatrice."

"Bella! Ciao Beatrice." The man took both her hands and kissed her on one cheek then the other, just as Mark had done to the old woman.

Beatrice stiffened. The man smelled strongly of cigarette smoke, garlic and wine and stood too close.

The old woman fired off a string of words, her hands flapping in Beatrice's direction and Mark said, "Speak English, Nonna. Beatrice doesn't speak Toscano, and it's all right."

Nonna's eyes narrowed. "Who is the family for Beatrice?"

Mark again spoke in what he'd called Toscano and said something she didn't understand.

Joe said, "Come, sit, eat." He turned and with a wave of his hand said, "This is the family, well some of them. Nonno Giuseppe Rossi." He indicated the mandolin player. "My father Guido de Luca." He held his hand towards a man with very shaggy eyebrows, then laughed. "There's a test afterwards for all the names." He placed his hand on the woman in the red dress's shoulder. "My wife Mia, and my son Bao."

Another woman came out of the house holding an enamel pot. "Ah and my Madre, Zarah de Luca," Joe said.

The woman cried out, "Marchio, I thought you weren't coming today. We started without you, but you are in time." She plonked the pot on the table. "Where is your brother? He never comes to visit us."

Joe said, "Mamma, come and meet Mark's friend."

The woman walked towards them, and Beatrice thought Mark looked tense, but all he said was, "Aunt Zarah, this is my friend, Beatrice."

The woman wiped her hands on her apron and stared at Beatrice. "She's beautiful. Too good for you, eh Marchio?"

She glanced behind Beatrice as if searching for someone, but Joe interrupted.

"Mamma, his name's Mark."

"Puah! He is Marchio and you; you are Giuseppe like Nonno. What for these names—Mark and Joe." She fixed her gaze on Beatrice and said sternly, "Are you alone?"

The question confused Beatrice, but Mark shrugged and said something to his aunt.

Zarah frowned and replied rapidly. Her tone sounded scolding.

Beatrice glanced from one to the other, wondering what they were saying, suddenly feeling unsure of her welcome.

Mark replied in the same language and his aunt waggled her finger then slapped his hand. But she turned and smiled at Beatrice saying, "No matter." She grasped Beatrice's wrist. "Come, you sit with me and Bianca. We find out what my nephew is doing so I can report to my sister."

Bianca had an amazing mass of straw-coloured hair. She smiled at Beatrice and opened her mouth to speak, but Aunt Zarah clapped her hands. "Come, some wine! Bianca, more plates, and glasses."

Bianca rolled her eyes at Beatrice before she walked towards the house.

Mark pulled up a chair next to hers and explained quietly that his aunt was cross with him because Beatrice's mother wasn't with her.

"But my mother's in England," she said in a low voice, trying to imagine her mother in this gathering. It would never happen, and that gave Beatrice a warm glow of triumph. This was all hers and her family couldn't take it away.

"Don't worry about it. It's just my auntie's way. She and my grandmother are a bit old-fashioned."

Beatrice lowered her voice. "What is this place? It said on the gate it's a guest house."

"Yes." Mark looked amused. "My aunt and uncle run this boarding house, mostly for travelling salesmen. My grandparents and Mia also help. Joe owns a garage in town, and his sister, Bianca, is a nurse at the hospital. I don't know the three blokes at the end of the table. They're probably staying next door."

Beatrice asked, "What's next door?"

"That's Jack's place," Mark said. "Well, when he's home, otherwise it's just a place where people meet or stay sometimes. Another couple of blokes share with him, but it's really Jack's place."

She wrinkled her nose in concentration.

He said, "Jack Henry. That bloke you were listening to that night in the street."

"Oh." Her eyes widened, and she glanced nervously at his family, before dropping her voice to a whisper. "The communist candidate?"

He gave her a wry look. "He's a good bloke. Wait until you meet him. You'll love him. Everyone does." He paused then said, "My aunt and Nonna both reckon he walks on water." He picked up a tumbler and half-filled it with wine, placing it in front of her. He leaned across the table, tore off a hunk of bread, and put it on her plate. "The soup's good. You'll like it."

Nonno Giuseppe picked at his mandolin and the sound sent goosebumps down Beatrice's arms. She watched the people around the table. The three men who Mark said were staying with Jack, look ragged and hungry as they eyed Zarah dishing up the soup. They looked so poor and out of place as if they didn't belong to the family gathering.

She leaned towards Mark. "The men who are staying with Mr Henry, who are they?"

He gazed thoughtfully along the table. "Probably off the rattler. Jack takes in everyone."

Beatrice pursed her mouth. "What does that mean, off the rattler?"

Mark paused and searched her face. "Really? You really don't know?"

She shook her head, her gaze flitting to Joe who had made a strange sound in his throat.

Mark frowned across the table at his cousin, then said, "Men who have no work sometimes cadge a ride on freight trains so they can get to the next town to find work. It's not so bad now, but for a few years, it was terrible. If they're caught, they end up in jail. The comrades in all the towns try to help. Here, they sleep at Jack's place and my aunt feeds them. My parents do the same at home in Herberton."

Beatrice peered sideways at the men, wondering at people who would take in homeless beggars and house and feed them. It was like something out of the New Testament. Now she understood what Mark meant by Jack walking on water. She wasn't sure whether she was shocked, although she should be at such blasphemy, instead she felt very insular and self-centred. Her life was insignificant and pampered. She felt ashamed and picked up her spoon to cover her confusion and her ignorance.

But she soon forgot herself as the food came out and the family talked. Never in her life had she seen such a variety of food at one sitting nor eaten so much. Never before had she sat down at such a noisy dining table with so much laughter and chatter. Everyone tried to speak in English for her sake, but they often drifted into their own language and then back to English, to the point Beatrice found it difficult to follow any one conversation.

Mia leaned over and whispered, "I know what it's like, just let it wash over you." She smiled and got up. "Bao needs a nap."

Beatrice tried to take Mia's advice, sipping her wine slowly, wary of its pungent aroma. It tasted of mulberries, but it made her eyes water.

All afternoon Mark translated, put morsels of food on her plate, explaining what each was, using words she had never heard and would not remember until the afternoon became hazy. Hours later, she realised it was growing dark, and in sudden panic, she whispered to Mark, "I have to get home. My family will worry."

"Of course." He stood up. "Nonna, Aunt Zarah."

Everyone at the table stopped talking and looked at Mark. Beatrice felt herself quailing at drawing so much attention.

He said, "Please excuse me. I have to take Beatrice home. For her, it's late."

They all stared at Beatrice.

Bianca asked, "Where do you live?"

Beatrice opened her mouth to answer but Mark intervened. "It's not far."

Aunt Zarah hugged Beatrice and said, "Come back and see us again soon." She placed her hand on Beatrice's cheek. "Now kiss Nonna and run home."

Beatrice hesitated but felt Mark's hand in the small of her back guiding her towards his Nonna, who said in admonishment, "Next time, you bring your Madre."

When they were in the car Mark turned to her. "Where do you live?"

My uncle's place is called Sunrise Sugar Estate. I don't really know where it is from here, but if you take me back to town I can direct you.

Mark was staring at her with a strange look on his face.

"What's wrong?":

"I know where Sunrise is. My gang cut there. Who is your father?"

"Arthur Langham. Why?"

Mark's mouth became a thin line and he looked away.

"Is something wrong?"

He shook his head and reversed the truck out of the driveway.

They remained in strained silence until they reached the turnoff before the farm.

Beatrice said, "Please stop here."

Mark jammed on the breaks and a cloud of dust billowed up covering the truck. Dark cane fields fanned out from either side of the road. The sun had already dipped behind the mountain range, casting the coastal land in shadow, and clouds scurried across the deepening sky.

He took her bike from the back of the truck and stood with it propped in front of him.

As she took it from him she asked, "Will I see you again?"

He shook his head. "Beatrice I am sorry. It's not a good idea."

"Why?"

He ran his hand across the back of his neck. "I had no idea who you were. I should have made the connections but I'm an idiot..."

"I don't understand…"

"Look, we're from different worlds." His voice was harsh.

Her face flushed as it dawned on her what he meant. "No. We're from the same world. Look!" She pointed at him and then herself, trying to lighten the atmosphere. "You're there, and I am here." Her hands went to her hips. "I don't know why you suddenly think you can't talk to me." Her eyes were on the verge of filling with frustrated tears, and she looked away, wiping her hand across her face.

"What's wrong?" he asked.

She sniffed, a little embarrassed by her outburst. "Nothing. Um. I just thought we could be friends."

"Friends? You must have lots of friends."

"I don't really know anyone here."

He said, "What about your friend Rainer, the policeman?"

"Oh, he's just, just …" She looked up at him. "My family know him, that's all. He's not my friend."

Mark frowned and looked at the bike before straightening his shoulders and saying, "Do you want to go to the pictures next weekend? They have a matinee on Saturday afternoon. I could meet you outside at 2 o'clock."

"I'd like that."

She mounted her bike and rode toward the farm, happy at his change of heart. She liked him and his family, but he was right. They were from different worlds, and she could never tell her family about him. He would have to remain her secret.

Every window in the house was lit, although that wasn't unusual, and half-a-dozen cars lined the driveway. She prayed no one had noticed her absence. As she let herself in the front door she hesitated before walking along the corridor and past her Uncle George's study.

The door was ajar, and she heard her father's voice. "Not sure you're right, old man. The communist message is becoming increasingly popular, and this will help their cause. Rather than starting a war, I think your job is to regain control over your members. It's just Ingham now, but already I hear Mourilyan Mill is planning to down tools and then we'll have a conflagration."

Another voice said something inaudible, but Uncle George interrupted. "By that time, the Bolsheviks will have taken over the union, lock, stock and barrel."

She stepped closer and heard her father say, "Never mind all that. We have to stop this now before it goes further. It's not just the mills around Ingham. My biggest concern is it spreading. If Mourilyan Mill goes out, there'll be more. What can you do, Clarrie?"

A voice she didn't recognise said, "Perhaps if the union steps in and takes the lead rather than this stand-off, we can get the men into the Arbitration Court. That way we can regain control."

"What! Encourage the union to support the strike?"

"In a nutshell, yes. While the men have taken matters into their own hands we have no control. Let the union appear to achieve something, and the men will fall into line."

Aunt Emily came around the corner and Beatrice hurriedly moved away from the door and along the corridor.

"Where have you been, Beatrice? We were worried," Emily scolded.

"Sorry, Aunt Emily. I took a shortcut home, but it was the wrong turning." She swallowed. "I'm so sorry to worry you, but I'm exhausted. I think I'll have a bath and go to bed."

Beatrice didn't want to talk right now. For once she craved solitude, and she felt guilty at all the lies that seemed to slip from her mouth with increasing ease.

Aunt Emily appeared animated in a way Beatrice had not seen her before, her gaze flicking critically across Beatrice's clothing.

She said, "My dear, Howard Rainer's here. I've invited him to stay for dinner when the meeting's finished. I thought you'd want to thank him for the beautiful bouquet he sent. Hurry now and change into something pretty."

"I'm not hungry." Beatrice felt trapped. She didn't want to encourage Howard, neither did she think she could fit in another crumb.

"But you missed lunch. You must eat, Beatrice. Are you coming down with something? Perhaps we should call the doctor."

"I'm fine. Just tired." Beatrice tried to move past her aunt.

But unusually, Aunt Emily remained assertively blocking the corridor. "No one likes it if you don't smile, dear."

Beatrice stopped, surprised. This was her aunt speaking, the one who on most days seemed not of this world. Before thinking she snapped back. "Yes, but nobody respects you if you do."

The look on her aunt's face made Beatrice wish she could bite back the words. She smiled brightly. "Sorry Aunt. I'll change now and be back down in no time."

She reached out and squeezed Emily's hand, then rushed upstairs to her room, dreading having to face dinner with guests.

10. Strike

Mark opened his eyes, stretched, and winced in the pre-dawn gloom. Every muscle in his body ached from the long hours of cutting he had put into the last week to make up for being away so much, and his body was paying.

The barrack room he shared with Finn was large enough for two beds and an old chest of drawers. The window opening was a square cut into the tin wall, intended to let air flow through the otherwise stifling box. A hinged corrugated iron sheet acted as a window covering, now propped open with a pole. The dying moon cast a feeble light in through the square, lighting up the beetles that struggled to free their feet from Mark's mosquito net.

A loud snore came from Finn's bed across the room and Mark sighed. He'd never get back to sleep now. His mum called snoring the song of beer and Finn was the maestro. He raised an arm behind his head as he listened to the mud-chooks screech in the distant forest, knowing he should get up, but he couldn't muster the energy to move. He shifted to alleviate the prickle from coir poking through the thin mattress ticking. But his aching muscles were nothing to the treachery unfolding.

The union had stepped in and taken over the strike once the Ingham blokes showed they were serious, but the low point was that twenty five of Frank's men were arrested for the fires at the Macknade Mill. Then Mourilyan Mill went out in support of their comrades.

Mark should have known his own union was up to no good when they ignored Mourilyan Mill's decision to down tools. It hadn't seemed to matter that the Arbitration Court agreed to allow the men to burn the rat-infested cane on the word of an inspector. Yet, the mills still stuck to their position on penalties.

After the Arbitration ruling, the union persuaded them that as a sign of good faith they should go back to work, and Mourilyan, Ingham, Macknade, and Victoria Mills did just that, although the men grumbled about the reduction in wages. All in all, they had won and more importantly, they had forced their own union to act in their interests. Mark was jubilant and had gone around the district with Jack, making sure everyone knew the result.

Then came the bad news. The court ruling regarding burning the cane only applied to the Ingham Mills. At the union meeting, the organiser shifted his feet but couldn't meet their gaze. That told Mark everything he needed to know. He watched the bloke wipe his hand across his mouth and mutter, we're working on it. What wasn't he telling them? Mark gazed around and saw the men wanted to believe the union.

After the meeting he'd gone back to work feeling the heaviness of failure, blaming himself, going over every detail to understand where he might have been unclear on some point. All the sugar workers were in danger, not just Ingham. But he'd failed them. They had elected him as the militant minority delegate, yet he'd done nothing to help the Goondi men. He'd failed them, just as the company had done.

Outside, on the barrack veranda, someone moved. Most likely Bert. He was always first up in the morning. Mark pushed the mosquito net aside. It wasn't yet summer but that didn't deter the mossies. Malaria, along with all the other diseases in the cane fields, had been bad the past year. The Cocsec smoke just didn't keep the pests at bay.

He stifled a groan as he swung his legs out of the bed and sat on the edge of the bunk. The stone-curlews, with their banshee wailing, seemed to channel the souls of the dead as the false dawn lightened the sky.

A screech from the lever of the hurricane lamp interrupted his reflections, and he heard Bert strike a match to light the wick. A creak and thump from the first room meant Danny was up. Another day had begun. Mark dressed and walked along the veranda in the faltering dark.

In the kitchen, Bert shuffled about laying kindling on the fire. Mark sat on a bench running the length of a scarred wooden table, watching Bert as he filled the kettle and placed it on the stove to boil. Next, he heated frying pans. A porridge pot steamed alongside. Mark's stomach rumbled in anticipation.

Danny ducked his head through the door, his eyes bleary from sleep. "Mornin," He greeted them, rubbing his right forearm. A pungent smell of liniment filled the room.

Bert picked up an egg whisk and nodded to the ganger. Mark shifted over for Danny who thumped down onto the bench and opened a tin of Log Cabin. He took out a paper and stuck it to his moistened lowered lip before he scabbed out a wad of tobacco and ground it between his palms. When he had the right leaf grind he peeled the paper from his lip to roll his first cigarette of the day. Cigarette's during the day, shag pipe in the evening. Tobacco was Danny's most faithful companion.

The kettle whistled, and Bert poured boiling water into an enamel teapot before plonking it down on the table.

Danny lit the rollie, inhaled, coughed, and wiped his mouth on his shoulder. "Sugar," he demanded.

Bert came back, banged the tin on the table, and said, "You'll have it kill you, one way or another."

Danny grinned at Mark as he took a bone-handled knife from the cutlery tin in the middle of the table to prize off the sugar lid. He poured a stream of golden grains into his mug and stirred his tea with the blade of the same knife. His face sobered. "Life kills you anyway. May as well take sweetness where you can find it."

"Ants have the same philosophy," Bert said and stomped back to the stove.

"Big words now. You swallow a dictionary?" Danny brought the rollie to his mouth between finger and thumb and sucked in a lungful of smoke.

Bert slapped steaks into a smoking pan. "Just put the damned lid back on properly."

The smell of frying steaks followed by bacon filled the room. The aroma mingled with the wood smoke from a leaky kitchen flue.

Through the open door, Mark could see the sky lightening as the sun breached the lip of dawn.

Danny noisily slurped his tea and smoked. When he finished his cigarette, he stretched and walked to the door before flicking the glowing butt in an arch. It landed in the dirt beyond the barrack. It was the same ritual every morning. First, Danny hitched up his trousers as he glanced at the sky. Then he banged his fist against the iron wall and shouted, "Get up you lazy buggers. The day's nearly over."

Mark heard the groans as the rest of the gang roused themselves. One by one, they filtered into the kitchen to sit along the benches flanking the table, some quiet with sleep still clinging to them, some stiff, rubbing liniment into sore muscles. All hungry.

"Where's Finn?" Danny directed the question at Mark.

Mark shrugged. "He'll be out in a minute."

Bert dished up and still Finn had not appeared. Mark got up and went to their room. He kicked the end of Finn's bed.

"Get up—my breakfast's getting cold."

Finn groaned and turned over. "My head hurts."

"Serves you right. You were blind last night!" Mark scowled at his brother's sweat-soaked hair.

Finn struggled upright and fought off the mossie net, pushing it to one side. "Fucking thing." His mouth pursed, and he frowned. "I don't think it's the beer. I reckon I'm coming down with something. I ache everywhere and I'm freezing, but my legs are on fire. I reckon I've got a fever." He placed his palm on his brow. "How do you tell?"

Mark peered at his face. "You look a bit weird. Your eyes look like they've been boiled in Kero. Maybe I should ask Bianca to come round to see you."

At the end of the day, when he returned to the barrack, Mark found a note from Bianca. It said, *I've taken Finn to the hospital, he's very ill. Come as soon as you get home.*

Finn was in a bad way. The doctor thought it was a milder form of Weil's disease. If that was milder, Mark didn't want to see serious. He sent a telegram to his parents. Then he wrote a letter to Beatrice.

They had gone to the pictures last weekend, and she had said she wanted to go to the beach. Mark had explained that the sea here was not like other places. There were crocodiles and deadly jellyfish. It was best to stay out of the water.

She'd just smiled so they arranged to go by ferry on the following weekend. But now Finn was sick, he'd have to beg off. He asked Bianca to deliver the note. At first, she refused, but he wore her down and she eventually agreed.

Every day after work, Mark went straight to the hospital, hoping Finn might have improved. He was in an alcove off the main ward, and mostly Mark just sat next to the bed while his brother alternatively ranted with the fever or lay unconscious and limp like a sweat-beaded rag doll. A faint whiff of rotten eggs exuded from the experimental sulphonamide drugs they were giving him.

Mark took in his sketchbook to while away the time as he waited for his brother to get better. Memories of their childhood filled his mind. Bet you my new ging, you can't hit that hare, the 10-year-old Finn had challenged. But shooting a bolting hare was one of Mark's talents, and he coveted Finn's ging.

Their dad had made it for Finn's 10th birthday. When Mark

asked for one, his dad said he was old enough at 11 almost 12 to have a go at making his own. Mark had tried, but it wasn't as good. His dad promised he'd show him how, but Mark figured he could just have Finn's ging now.

So, he shot the hare with his dad's old .22 rimfire rifle, the bullet going in just beneath the left shoulder blade.

How do you do that? Finn had demanded.

Mark had shrugged and explained it like his father had explained it to him. It's about the breathing. Keep your eye on the spot you want to hit then go long and just ahead of the hare, so he'll run into the bullet. Keep steady and then pull the trigger between inhaling and exhaling. You must stay stock still and adjust for the distance, wind rain and that sort of thing.'

How, Finn had demanded.

Mark had shrugged.

Finn was always restless and on the move. He had no patience for practising things although he was always game for a new adventure, dragging Mark into situations he would not have volunteered for otherwise.

Mark took the sturdy slingshot that Finn held out, feeling the smooth wood of the Y fit firmly in his hand as he pulled back the rubber sling.

Finn had picked up the hare to take home to Mum to cook for dinner, preening unashamedly when later she praised his marksmanship.

Mark had let his brother take the credit, while he placed the slingshot in his drawer. But his ownership hadn't lasted. The next time he went to get the ging it was gone, and he knew Finn had repossessed it. When Mark had complained, Finn had said, Finders keep. Losers weep.

The memory caused Mark's eyes to smart. Finn couldn't die. He blinked and ran a hand over his face. His throat felt tight, and his chest constricted. His mother had told him his real dad had died of some mysterious disease. Not that he remembered, but he couldn't lose Finn as well.

The visitors' bell sounded, and a nurse came in and told him he would have to leave.

Mark tore out the sketch of Finn holding the hare and left it on the table next to his brother's bed.

The nurse said, "He'll be all right, you know." She picked up the sketch. "Oh look, I can see it's him when he was a kid." She glanced up at Mark. "You know the doctor says he'll recover. Your brother's strong and healthy and he got here quickly. So long as the disease stays out of his vital organs, he'll get better."

Mark nodded but didn't trust himself to speak.

A few days later, Mark waited on the station platform with his mum, while his dad retrieved the luggage from the guard's van. He leaned his back against the sun-blasted ticket office wall, and lifted his face, eyes closed, relishing the warmth on his skin. The shriek of a guard's whistle interrupted his reverie.

A small boy, with white-blond hair, ducked between the train couplings to avoid the angry guard. He dashed across the tracks to disappear into the trees at the top of the embankment, a fishing rod, fashioned from a stick, carried over his shoulder like a rifle.

A loaded trolley, heading towards the luggage van, clanked

across the uneven station platform cutting off Mark's view of the kid. The porter pushing the trolley was a squat, swarthy man of middle age. Another immigrant he guessed, newly arrived from Sicily. He glanced down at the man's shoes and saw his boot stitching had been repaired many times.

A woman scuttled after him, carrying a threadbare carpet bag, leaning to one side as if it was heavy. Mark could tell by her clothing she was local. Her mud-splattered boots and legs indicated an early morning walk along unpaved bush roads. Her corset-pink hat and matching jacket blossomed with starbursts of scrubbed grey mould. Lank blonde hair escaped in tendrils that stuck to the grimed sweat on her neck.

She yelled at the porter to wait, and when he appeared not to hear, she shouted, "Oi you! Dago—your ears painted on? Stop, why don't ya!"

Mark's mother sucked in a breath and covered her mouth. Mark straightened. The porter stopped and turned towards the woman in pink.

The Sicilian's nostrils flared white-rimmed, and his jaw clenched.

Mark took a step forward, but his mum placed a hand on his wrist.

"Stay out of it, son."

The pink woman marched up and thrust her chin towards the porter's face.

People stopped to watch. People who moments before had been talking and laughing together, milling about on the platform saying their goodbyes to passengers, had stopped talking and just stared at the porter.

Over by the ticket office, a matron in black widow's weeds voiced a common opinion. "They should all be deported."

The crowds seemed to move closer together, their disapproval hanging in the air above the platform like a malarial miasma.

Mark felt the lava bubble in his stomach expand. Shaking his mother's hand from his arm he strode towards the porter.

The porter glanced across at the station master's furious face, and then slumped and muttered an apology to the pink woman. "Chiedo il vostro perdono, signora." He held out his hand for her carpetbag.

Mark stepped between him and the woman. He took the bag from her hand, staring into her narrowed eyes. "Please, allow me." He grabbed the bag and slung it onto the trolley.

The woman in pink stared back, slack mouthed before she said, "Filthy foreigners."

Mark turned his back on her and said to the porter, "Benevento in Australia, you're very welcome, mate." He shook the man's hand and said, "Non badare all'ignoranza." Then just loud enough for the pink woman to hear, he translated, "Don't mind their ignorance."

The station master was bearing down on them, alarm now written across his face, but Mark's father headed him off by placing his two suitcases into the station master's path before asking, "Can you tell me how to get to the hospital?"

The station master glanced at the porter but stopped to answer Mark's dad's question.

Mark grinned at the porter.

The porter nodded and turned away. His knotted arms reached forward to push the trolley, back muscles tightening to stretch his waistcoat across his shoulders exposing fraying seams.

Mark smiled at the pink woman.

She scowled, turned her back, and flounced off.

He hurried towards his dad and picked up the two suitcases, saying to the station master, "No worries mate, I'll show him."

With his parents following, Mark strode toward the station exit. His dad was still laughing when they arrived at Mark's truck.

His mum scolded. "You should have stayed out of it. You were rude to that woman, and I didn't bring you up to do that. No matter what she did, her wrongdoing does not make your rudeness right."

Mark's eyes grew serious. "Sorry, Mamma."

Rage gnawed at his stomach, but he knew his mother was right. Retaliation wasn't the way to go, not even the politely passive kind. The only way to get these Britishers' respect was power, and in this place, those with power owned land, a lot of land. It was a situation he would find a way to emulate.

When they arrived at the hospital, Mark's parents stood in the spartan white alcove and gazed at Finn with worry etched in their faces.

His dad looked up and gave Mark a bleak smile, but he seemed aged as he sat down by Finn's side and took his hand. It struck Mark that Finn was their dad's only biological offspring. He wondered if that made a difference. Did it even matter?

Finn groaned, and his closed eyes flickered and writhed as if live things squirmed under the lids. His arms had a mottled deep maroon rash as if bad blood congealed under the skin.

His mother brushed Finn's sweat-soaked hair back and bent to kiss his brow. She had tears in her eyes.

Mark felt his throat constrict. "I'll go and find a doctor to talk to you."

At the end of the visitors' hour, Mark walked with his parents down the hospital steps. The sun dipped below the mountain range leaving only a burnt-orange smudge in its wake.

His dad stopped and lit his pipe, striking a match against the rough outside wall. The red phosphorus flared, and he sucked twice in quick succession, sending the sweet smell of Mark's childhood into a thin blue cloud that drifted and spiralled into the air over their heads.

His dad shook out the match and said, "He'll be right. He's a tough lad."

His mother's eyes glistened with restrained tears, and his dad put an arm around her shoulders. "He's a survivor, Gina. Remember the last time."

Her face grew grave. "That was your fault, Erik."

Mark's dad shrugged. "Some have to learn the hard way."

His father was right. Finn never learned his lessons easily. When he was 16, their dad had stumbled on a copper lode while out on a prospecting foray. He had pegged the claim and had taken the opportunity to teach his boys about explosives, showing them how to use ammonium nitrate and fuel oil to blast apart rock. At the last-minute Finn, determined to see their handiwork in action, decided he needed a better vantage point.

He'd got away lightly that time but still ended up in hospital with a burst eardrum from the shock wave, and a cut to his cheek where a rock had bounced up and hit him. The scar on his cheek had faded now and gave him a lopsided smile that women seemed to love.

Mark's parents stayed with Uncle Guido and Aunt Zarah for 10 days, until they knew Finn was out of danger, but it would be weeks before he could leave the hospital. Every evening while Mark sat by his brother's bedside sketching, he jotted thoughts in the margins of his drawings.

Finn was lucky he would recover, but what about the blokes who never did? Or the ones who did and couldn't work again. He wasn't even sure Finn would ever again manage any hard graft. The doctor said it might take months for Finn to recover, and still, they had not won any agreement to compensate the men or declare Weil's an industrial disease.

What could he do to make the industry listen? A steel band tightened around his head, and he got up and walked out of the hospital. They had to do something and maybe Jack was right revolution was the only way to force change.

A month later Finn was discharged, and Mark took him to Aunt Zarah's to recuperate. Then he wrote to Beatrice, apologising for standing her up, and asking her whether she would like to go to Flying Fish Point on the Mandalay ferry.

Foolishly he said he'd bring a picnic, but as the day came closer he wished he hadn't said the bit about the picnic. What the hell did he know about organising picnics? He asked Bianca to help.

She laughed at him in disbelief but then changed her mind. "I tell you what, I'll make the picnic if you take Finn with you. He needs to get out and get some sun on him. He's driving Mamma crazy."

Mark groaned. "It's supposed to be romantic. Not an invalid's outing."

Bianca placed her hands on her hips, her mouth a stubborn line. "Anyway, you can't take a woman like that on a picnic without la dama di compagnia. It would shock your Mamma."

Mark stopped. He didn't think his mother would worry, but Aunt Zarah would. "All right, you come and be Beatrice's chaperone."

"Hah! I must make the picnic, look after your brother, and chaperone your girlfriend. What do I get in exchange?"

"Please Bianca. You'll have my undying gratitude."

"I'll want more than that. But it can wait until you have something worth wanting. Now you have nothing." She grinned at him.

"You're an evil woman." Mark's shoulder's lightened. A trip to the beach with Beatrice was just the thing to take his mind off the worry of the past couple of months and it would be good for Finn to get out and about. He was still as thin as a cane stalk and hadn't yet regained his old vitality.

11. Publication

Beatrice hummed with suppressed excitement. Mr Groom had published her piece on the October federal election for the seat of Herbert, along with statements of each political perspective. Of course, Mr Martens won the seat for Labor and Mr Lyons, who Mr Henry had called a fascist, was returned as Prime Minister.

Next to her piece was a funny caricature of Mr Martens, foot resting on his vanquished opponents, while in the background Mr Henry, as the Pied Piper, danced ahead of the workers, leading them away from Labor's triumph.

The cartoon was signed *Sisyphus,* but it was signed within the drawing not as a byline. She pursed her lips. Sisyphus, according, to Homer's Iliad, was a trickster who receives eternal and repetitive punishment for trying to cheat Death. She would like to meet that cartoonist.

The paper did not give by-lines, but it didn't matter. The story was hers, although like the cartoonist, she had sent it in using a nom de plume: *A View from the Sidelines!* By S. B. Anthony. Beatrice was a great admirer of the American founder of the National Women's Suffrage Association, but she thought the name obscure enough in Australia to be mistaken as just the name of a journalist— a man of course. She hadn't thought of using a name from mythology, but even so, a name wasn't used on her piece.

She replaced the paper on the hall table and hugged herself as she gazed at the copy with pleasure. She was dying for her father to read it and she imagined, when he did, he'd finally realise that she had grown up. She wasn't so naïve as to think he would have an instant change of heart, but perhaps he might begin to see her in a new light. A grown woman with her own mind and her own thoughts.

Things were starting to go so well. Not only did she have her opinion piece published, but Mark's brother was out of the hospital and Mark had asked her on a picnic. All she needed was an excuse to get away for the day, and Bianca had provided the very thing.

When she heard her father arrive, Beatrice went into the hall to meet him. "Hello, Daddy." She held her cheek for his dry peck. Then she drew in a breath and said, "I would like to use my time in a more useful way and thought I might volunteer at the hospital. My friend Bianca ... you remember Bianca, the nursing sister? ... Well, she is taking some invalids for sun therapy at the seaside and asked if I might be available to help. It's the latest thing in health cures, you know."

Her father said, "So I've read." He picked up the newspaper and walked towards the drawing-room. "Let Ida know she can serve afternoon tea, will you?"

After tea, Beatrice held a book on her lap. Aunt Emily embroidered. Uncle George looked through his stamp album and her father read the paper. The room was silent except for the ticking of the grandfather clock out in the hallway.

Suddenly her father exhaled loudly. "Good grief. Why does Groom publish this tripe?"

"What's that, old boy?" Uncle George said.

"It's obscene. Actually, it's seditious."

Beatrice pressed herself into the chair. Was that her article he had read or something else? What had she said that made him so angry?

He handed the paper to Uncle George. "What do you make of that?"

Uncle George read the article and Beatrice held her breath. Then he said, "Bolsheviks have no right to run for the Australian Parliament. Godless heathens. You're right. Spouting equality between men and women and the races is tantamount to inciting insurrection." George paused and then said, "I know Arthur we don't always agree, but I think this is one area where we can work together. You don't live up here, but this menace is getting worse. Personally, I didn't defend the Empire during the Great War so we could have this kind of carry on. It's time we cleared out these Bolsheviks for good. There are nests of them, and they're multiplying. I shall have a word with Groom about what he prints in his papers, but I'd like you to meet some of my like-minded colleagues."

Beatrice placed her hand against the thrashing pulse in her neck. Thank goodness she hadn't used her own name, but why the anger?

It seemed a little extreme. After all, she had just reported on the campaign and mentioned Mr Henry's speech, a pretty mild account without the colour on the street. Perhaps it was the drawing that had so riled her father.

Her father glanced across at her, but she pretended to be absorbed in her book.

Aunt Emily put her embroidery aside and got up. "I shall see how cook is going with dinner."

Her father waited until her aunt left and said, "I'm interested. I'll need to remain in control of the old tiller a while longer, so I will be returning next harvest. If it's all right with you and Emily, I would like to stay on here."

"The cane growers will be delighted. Perhaps it might be an idea to come along to the Brotherhood meetings. That's where much of the real business takes place."

Beatrice's father sounded surprised. "I thought your church didn't approve."

"Oh, I don't know," George said. "It's different in Australia, not like that Semitic lot of Bolsheviks in Europe."

"Not sure if it is, George. That might just be the Spanish newspaper *Acción Española* talking. I read that translated article in Sydney, but I don't agree. Freemasons around the world are very similar to those here and I'm certain there is no Bolshevik or Jewish conspiracy within the Brotherhood, at least not in my neck of the woods."

George said, "Regardless, here we're merely a business community supporting market interests for the good of the Empire. The church has nothing to fear. In fact I told Archbishop James Duhig, not a month ago, it's people like us belonging to these different groups that protect the church. Our concern is for the purity of the nation, and Christianity's safety, first and foremost."

Her father lowered his voice. "It's Australian market security that worries me. If the men demand higher wages or compensation for the disease, we'll no longer be able to compete with sugar from around the world."

"The government will just have to raise tariffs."

"Higher tariffs aren't the answer. Look at the Americans: no sooner had they introduced tariffs than it instigated a Cuban uprising, and then they blamed American tariffs for the Depression. I was to have gone to Cuba next year but who knows what will happen now they have an army sergeant running the place, although he might make it easier for us if it suits him, I suppose."

Uncle George closed his stamp album and got up to replace it in a glass cabinet. "The lower classes seem to think they have a right to seize power whenever the mood takes them. Look at the miners in Spain. I invested heavily in Rio Tinto and with things the way they are, who knows what the Asturias miners will do next. My son Charles said he'd look into it for me, but lord knows what he'll be able to do against one of these so-called Soviet collectives."

Her father nodded. "I too... I plan to make a trip to Spain to sort out some of my investments. Perhaps Charles and I can put our heads together. He knows many of the right people now and of course, there's always my father-in-law's influence." He paused and shot another glance in Beatrice's direction. "Beatrice dear, can you run along and help your aunt."

Beatrice put her book down and walked out of the room, but as she left, she heard her father say, "Much of the investment is backed by Beatrice's endowment..."

Beatrice swung back to the doorway.

Her father glanced at her and said, "Run along then dear."

She frowned. "But you are talking about my inheritance. I want to hear."

"Not really dear. This is men's business and doesn't affect you. Now run along. There's a good girl."

A surge of retaliatory fury remained trapped in her well-mannered throat, and although she dawdled near the door to eavesdrop, there was no more conversation about her inheritance.

Instead, she heard her uncle say, "The Spanish Catholic party's leader, Gil Robles, advocates a response to the Asturias miners in a similar manner to what Chancellor Dollfuss did earlier in the year in Linz and Vienna. I think Australia might learn from such leaders."

Her father replied wryly, "Wasn't Dollfuss murdered for his troubles."

George said. "Ah, but that was for banning Hitler's Nationalist Socialist Party in Austria, not for stamping out the Stalinist socialist uprising.

Her father cleared his throat. "Well, the one thing we must insure against is that these socialists of either calibre don't get elected in Australia. They must not be allowed to gain any more popularity with the common man. Clarrie thinks they're trying to take over the union. That ridiculous caricature in the paper seems to support that point of view. We'll have to do something to discredit these Reds. I shall speak with Howard. Perhaps the intelligence services might come up with something."

So, Sisyphus had captured her father's fears in a few pen strokes. How she wished she had such talent. She walked towards the kitchen, her concerns over her inheritance forgotten as she tried to understand that last bit of the conversation. It was so confusing.

Her father and uncle used the term socialist interchangeably. Yet that couldn't be right because Hitler's national socialist politics were the antithesis of those of the communist socialists. She had thought the Nazis were fascists, similar to Mussolini's Italian Fascism, but Italian Fascism was corporatist not socialist.

She understood British liberal capitalism was a combination of a philosophy of the primacy of the individual along with a set of economic principles, so perhaps all the other isms were understandable by first deciding if they related to philosophical beliefs or economic principles or a combination of the two.

She would need to go to the library and look up the differences. If she wanted to write articles for the newspapers she'd better make sure she understood the concepts and the variances that lay between them.

12. The Picnic

As the year turned, Mark's gang cut out their last field of the season. The monsoon had yet to arrive, and he still had not found a job to get across the slack, or at least nothing that paid a living wage. He decided to take Finn home and work the tin dredge with their dad for a few months. Tin prices were beginning to pick up again.

Finn hadn't fully recovered and wasn't able to do any physical work. Lazing about was driving him, and consequently their Aunt Zarah, crazy. So, going home was most probably the best option.

Javier Cruz had suggested Mark go with him to Brisbane to work in the shoe factory during the off season. You're a sure bet: non-smoker, so no lost production time. The fucking capitalists love that. Javier had grimaced, shrugged, and then taken out his tobacco pouch, adding, maybe it's better to pick fruit at Stanthorpe. At least the farmers don't give a damn what a fellow gets up to so long as he does a fair day's work.

Mark had entertained the idea although he'd never been to Brisbane. In fact, he'd never been outside of the region and while Javier's proposition was tempting, he shook his head. He would have to take Finn home.

Beatrice was going back to Sydney in a week, and Mark had contemplated going too. At least then he might see her, but jobs were still scarce, and he couldn't risk it, not if he wanted to have the money for the farm, and he reckoned he'd found the perfect place, in the foothills up the Palmerston Highway.

On the day before he left Innisfail for his home in Herberton, Mark once again took Beatrice to Flying Fish Point on the Mandalay ferry. He asked Bianca if she would come too, both as a chaperone for Beatrice and to look after Finn, who hadn't let up complaining that Mark was ignoring him since the last time they'd gone to the beach.

When he'd asked Bianca, she'd narrowed her eyes and said, you just want me to make the picnic again.

He'd squinted at her guiltily. Will you?

She had gazed at him for a full minute before replying. I'm keeping a tally on all these favours. Don't think I'll forget. She walked away singing, I'll be a rich woman soon, and you'll be my slave. At the door, she stopped and swung around. Make sure you choose a day I'm not on duty. I am not swapping shifts again to suit your love life.

The day Mark had chosen arrived, and it was as hot as any January day he could remember. A rare cloudless day in the middle of the wet season. The sun scorched the sand to blast-furnace heat, and the wind drove desert air across the Great Dividing Range.

At the beach, Mark and Beatrice left Finn, who was still very weak, with Bianca and the picnic under shady trees, and went off to paddle ankle-deep in the frothy waves. Mark refused to go into deeper water for fear of crocodiles and jellyfish and begged Beatrice not to consider it.

Still, she insisted on lying down in her bathing costume in the shallow water. "To get cool," she said, laughing at his worried frown. "You stand guard and watch for Mr How Kee's monsters."

A few months ago, the newspapers had reported that Mr How Kee had seen something he described as a monster when he was out fishing. There was speculation around the town that it was a Japanese submarine, spying on Australia. No one else had seen anything.

Beatrice joked that Mr How Kee must have visited the opium den in the Chinese quarter before embarking on the fishing expedition.

Mark was sure Mr How Kee hadn't imagined it. He agreed it might have been a Japanese submarine scouting the coast. Just as plausibly, it may have been a floating tree or even a whale, but rumours abounded of an imminent Japanese invasion.

While Beatrice splashed in the warm waters with the sunlit shallows reflecting in her gleeful eyes, he kept watch. It dawned on him that he felt so at ease with her because she seemed to skim across the ocean of life, embracing the wind in her face with the same exuberant abandon as Finn. Except hers was a softer and a more inveigling energy than Finn's hard recklessness.

Whereas Mark turned over and examined every step along life's path. What did that say about him? Did he need responsibility to make him feel useful or was he drawn to their spirit of adventure because his was so tempered by reflection? Finn accused him of dourness. Perhaps his brother was right.

Beatrice's skin soon reddened, so he suggested they take shelter beneath the giant rainforest trees growing beyond the high-water line. They walked further along the beach away from his brother and cousin. Beatrice had brought a small towel, and he laid it down for her to sit on, while he sat on the sand next to her, leaning back on his hands, his legs stretched out.

The sea seethed, its colours graduating from turquoise to a deep and distant purple, while he talked about inconsequential things to avoid telling her he was leaving the next day. Was this the end? He hoped not. She said she would return with her father for the next season but would she? After taking up again with her old crowd in Sydney she might change her mind.

On the horizon a ship sailed south, its twin stacks trailing tendrils of grey smoke stark against the bright sky. Soon, she would be on a deck just like that one, sailing away perhaps forever. He forced away dark thoughts and gauged the incoming tide as it washed waves up the beach, leaving behind salt spume spluttering over the multitude of crustacean burrows.

Beatrice inhaled sharply, jerking him from his melancholy as she said, "I had an article published about the election. Mostly about Jack's campaign."

"Congratulations." Trepidation crawled across his neck. He shook it off and smiled at her. "I wish I'd seen it. How did it go?"

She couldn't be aware of how some people reacted to ideas of Communism. Pagans, barbarians, devil worshipers and other worse things he'd heard Jack called as if atheism was a dirty word. He was used to insults—heard them all his life, although mostly at school about his cultural heritage, but publicly supporting the communists was a different ball of wax and he wished she'd take more care.

She hugged her knees to her chest. "It made my father furious."

Mark frowned. "What did he do?"

Her eyes flickered towards him and away. "Oh, nothing to me. He doesn't know I wrote it. He just ranted at my uncle. I think his anger was stoked more by Sisyphus's cartoon of the Pied Piper that accompanied it."

He hadn't known they had published his drawing. Hopefully there would be a cheque in the mail."

She paused, then with another quick sideways glance she asked, "Do you know who Sisyphus is?"

Mark didn't reply.

She said, "I suspect he's a communist. Are you a communist, Mark?"

He scrutinised her face. "No. I'm not a member but I understand why they believe what they believe, and support some of their goals."

She folded her legs sideways and turned to face him, her eyes full of curiosity. "What goals?"

He pulled in his legs and leaned forward. "I'm committed to equality; I just don't want a violent revolution to achieve it. I don't want to overthrow anyone, but I also don't think the current system is fair."

"What do you mean?"

"Well, the establishment in liberal democracies preach individual meritocracy and tolerance, particularly for other people's beliefs, but then use devious means to coerce people into doing what they want. If you don't do what they want, they make sure you're either discredited or excluded in some way. Merit and tolerance in the capitalist system is only for those who conform to the standards set out by the rich."

He stopped speaking and relaxed his grip on his knees, sliding out his legs to dig his bare feet into the sand, resting back on his elbows before he continued. "In my view, anything that requires coercion or ends up excluding people who hold other beliefs, can't be good." He glanced at her and smiled. "Listen to me philosophising. I sound like Bert banging on about the fascists and the Nazis in Europe."

"No, please. I want to hear what you believe in?"

Political conversations with women were a new experience for Mark and it made him nervous. He toned down the rhetoric. "My dad tells a story about an old mule with a fly on his back. The fly sat there all day, while the mule toiled from sun-up to sun-down and then at the end of the day the fly said, look how hard we worked!"

He gazed at her trying to see beyond the polite curiosity, to gauge whether she was really interested or was humouring him, but she concentrated on piling up sand in an ever-growing mound. He watched the sunlight playing across her face, and wondered why she, who had everything, even cared.

A sharp sound of a branch cracking caused both of them to pause and turn towards the noise. Further along the beach a very large black bird, with a blue head and red neck, stepped out of the forest.

Beatrice inhaled. "What's that?" she whispered.

Mark stood up, but the bird spotted his movement and in terror scrambled back from where it had come, its retreat snapping twigs as it crashed back through the foliage. It was immediately hidden in the shadows.

Mark relaxed and grinned. "It's a cassowary. Like an emu, but from the forests."

"Are they dangerous?"

He sat down again. "They can be. I wouldn't get too close."

"This place is so strange, sometimes I wonder what country I'm in, or if I even belong here."

He nodded. "Do any of us belong here?"

That realisation had niggled all his life, but she interrupted his thoughts.

"That's funny. Birds aren't like us. They don't own things." She shook her head and piled more sand onto her mound.

"Maybe individual ownership is the problem." Mark thought of his desire to own his own farm.

But Beatrice had gone back to their previous conversation. "My father is afraid the communists will start a revolution in Australia." She patted the mound as if shaping it.

Mark frowned. "Did he say that?"

"I heard him talking to my uncle. He said the socialists all over the world are causing trouble and he's afraid there will be bloodshed when they overthrow governments, and the world descends into anarchy." She began to scoop a trench in a circle around the mound of sand. "That would be so unproductive." She said the last bit in a haughty tone and laughed as if mimicking someone.

The mound she was building looked surprisingly like a castle.

He said, "Some form of government is always needed to instil the rule of law, but it also needs to concern itself with equity in distribution. But your father need not worry. Jack says that a socialist revolution doesn't have to be bloody, it can be democratic. He reckons war is a tool of imperialism to expand markets. It's not the communists' preference. Their goal, or at least their stated goal, is to enfranchise all people and redistribute surplus more evenly. Although I am not convinced that is what would occur if they did start a revolution. There are stories coming out of Russia that show Joseph Stalin doesn't practice what Jack preaches. Jack says the stories are western propaganda, but I tend to think anyone who has too much power is bound, eventually, to abuse it."

"No matter if it is democratic or bloody, my father will never give up what he's got, not even for the majority. Anyone who wants it will have to fight him and take it by force."

A smile quivered at his mouth's corners. "You wouldn't want me to fight your father, would you?"

Beatrice pulled her mouth to one side and glanced at him from beneath her eyelashes. "Isn't that what you did with the strike action in Ingham a few months ago?"

He fell silent. How did she know he had been involved at all?

"The thing is you can refuse to work for my father if he won't listen, but it's different for me."

"It's not that easy, but you also have the option to walk away."

She scowled. "But he would cast me out. I'd be destitute or worse, he would have me locked up in an asylum." She shuddered. "Oh! Never mind. Pass me that stick by your foot."

"This one?" He grinned and held up the stick.

She took it from him, stuck it into her sand mound, and sat back. "Do you like my castle?"

He smiled. "Very impressive."

She pushed it over with her feet. "I used to love building castles when I was a kid, but this one wasn't very good. You need a bucket to make a good castle." Then she said, "Is that why Jack said all the different people, like the Italians, and Greeks, and Aborigines and everyone, men, and women, have to work together and support each other?"

The non sequitur threw him, but he thought about how he could answer her question. "Giving people labels is divisive. It forms subgroups of people, who we can blame because they are not one of us. What Jack meant is that first and foremost we are all humans, and in order to make a difference we should stand together as a class to fight injustice. I think it is more complicated. The problem is that a capitalists economic practice seeks to maintain an unemployed buffer, leaving the unemployed, who are only too eager to get a shot at a wage, as a reminder to workers of the fragility of their existence. But in a way Jack is also right. If we don't all stand together they'll find ways to exploit us, laying blame on the victims, such as blaming immigrants for taking peoples jobs. If workers act together they are stronger and can take on the establishment. It's a more equal fight. That's what unions are for, to even out the power balance."

"Like the mule with the fly."

He gazed at her. "Sort of. But all we unionists want is to redress the balance. The thing I like about a liberal democracy is the idea of multiple coexisting beliefs under a banner of tolerance. Communism is a great idea for humanity, but it will never work because it's coercive, favouring one belief, and only one, over all others."

"Like religion."

"If you like. But with liberalism people have to fight for their beliefs, but once those are accepted by a large part of society, liberalism happily folds new beliefs into existing social conventions. Something the government could easily do with their economic principles, ensuring all men have a decent standard of living."

"Huh! What about women?"

"Women as well."

"I really can't imagine my father and uncle accepting your point of view. I think you are fighting a losing battle, and they would never allow women equality." The thought seemed to amuse her for she laughed before she continued. "But I do agree, wealth should be distributed more evenly." She lapsed into silence, a frown forming between her eyes as if deep in some private thoughts.

The sunlight, seeping through the leaves, dappled her skin with its diffused light, and he felt a surge of something soft and alien wash through him. The sand from her broken castle was speckled across her arms and face, and he leaned over to blow some grains from her shoulders, concerned that the glow blooming on her skin would soon turn to blisters.

How his mouth found hers he didn't remember, but he pulled away, stuttering a mutilated apology.

Her smile as she gazed up at him caused a rush of emotion so confusing he had a sudden urge to run. He turned away, blood thrumming in his ears as he stared, unseeing, across the sea. His world narrowed, reduced to an isolated sliver on the wrong side of the gulf that separated them. How on earth had he imagined they could be together?

Her voice broke through his reeling thoughts. "What's wrong?"

He couldn't tell her. He wasn't even sure he knew. This desire was an entirely new sensation, at once a desperation to completely possess, but at the same time a yearning to merge himself with her. Yet it was all overshadowed by the certainty of ensuing retribution once her father found out who she was seeing.

Beatrice sat up and touched his forearm. When he didn't move, she ran her palm up to his shoulder and cupped the back of his neck. It was like the recoil from his dad's Krag-Jørgensen, and suddenly she was on her back, her mouth under his, soft and opening beneath his lips as he tasted her warm eager slipperiness. All his tension and doubt dissolved into the sublime optimistic promise of her mouth.

"Coo-ee, Mark!"

He heard Bianca's voice as if from a distance, and reluctantly broke contact with Beatrice's lips.

Bianca walked towards them. "Be more discreet, you two. A family with children has just arrived. Now, come and have some lunch. Finn won't let me read my book; says he's bored and keeps flicking sand at me."

Mark swallowed to ease the tightness in his throat as he stood up and dusted the sand off his shorts. He glanced at Beatrice, but she hadn't moved, just lay back languidly, smiling up at Bianca.

He held out his hand to pull her up. For a moment, he held her close taking in the smell of her, the softness, the heat from her sunburnt skin, the scent of her hair, and he never again wanted to be anywhere else.

The distant laughter of children brought him to his senses and reluctantly he released her. Beatrice bent to pick up her towel, then she linked her arm with Bianca's and strode off down the beach, the frilled skirt of her bathers flipping and dipping with each step.

Mark followed, admiring the certainty of her long stride. He would have to tell her he was leaving tomorrow and do it soon. He shouldn't have kissed her. Their relationship was dead before it had started.

1935.

13. European Skirmishes

Hans Oster, Deputy Chief of the German Abwehr, ran his hand across his thinning hair before continuing. "At this point I think we can all agree that whatever happens, the Soviets cannot gain further momentum."

Denton leaned forward and picked up his brandy glass, covering his surprise at his companion's confidence. Winston Churchill sat back casually puffing a cigar as if the statement made no difference to him. But Denton knew he was all ears.

The three men were sitting in a small alcove off the club's guest area, where they would remain undisturbed. Outside a winter heatwave carried over the last summer's dryness into the early months of 1935. Roses and daffodils bloomed across England as if spring was already here, and a vase of the flowers sat on a sideboard filling the air with their scent.

Denton had been receiving reports of German rearmament for a while particularly submarine building. Wilhelm Canaris, the new head of the Abwehr, Germany's spy agency, had been involved with secret submarine building for years, first in Japan and more recently in Spain under the cover of the former dictator, Primo de Rivera's so-called New Armada program.

Denton said quietly, "That's a bold move," and with studied nonchalance, he took a small sip of his brandy before glancing across at Winston.

Both of them thought Britain should be taking a tougher stand against these European dictators, and sanctions just weren't going to cut it. You don't stop a bully by giving in to their demands.

To make sure of what Oster was telling them, Denton stated the obvious. "If Adolf Hitler resurrects the Luftwaffe, Germany will be in violation of the Versailles Treaty."

Hans shrugged. "What will Britain do?"

The men sat in silence, each loath to answer. Indeed, what would Britain do? Germany wanted an agreement with Britain but for the past six months, Hitler had been making overtures towards Italy, which Denton was certain had something to do with his plans for annexing Austria.

The question he'd been trying to answer was did the Germans, with their new submarines, also harbour plans for the Mediterranean? Was this some new three-way pact developing between Germany, Italy, and Spain?

If that was the case, it was a grave concern for Britain and for European stability. If this new information about plans for the re-establishment of the German air force and potential conscription, was already underway, it was of even greater concern.

"What is it you expect from us, Hans?" Denton asked.

"At this point, it is simple curiosity, will Britain agree to a British/German navel agreement?"

"You know that plans are being made, so what's really behind this."

Oster sighed. "Some of my colleagues are concerned. Operation Hummingbird and the extrajudicial killing associated with the Röhm Putsch, particularly the assassinations of political competitors such as the former Chancellor, have caused some of my colleagues to reevaluate our positions. Although do not misunderstand my meaning, we are first and foremost loyal Germans, but you will understand there are some activities that cannot be countenanced by a civilised country."

Denton nodded. "Where does Canaris sit with all this?"

Hans smiled. "We have the beginning of an understanding. You realise none of us wants another European war."

Denton had his doubts. Canaris had been an advocate of Hitler's expansionism, and the man was fiercely anti-communist, wanting to build up military strength against any potential Russian designs on Germany's eastern borders.

That he was using Spanish cover for his submarine building activities wasn't a surprise. He was well known in Spain from his time in the German embassy in Madrid. What worried Denton more was that he was also very friendly with people in the British armament firm Vickers, who also had factories in Spain.

Moreover, Vickers had prior form. They had actively pursued an arms race between Britain and Germany before the Great War. What Denton needed to know was, what Spain and Vickers were planning with the Germans, particularly in terms of rearmament and how their plans might impact Britain.

That night Denton decided he needed to visit his old friend Jacobo Fitz-James Stuart, the Duke of Alba, and a well-connected Spanish grandee. It was always better to make such inquiries as unobtrusively as one could. He would pay a visit to White's, or the Marlborough room, where he was sure to find Jacobo. He would know what his government was up to.

Some inner intuition warned Denton that Vickers was already up to its eye teeth in activities he needed to know about. Perhaps he should also revisit the Athenium Club one evening and see if he couldn't have a word with General Sir Herbert Lawrence, the chairman of Vickers.

Vickers, Canaris, and Spain were giving Denton indigestion. He'd recently received a report that the Spanish War Minister, José María Gil Robles, was about to appoint Francisco Franco as head of the army in recognition of his barbaric crackdown on the Asturian miners' rebellion last year.

Gil Robles, Canaris, and Franco were well known to each other and somehow these issues fed into a red flag raised on the sill of Denton's consciousness. He needed to know if the Spanish were planning on re-establishing relations with the German Military and if so, to what purpose.

All these men had one thing in common and would argue for increasing militarisation as a defence against encroaching communism, but Denton wondered if that wasn't just the bogeyman set to frighten the children.

Stalin was having too many of his own problems to look elsewhere, and he feared German rearmament as much as the rest of Europe. He'd recently approved a policy where the Third

International would create popular front coalitions of left-leaning parties as a bulwark against Nazism and Fascism. Perhaps that was the problem. The world's political and social polarising had finally coalesced into solid and opposing shapes.

Denton arrived at his preferred club where he had taken a room. He'd been sleeping there more and more as his domestic situation became untenable. His daughter had not yet returned to Australia, and Denton was worried she never would.

She had taken it into her head to set up a charity to collect for the poor people of Quetta, who had been devastated by an earthquake that had destroyed most of the city. There had been talk of forty thousand dead, but Denton advised her that the 1st Queens Battalion was there to help, and she had a duty to her family.

She shrugged him off with what seemed like a certain evasiveness, and he began to worry that her marriage was seriously in trouble. Then she had gone off with friends to holiday in San Sebastian for weeks, leaving her nephew Charles West to keep a watchful eye on the charity in her absence.

Who she had gone with she didn't say, but Charles was busy with his new job with *The Times* and only called in sporadically? The trouble was, she had made Denton's home the charity's rallying base and function rooms, and his valet had had enough of all the people ringing the doorbell.

Symonds threatened to resign, so Denton had given him leave to go and visit relatives. But now Denton couldn't go home without running into characters, whom he had never previously met and did not wish to know. So, he moved quietly into his club. Domestic issues were, he supposed, why London clubs were still so popular.

He did wonder what his daughter was up to and was tempted to turn to his intelligence resources to find out, but he suppressed such unprincipled thoughts. Besides, if she found him spying on her activities she would never speak to him again, and really Denton didn't want to know if his daughter was having an affair. That was none of his business.

14. Retribution

Mark realised he had been an ignorant dupe thinking he might ever become a cane grower. His dad was right, reckoning the only way you could join their club was to be born into it. The rest was an illusion, a hoax to keep you under the boot, believing that if you worked hard enough you could make it. The great Australian dream was a fantasy. The victory he had felt so nearly within his grasp, snatched away by a lie. It was one history had seen before, and something to which this land had long borne witness.

It all began at sign-on for the 1935 harvest. Mark had arrived back in Innisfail before the new cutting season had started. The sign-on took place at the Goondi Mill, and he stood in the queue with Danny and the rest of the gang as they waited for their turn to sign the Gentleman's Agreement for a new season.

Beneath his feet lay the wounded soil of those who came before.

This land's blood and violence covered by a thin layer of dirt. The native and the slave, never given the status of enfranchised men. The great lie of the imperialists once more exercising power over the immigrant and the worker. He raised his gaze.

Overhead, limp, and empty skins of the night tiger festooned the rafters with their serpentine decorations, shed during the comparative peace of a mill rendered silent during the growing season. Mildew grew on old bagasse mounds scenting the air with the sharp and earthy odour of rotting wood. Weeds sprouted alongside the tram lines. Along the fences, chains of cane beetle shells clung to each other, waving emptily in the breeze. But Mark knew the place would soon be back, a bustling hive of magic that turned a grass stalk into the sweetness that powered the local economy.

He hadn't seen Beatrice since she had left to go back to Sydney. When he'd said goodbye at the end of January, she had lost her usual gregarious charm.

Will you write to me? She'd had tears in her eyes.

He had rubbed his palm across the back of his neck, not knowing how to handle her tears, not even sure he believed in her continuing steadfastness.

And send drawings of your home, she had demanded.

He had taken both her hands in his, and before he knew what he was really saying, he had asked her to go home with him.

She'd given him a sceptical look, but he couldn't say more. What did he have to offer? She had promised she would come back with her father when he returned in May.

Mark had spent the summer thinking long and hard about asking her to marry him. If they were to make a go of life together–

if it wasn't empty promises—he'd have to have more to offer her than the life of a cane cutter.

And now he had and was bursting with the news, which he could hardly wait to tell her. He'd bought a farm up the Palmerston Highway. It was 65 acres, covered with jungle, except for about 20 acres cleared by the former owner. The land boasted a dilapidated shed, which had once served as the family home.

It wasn't much, but it was a start. A season or two in the cane and he could put down a small crop of sugar in the clearing, then build a proper house and clear more land. If his plans worked out, he would ask her to marry him. Except, he didn't know why she would give up her grand life in Sydney to be his wife.

It amazed him when he began to get her letters, almost every other day. He was stunned that she seemed to like him at all, but a relationship couldn't survive if she went back to Sydney again, and he could only see her on rare occasions. He sighed. He couldn't think of that right now. The queue had shortened, and Danny was next up.

The bloke at the sign-on desk said, "Wait up, your gang has foreigners. They need to come back tomorrow."

Danny asked, "Why's that, then?"

Mark scrutinised the cane inspector. The man's ginger moustache drooped like a mangy rat tail across his top lip. He was new, and Mark didn't know him.

"Tomorrow's foreign gang sign-on. Today is just for Britishers." He tapped his finger on the folded newspaper under his freckled forearm. It showed an advert for the sign-on, the same one Mark had seen in Herberton a week before.

Mark heard the warning in Danny's words, although his tone

was reasonable. "You got mates waiting to join a gang then, have you?"

"As a matter of fact, two local blokes with union tickets are looking for work." The inspector aimed his pencil at two men who stood away to the side of the queue.

"Britishers?" Danny asked and rocked back and forth on the balls of his feet.

"Yeah."

"Locals, you say," Danny said looking at the men. "I don't recognise them."

"Well, from Brisbane anyway."

"So, local Queensland Britishers?" Danny's big head nodded slowly as if thinking this over. "Ever cut before?"

"No, but they're keen."

Danny's voice dropped to a deep softness. "So, good blokes who cut all last season and did a damn fine job must back off for Britishers, who have never cut a day in their lives." His tone became harsh. "But want a crack at it. Soft Brisbane boys!"

"Don't rattle your dags, chum. It's the agreement: Britishers first."

Danny's face went red. "A fuckin snagger," he said. "You want the cane cut, or not?"

"Aw, come on chum. Don't be like that," the man said.

"Be like what? Be like I want my gang to work with me, not give some soft coves a go only to be left stranded because they can't hack it after a week. Then what do I do? You'll leave me in the lurch like last year. The only bloke I could find willing was Mark here."

"These men won't let you down. And you can't have two foreigners in your gang when Britishers are available. You've been around long enough to know the rules."

Danny frowned. "Two foreigners, you say. And who are they?"

The man glanced down at his list. "Anders and Manzoni."

Mark's heart sunk. He would have to go back to the tin. He couldn't go back. And there was Beatrice and the farm. "Hang on..."

Danny put his hand on Mark's arm and glared at the man.

Someone called out, "What's the holdup?"

Danny turned the face of Thor on the men in the queue, and they backed off.

Bert looked questioningly at Mark; astonishment written across his usually solemn patrician features.

Danny said, "So!" He rose on the balls of his feet and then settled back. "Mr Anders is a foreigner, is he?"

"That's right mate, according to the Gentleman's Agreement."

"And Dr. Manzoni?"

"Yes, I said so, didn't I."

"So, what about Mr Cruz?" Danny looked at Javier and said, "Sorry mate, got to make a point."

Javier shrugged but fixed his gaze on the man behind the desk.

"No, Mr Cruz is all right. He's an American and fits into the British category."

"So, what about me then?"

"Don't be daft Danny. You're British."

"You think so? But I'm born in Holland."

"Oh, that's all right. Dutch, American, British are the same. All white men."

"So, now you're telling me that a chum, who has lived here all his life just 100 miles from where we stand is foreign, but me and Javier, arriving from overseas as adults, are not."

"Look. I've heard of your gang's reputation and it's a good one, but I didn't make this agreement. I just carryout the rules, and Anders and Manzoni are on the list as Italians and will have to come back tomorrow for the foreign cutters' sign-on."

"Fuck your sign-on, mate. Goondi's loss. My gang goes with me."

"Hang on, don't lose your hat." The inspector stood up. "The rest of your chaps are fine, but we've got to tighten up."

"Fuck that. I'll sign up the gang to Mourilyan Mill. Tell that to the Goondi cane growers. The best gang they ever had, and your stupid rules are going to lose them. Just tell Mr Hudson to shove his sign-on, preferably somewhere the sun don't shine. Come on, boys. We're going."

Mark stepped in, knowing an argument wouldn't help. "Wait Danny. I'll be no different at Mourilyan and we're holding up the line." He pointed at the queue of men, some watching the argument with interest, others trying to ignore it. "Let's sort this out later. You blokes sign on now, and Bert and I will sort something out tomorrow."

As he walked away, Mark felt the lead of failure, saw his farm ownership fading. To imagine anything else was his own conceit: a nose pushed against the glass barricades gazing hopefully through the defences put in place by the rich: subtle and corrupting. Jack was right all along, and he was an idiot.

Later that same day, Mark and Bert waited at the Goondi pub while Danny went to the union office to argue their case. Bert paced up and down the veranda, his footfalls an eternal metronome marking off time.

Mark sat on the bench that ran along the outside wall, trying to remember the contours of Beatrice's face, the shape of her nose, her laughing eyes, her generous mouth alternatively polite and passionate. They had arranged to meet by the river, and he squinted at the sky to see what time it was. He would be late, but perhaps it was foolish even to think of going. He had nothing now to offer and had probably lost the deposit he'd put down on the farm.

Bert stopped pacing and swung around to face Mark. "This is a very strange situation. I'm not sure what to make of it. Fair enough, I must wait until tomorrow, but why you if you are naturalised?"

Mark shook his head. "Shearing chums. No money in wool at the moment."

Bert pursed his mouth. "I've reflected on this and perhaps for me it's an opportunity." He paused for a moment. "I'm well qualified and too old for this job. Zarah has been good to me with the baking job over the last few months and working for Jack on the newsletter translations has been fine. But I need to go back to teaching. To make a career again. What do you think?"

Mark shrugged. "If that's what you want."

Bert said. "I think it is. I will advertise in the newspaper and try for a job as a teacher or tutor somewhere, maybe in Cairns or Townsville, maybe even Brisbane or Melbourne."

"What about the gang?"

"Danny has a good argument for you, but for me, they see me as a foreigner, albeit I have applied for naturalisation as a British subject. You will get in. It was just that man making jobs for his friends. That's why he picked on you."

Danny walked along the road towards them, his shape looming dark against the fading western light. "Good news and bad news," he called, his face held in grim lines. "They've relented on you, Mark, but Bert mate, they won't budge. I spoke to the organiser, and he said the cane inspectors have got orders from the mill to tighten up since the strike in Ingham last year. All the CSR mills are following the agreement to the letter, now. The growers think the communists are trying to take over. Bert, your name was on the list of members, and Mark, the organiser told me the company wants to get rid of you. They reckon the Ingham strike last year was down to you. Anyhow, the union supported you so you're sorted, but Bert, mate, I could do nothing. You'll have to come back tomorrow."

Mark's relief was tinged with concern for Bert, but Bert placed his hand on Mark's shoulder and said, "I am happy for you, my friend." Then he shook Danny by the hand. "Thank you, Danny. You are a good ganger. The best, but my future is not in the cane. I have decided. In the meantime, I continue baking bread for Zarah if she'll have me, and Jack will be pleased I can continue with the district newsletter."

By the time Mark got to the river, he was late by more than an hour and the place was deserted. It was disappointing, but even if she had come, she couldn't have waited. His limbs felt heavy as he climbed back into his truck and drove to Guido's. The day he had looked forward to for months now left a taste of river mud in his mouth. He had a job and should be exuberant, but he was worried about Bert. Despite the ongoing work, he couldn't summon the enthusiasm to join the gang at the pub.

When he walked in through the kitchen door at Guido's Guest House he saw Beatrice sitting at the table with Bianca and Aunt Zarah. They were shelling peas and drinking Uncle Guido's lemon liqueur.

"Beatrice! You're here?"

She jumped up from the table, her cheeks pink. "I waited by the river all afternoon." Her tone was accusing.

Bianca rolled her eyes and said, "Well you might have to wait a bit longer. Jack asked me to tell you Mark, he needs to speak with you urgently."

Mark shook his head, grateful but astonished that she had come to the guest house to find him.

Beatrice slid her hand into his, the soft warmth buoying his flagging spirit after the enervating day's events.

She said, "I'll come with you."

They went next door. Jack was sitting with Bert on the veranda. Both men stood when they saw Beatrice.

Jack said, "Mark. Good to see you mate, and Beatrice, you're back from Sydney. How was it?"

"Lonely. I missed you all." She smiled at Jack and hugged Bert.

Mark shook the men's hands. "Bianca said you had news."

Jack pushed his chair towards Beatrice and then sat down on the doorstep. "You missed the meeting in May, and I just wanted to let you know what happened because you were re-elected as the rank and file delegate in absentia. We need to work together. Do some planning about how we will handle the burning issue this season."

"I don't think I'm much good as delegate. The company won't listen to me. In fact, they are trying to get rid of me."

Jack nodded. "Bert was just bringing me up to date on today's troubles."

Mark squatted on his haunches.

Jack said, "But there's worse. The company's trying to get the court ruling from last year's hearing overthrown. The growers are refusing to burn. We will have to join forces to..." He glanced at Beatrice and ran his palm over his mouth.

"My uncle and father?"

Jack nodded. "Maybe you shouldn't be here, shouldn't listen in."

"No. I want to. I think what my family's doing is wrong. I want to learn more. Maybe I can help."

Mark shook his head at Jack, and said, "You can't go against your family, Beatrice. That's not right either."

Jack changed the subject. "The good news is that Dr Cotter discovered the bacteria causing the rat's disease. It's a particularly bad form of leptospirosis but he's pretty sure burning cane before harvest will kill most of the problem. Although the company blames you for causing the strike in Ingham last year, we must continue the campaign to allow burning as a prevention. They're pushing to extend the Gentleman's Agreement, but that's a ruse to expel immigrants from the industry."

Mark nodded.

Beatrice scowled and took a breath, feeling torn loyalties even as she said, "It's worse than that. My father and my uncle were talking about having the Communist Party outlawed."

The men stared at her.

"How?" Jack asked.

Beatrice shrugged. "While we were in Sydney, I heard Daddy

speaking to his friend Mr Menzies about uniting all the non-labour parties to crush, not only Labor, but also any other workers' parties and the unions. Mr Menzies wants the union controlled and the Communist Party banned completely."

Jack laughed. "He'll have a hard time getting that across. The labour movement is becoming stronger by the day. But I know Menzies. He's the bloke who wants to keep unemployment levels up, which will serve to keep a lid on wages so companies can make more profit. When Ted Theodore said the Government could pay for full employment, Menzies and his cronies shot him down in flames, claiming some rot about inflation."

Mark took Beatrice's hand. He could see the apprehension creased into pleading lines around her eyes. "You need to be careful, Beatrice. It's better if they don't know you have anything to do with this."

Jack said, "Same goes for you, Mark. If Beatrice's father hears about you taking the fight up to his company, bang go your prospects for his daughter's hand."

Beatrice tilted her face towards Mark in astonishment. "Were you planning to consult me?"

Mark had a sudden coughing fit. Damn Jack and his big mouth. The bloke was grinning like a gargoyle. He straightened up and leaned on the veranda railing, staring out into the evening gloom as he recovered his breath. But at that moment he knew he would have to choose which path his life might follow.

Over the next few weeks rumours abounded about the cane growers refusal to allow burning. The union said they were trying to get the matter before the industrial court, but nothing came of it. The more fearful of the disease the men became, the angrier they got. Mark had spent the past weeks after work every evening, speaking with the cutting gangs from different barracks and even catching up with the mill hands when he could.

Goondi men were loyal to their union and despite Jack's pleading that they could take the decision into their own hands, Mark hesitated to go against the union, despite their apparent inability to gain traction with the company or Cane Growers' Association.

He saw Beatrice infrequently but when he was able, they met secretly, usually at Guido's Guest House or at Jack's place. Fear grew in him that, one day, someone would see them together and tell her father. Beatrice smiled at his caution saying she didn't know anyone in Innisfail.

But she did, and more and more people came to recognise the woman who was not only George West's niece, and Arthur Langham's daughter, but was rumoured to be heir to her British grandmother's fortune and was supposedly related to British aristocracy. There was even a write up in the social column of the newspaper about her.

Mark had asked her about that report, but she had shrugged and said it was all an exaggeration and didn't everyone claim some distant relationship with the aristocracy.

Mark shook his head. With the exception of some of his mother's fantasies, he'd never met anyone who claimed to have links with the aristocracy.

Beatrice had laughed and said, and neither do I. But afterwards, she received so many invitations she had less free time than Mark, and he swore she spent more time with Bianca than with him.

Beatrice had taken up volunteering at the hospital. She said it was so she could get away more easily to see him, but Mark also knew Bianca's persuasive powers.

When they did get time together, they discussed plans for the farm, imagining being together freely without hiding from her family. Mark repeatedly wondered at the good fortune that had brought her into his life.

But as the 1935 season's days passed into weeks, his problems intensified and to some extent, it was his own doing. It was as though his life ran along parallels. On one track was Beatrice, and Mark's desire to be an appropriate suitor. On the other, was his duty to the men. Mark needed to see to their wellbeing, and it was the latter track that set Mark on a collision course with Arthur Langham.

15. Industrial Action.

In a shallow oxbow of the North Johnstone River, a weedy paddock was next on the schedule for harvest. The cane was a tangled mess. Cutting it would be fraught with traps, both snakes and rats and even the odd crocodile. Mark recalled the one at Stitts farm last year—15 feet and a stomach full of chook feathers. It took five bullets to kill it.

He glanced at the western sky brooding above the mountains. Forked lightning chased clouds that scuttled across the range bringing columns of rain. The scene was startlingly beautiful, an orchestra of light and shadows, but it was so familiar Mark was only interested in what it meant for the weather. If the rain arrived this morning it would make cutting even harder.

Danny had requested the cane inspector authorise a burn as per the court ruling from last year. The inspector arrived with his shiny knee-high riding boots, solar topee and long gloves protecting him from any possible contact with germs. His cursory glance across the paddock before he shook his head, told Mark how it would be.

He tried to argue but the bloke just scribbled something on his clipboard and said, "Can't see any problems here."

Danny cursed and said, "Any man in my gang gets sick, you'll pay."

After the Inspector's pantomime, Mark realised the company wasn't even trying to take precautions.

Over the next few weeks Mark increased his efforts, asking other cutting gangs to test the system by requesting a burn permit where there seemed good cause. Soon most of the cutters realised the truth.

Mourilyan Mill was the first to down-tools and the mill hands declared the cane black. Weeks passed and the protest spread to the other mills. Tully, South Johnstone and even Hambledon Mill near Cairns stopped work. Mark spoke to the marine workers and the railway workers who agreed to support the strike.

Eventually, he also persuaded the Goondi cutters and mill hands to go out, but it wasn't easy. At the meeting one night, he explained the inspectors were a smokescreen to convince the court the company was doing all it could. As they had seen for themselves, it was impossible to get a permit to burn.

The vote to strike was won by a slim margin but the Goondi men agreed to down-tools and join the other mills in the strike. Yet despite the vote, Mark was horrified to learn that the union refused to acknowledge the men's grievance or their decision and would not countenance the strike.

The following Saturday, Beatrice told Mark her father had been in Clarrie Fallon's ear about the strike being a communist plot to overthrow the union. Clarrie Fallon was the Australian Workers' Union state secretary. Little wonder the union was against the strike.

When Mourilyan Mill downed tools, her father was prepared for the battle and ordered the mill closed. He then ordered all the cane transported to the Goondi Mill, where a group of farmers had volunteered to operate the mill.

She frowned. "My uncle has suggested calling out the Old Guard."

Mark had heard of the Sydney-based fascist outfit called the New Guard, but he'd never heard of an Old Guard.

That night he asked Jack what he knew.

Jack's lips thinned. "They are a secret quasi-military operation sworn to oust communism, sanctioned by the Bruce Government a few years back."

He then told Mark a story about how, in '32 the Old Guard plotted a coup to remove Premier Jack Lang in Sydney, but Governor Game beat them to it, sacking Lang instead. "They carry on about us wanting to overthrow the government, but it was precisely what they were prepared to do. Funny how those who shout loudest are usually the guilty culprits."

Mark became increasingly concerned. "How far do you reckon they'll go to re-establish control?"

Jack put his hand on Mark's shoulder and said, "Mate, they are just dithering old fools, who like playing with guns. Although there are rumours they are funded by the company. But never mind that. Focus on what matters."

What mattered now was the strike.

Despite most of the members voting to down tools and force the industry to allow them to burn, the union continued to refuse to countenance the strike. Without union support, relief was not forthcoming, and with no wages, the men's commitment was a fragile thing.

Mark recalled his earlier brag that if the union wouldn't help, the militant minority group would take it into their own hands. He'd have to make good on that promise but how?

The communists came to his aid. They went about setting up relief committees. Jack's place became the strike headquarters. Beatrice insisted on helping and wrote dozens of begging letters for Mark's signature. Mark spent hours on the phone contacting unions from across Australia. Many promised to send financial support to the rank-and-file strike fund.

Then, the court summoned all the men to a secret ballot.

So, that was to be their strategy; divide and conquer. Mark spent days speaking to members, persuading them not to cave into threats, and to remain solid. After all, this was a fight for their lives. They had to rely on each other for they were pitted against the might of the state, the company, the cane growers, and their own union. This was to be their David and Goliath moment, their Battle of Agincourt.

On the morning they were ordered to attend a quickly convened industrial hearing for a compulsory secret ballot, Mark waited at the southern Innisfail tram stop, opposite the Riverview Hotel.

The day had dawned warm, the sky cloudless and only a light breeze ruffled the palm trees that lined the river. The river water reflected a cerulean sky as it lapped and slapped at the wooden jetty. The only blemish was the sweet smell of sugar that lay in a bitter blanket across the town as volunteer labour manned the mill.

Soon men began arriving by the lorry load. One worker had brought along an accordion, and he played cheerful tunes to pass the time as they waited for the others to arrive. It gave Mark an idea, which he shared with the waiting men.

Once they were all gathered, more than 1000-strong, they raised their homemade protest banners. Mark thrust his sign into the air and in response the men around him wobbled their own banners. Then at Mark's signal the accordion player struck up chords for *The Red Flag*. Voices joined in, and in phalanx formation the men marched on Regent Theatre where the magistrate was to take the ballot.

With each line of the song Mark's determination grew. They came to the junction of Rankin and Edith Streets, but the road was blocked. Khaki-clad police, arms linked and guns at their hips, formed a barrier across the road.

Mark swore under his breath. "What the fuck is this now, a war?" But he sent word through the lines. "No violence, obey the law."

They were on the side of right. Their demands were reasonable, their concerns, not for profit, but for their health and to support invalided men like Finn.

A sergeant shouted at them to surrender their banners, and in silence, the men complied. The accordion player struck up the notes to the old international workers' song, *Solidarity Forever*. Immediately a sergeant confiscated the accordion, glaring at its owner as if daring him to challenge police authority.

Only once all their banners were surrendered did the khaki cordon move aside so they could proceed to Regent Theatre. No one said a word to the police, and Mark felt his chest swell at their discipline.

He took a step forward and thrust his right fists into the air. The men behind him followed suit and marched forward, the tramp, tramp of their boots the only accompaniment.

They stopped in front of the Theatre and Mark raised his voice. "Then raise the scarlet standard high,"

A thousand men's voices joined in. "Beneath its folds we'll live and die!"

The day turned into a minor victory for the workers who refused to submit to a secret ballot, no matter how much the court threatened to fine them. They had to attend by law, but not even the law could force them to vote in a secret ballot. They simply refused to write on the pieces of paper dealt out to each of them.

Eventually, a frustrated magistrate allowed them to leave, and jubilant men gathered at the pubs. Those who still had money shouted others a beer. The publicans knew the men would earn again and gave credit. As the evening drew in, Mark sighed with relief that the day was really over, and all had gone as planned without violence. Yet he also knew this was a minor skirmish.

They still had a long way to go, but he kept his thoughts to himself. Now was the time for the men to celebrate. He found Danny, Javier and Bert smoking and drinking beer in the yellow light that spilled from the Queen's Hotel.

Danny said, "Mate, the bloody union have seriously failed us. They are still refusing to sanction the strike. Even though it's as obvious as a dunny in the desert the members want this."

Mark nodded. "I think it might be Clarrie Fallon stopping the union from supporting us. He doesn't like initiative taken outside his control; demands absolute loyalty or you're finished. But other unions are sending funds, and other sugar regions have pledged support. Money is flowing in from across the country, and we have a fundraiser at the Innisfail Park tomorrow night to collect for the families who are doing it tough. If the industry and union won't do right by the men, the rank and file must."

Danny said, "Fallon doesn't give a toss that the bloody rats' disease is playing Two-Up with our lives. How's Finn doing, Mark?"

"He'll be all right, but he'll never do a day's labour again. He gets puffed out with the slightest effort. Dad's got him into the tin buyer's office, bean-counting for a pittance, and he's not happy." He rolled his head on his neck and winced. "Well, I'm off to get a feed out of my auntie." He nodded at Bert. "You coming, mate?"

Mark turned away and as he did, he heard shouting. A Chinese shopkeeper ran down the street, waving what looked like a heavily carved walking stick.

Mark tried to see what he was running from, but a dray pulled into the road, obscuring his vision. Then Mark saw the child.

A boy, barefoot in britches, clutched something to his chest as he ran. Whatever it was, Mark assumed he had stolen food from the man's store.

Bert pointed and looked at Mark as if for guidance.

"It's nothing, mate." Mark turned to walk in the other direction.

Bert shouted. Mark looked back. The boy dashed onto the road:

into the path of the oncoming dray. The shopkeeper stopped, his face registering horror at the impending collision.

The kid dropped his bundle and stooped to retrieve it.

Mark found himself running. Time slowed. His vision sharpened. Blood pumped through arteries, fuelling muscles. His feet barely touched the ground as he took the 20-yard run in what seemed like half-a-dozen steps. He grabbed the kid's dungaree straps in one hand while the other scooped up the parcel.

Streetlights flared in his peripheral vision, and he ducked sideways as the horses reared, their hooves flailing above his head, their black silhouettes surreal, not of this world, unable to hurt or damage. Or at least for that split second of conscious thought, he was invincible.

The drayman swore and sawed on the reins to control the team, but Mark dashed past before the hooves descended. He dumped the boy on the pavement outside the shuttered newspaper office and took a breath.

It was a moment of supreme and intense exhilaration that he had never felt before. Addictive. Now he knew what his brother sought all his life, and it struck him that for Finn to know he would never again feel so alive, sobered Mark. Perhaps Finn's moaning that his debilitation was worse than death, held some meaning. He would never dismiss his brother again.

The shopkeeper walked carefully towards Mark and the boy; his walking stick lowered.

The boy tugged at his clothing, pulling down his shirt to cover his exposed flank where one strap had given way and his dungarees sagged.

"Now look at what you gone and done." His pale hair and lashes almost luminescent in the streetlight as his face crumpled with concern at his ripped clothing.

Mark noticed the shirt still bore traces of a flour company logo. He knew that for some families this was a Depression necessity when flour bags were all the material a family could afford. The kid looked up at Mark, and even in the poor light, Mark could see the ravages of hunger in his face.

The boy said, "Please mister, can I have my dog?"

Mark looked down with surprise at the squirming bundle in his arms, realising for the first time it was a puppy and a live one at that.

The shopkeeper's face changed from wary to angry. "Not yours. You're a thief!" He glowered at Mark. "That boy stole the dog."

Mark shifted the puppy into the crook of one arm. "How much?"

The shopkeeper tilted his head to one side.

The kid's eyes were intelligent and sharp, his face defiant. "He was going to cook it, mister."

Mark laughed in disbelief and glanced down at the boy to see whether he was joking.

The shopkeeper was indignant. "I buy that one for guarding shop."

Mark said, "Buy another one."

"Five shilling," the shopkeeper said.

"One," Mark said.

The kid said, "Mister, e's a bitser, ain't worth a bob."

Mark ignored the boy and reached into his pocket. "One shilling or forget it."

The shopkeeper shrugged and held up three fingers.

Mark flicked him a florin. "Sorry mate, it's all I have."

The man walked away grumbling.

The kid stretched out his hands, but Mark said, "I bought it. It must belong to me."

"Oi, I stole it." The kid's face expressed indignation.

"Yes, you did. Funny that." Mark paused, gazing at the child. "How will you feed it?"

The boy's stare challenged Mark with its scorn. "Rats, chum. Dog's a good ratter." He said the words as if Mark was a bit slow-witted. "He's an earner."

"Where's your father?"

The kid screwed up his face and stared at Mark. Then he said, "'E's dead. Rat's disease got him. I hate the blighters. That dog can flush 'em out so I can kill 'em with my ging." He pulled it out of his pocket with pride. "My dad made it."

"Your dad was a cutter?" Mark asked.

"Yep, Johno Johannsson. Did you know him?"

Mark shook his head. "No. Sorry. What's your name?"

"Orville," the kid said.

"How do you do, Orville?" He gazed speculatively at the boy, wondering whether this was the son of the man whose place Mark had taken in the gang last year. The Johno who Finn had said they had found running naked down the streets.

He held out his hand. "I'm Mark Anders. Your dad was one of us, so he's entitled to relief. Tell your mother to come to Guido's Guest House and ask for me." He handed the puppy to the boy.

The kid grabbed it, ran down the road and disappeared into an alleyway.

Mark walked back across the road to Bert, wondering what the hell he could do for the boy. He had to do something. The kid was starving. He wished he could think as creatively of an earner, other than killing himself in the cane. If the boy's dad was dead the family had no chance. They'd been left to manage on the proceeds a 10-year-old boy could make from a stolen puppy.

Anger surged through him. Weil's must be made an industrial disease and the families looked after. Maybe Jack would have some idea about what they could do for the Johannsson family.

"You nearly got yourself killed by the horses, comrade," Bert said as Mark joined him.

Mark looked at Bert in surprise. "It's nothing. The kid's an odd one though. Clever little bugger."

Just at that moment a man in a double-breasted grey oxford jacket, striped trousers, a Homburg on his head, walked down the steps from the bank building. He swung an ivory-handled walking cane. His black leather shoes gleamed in the streetlight as the cuffs of his trousers flew back and forth, polishing off the dust as soon as it landed on the patent surface.

"Young man," he hailed Mark. "I saw what you did, saving that child. Commendable."

Mark stopped. "Thank you, sir, but it was nothing." His brain thrashed for the right words. "Mr Langham?"

"You know my name?"

"Yes sir. I know your daughter."

Langham peered at Mark in the dim streetlight. "You look familiar. Have we met?"

Mark didn't think it was a good idea to remind Langham of where they'd met, so he ignored the question. "Miss Langham volunteers at the hospital where my cousin Bianca works."

"Ha! Very good. Yes. Bianca, blonde hair. I've met her. And what do you do, Mr... ?"

Mark glanced at his feet and hesitated. Then he looked Langham in the eye and said, "I have a farm up the Palmerston, Mr Langham."

"A farming man, jolly good. Cane?"

"Not yet sir, but I plan to have a crop in next year."

"Well, good luck then and good evening to you."

Mark stepped closer. "Mr Langham, I was wondering if I might call on Miss Langham one day?'

Langham held up his cane for his driver to bring up his car.

Mark said, "Sir..."

But Langham ignored him and climbed into the vehicle. The chauffeur shut the door and got back into the driver's seat before cruising away.

Mark swore under his breath as he watched the car disappear over the hill.

16. Accusations

Beatrice was on the veranda reading a letter from her mother, who had apparently left London and was on her way to San Sebastian on the Spanish north coast. A surge of envy flooded through her before she remembered that if she hadn't come here with her father, she would not have met Mark.

She really liked him, but seeing him was getting trickier, with all this industrial carry on. She couldn't understand why her father didn't just negotiate a middle ground with the men, but if the other growers were anything like Uncle George, this was more than just the industrial dispute. It was something else altogether.

She laid the letter in her lap and gazed at the garden spread out before her. The outlandish landscape had become familiar to the extent she could now appreciate its beauty. In a little grove, off to the side, lay a pond into which a Grecian-style statue poured water.

Behind the pond was a love seat on the back of which sat a currawong. It was a romantic setting and Beatrice wondered who had built the seat and why. She'd never seen anyone using it other than the currawongs and bush turkeys.

The letter fluttered in the breeze, and she folded it and replaced it in the envelope. It seemed her mother had got herself involved in a charity, collecting money for people on the Indian subcontinent, although she had left day-to-day operations with Cousin Charles. So, going off to San Sebastian seemed a little odd. Then again, work to her mother meant directing others, while she acted the Lady benefactor.

Still, directing a charity made Beatrice quite envious. Her mother had set herself up in a career, and Beatrice wondered why her father didn't object. Perhaps because like volunteering, running a charity wasn't paid work. Yet, it meant her mother had delayed her return to Australia for a while.

Surely, that would make her father complain, but he seemed unphased by his wife's continuing absence. She wondered if they had quarrelled although she had never seen her parents have the slightest squabble. Her mother always seemed to agree with her father, in everything.

It was late afternoon, and a mosquito whined in her ear. She stood up and took a last look around the garden. The air seemed suffused with the sepia glow of a coloured photograph. A shrub, covered with little white flowers, filled the air with its scent. A butterfly, deep emerald and black, zigzagged through the trees. It was larger than her hand. Really, this was the most beautiful place once the immediate sense of strangeness wore off.

A car turned into the driveway. It was Howard. Beatrice pursed her lips. She had been avoiding him, making excuses that she was too busy volunteering at the hospital, even though her duties there, were few.

He took the steps to the veranda in a bound and said, "I'm so pleased you're home."

"I wasn't expecting you."

"No. I'm here about your uncle's report of missing cattle."

"Did you find them?"

"Not yet, but rest assured we will."

"I would have thought that was a regular police matter."

"Depends on who stole them and why, but I have my suspicions."

She led the way to the drawing-room where Uncle George was in the process of mixing sundowners for himself and Arthur.

"Ha! Howard my boy, drink? Not on duty still?"

Howard looked at his watch. "It's after knock-off time, so thank you, I will."

"May I have one, Uncle George?"

Her father frowned. "A small glass only, George, with plenty of soda."

Uncle George handed her a diluted whisky and soda and said, "I've ordered a new vehicle—an American Cadillac. They have all sorts of safety features apparently, so I thought I should give the Americans a try. It should be here any day. When it arrives, your aunt can use the Bentley, and you might make use of her little Morris rather than gadding about on the bicycle. Arthur tells me you're likely to be here a while given all the disturbances. I understand you are volunteering at the hospital. Jolly good show. A motorcar will help."

Howard glanced at Beatrice. "Your uncle is very generous."

She looked down and frowned, wondering whether Aunt Emily was to have some say, but she hid her irritation with a smile. "Thank you Uncle George. With the rain, a bicycle can be very trying, but won't Aunt Emily mind?"

Uncle George looked astonished. "I can't for the life of me imagine why she should."

Beatrice took the whisky and walked over to the French windows.

Howard remained with her father and uncle. He said, "The Cane Grower's position seems to be holding."

Uncle George nodded. "This business does no one any credit. The sooner the men realise how much we all lose by their actions, the better. They seem to give little consideration to the pain and suffering they are causing to the hard-working farmers, and the town's economy."

The electric light flickered, browned, flared, and then steadied.

A scampering sound followed by scraping in the ceiling caused the men to look up.

Howard asked, "Do you have rats?"

Uncle George shook his head. "I wouldn't put it past the communists to cut the power. It's the subversive sort of behaviour they saw in Austria last year." He paused. "Howard, we must know what the government is doing about it. This Bolshevik business can't go unchecked. I guarantee this strike is a prelude to full-blown insurrection. Part of Stalin's globalist plot?"

Howard took a long drink of his whisky before he said, "What can we do? The Party is not outlawed. All my men can do is monitor the situation unless one of them breaks the law."

They break the law of decency by breathing. "Uncle George grimaced. "It's time we banned the blighters."

Beatrice's father walked over to the humidor, took out a cigar and snipped off the end. "The political will is lacking. Too many sympathisers. Would you like a cigar, Howard?"

"Thank you," Howard said, "but what's to sympathise? I must admit I blame the foreigners. I spoke to Inspector Toohill at Ingham. He's convinced the Black Hand is behind much of the trouble. If we'd do more to limit foreigners coming here, we'd have less of a problem."

Uncle George said, "I spoke to the cane growers. They think it's the Bolsheviks stirring up disgruntled illiterates who are angling for easier work for the same money. Burnt cane is so much easier to harvest. What do they care if the sugar content is lower, and the industry loses profits?"

"I think they have a more sinister motive," her father said. "I spoke to Clarrie today, and he thinks it's the communists trying to take over the union at the direction of their headquarters in Sydney. He said they're attempting to undermine union prestige and have hoodwinked the workers into following them. Unless we stop it, I think you're right, George. This could lead to revolution. That's the communist agenda and smaller issues have triggered worse abroad."

Howard smiled at her father. "If it hadn't been your brilliant idea of summoning the men to a meeting with secret ballots, they might have intimidated more men into this strike."

Beatrice cringed at Howard's efforts to ingratiate himself. She'd thought he'd come to see her, but perhaps he visited so often just to get close to her father and uncle.

"Not my idea, but a good one all the same." Her father shook his head. "The company is haemorrhaging money and it's beginning to hurt."

Her uncle said, "I spoke to Bill McKinnon from the chamber today. The businesses in town are complaining. No one's spending, and tourism has hit rock bottom. It's hurting the local economy. I can try to rally the Blackshirts to help with the harvest, but we must organise and arm ourselves in case of insurrection."

Beatrice rolled her eyes. They were discussing the strike as if it was a prelude to a revolution rather than a protest by men who had good reason to complain.

She took a rather large gulp of her whisky, and said, "Wouldn't it be better to speak with the men and try to find a compromise?"

Her father looked at her with astonishment contorting his features, and then he frowned. "It is unbecoming to involve yourself in such matters, Beatrice."

Howard interjected in what seemed like a gallant attempt to change the subject and reassure her father. "The strike can't last much longer. Police are arriving from across the state as we speak."

Her father sighed. "I'm sure you're right, Howard. The company has already arranged volunteer crews from New South Wales. There are hordes of men without jobs desperate to work, even if the strikers aren't. They'll soon be begging for their jobs back."

Howard stroked his thin moustache with a fore finger and said, "Surely, sir, you won't take them back."

Her uncle nodded. "Quite right, my boy. The sooner such troublemakers find it impossible to get work in these parts the sooner they'll go back to where they came from, preferably Italy. They should all be deported. Let Mussolini deal with them."

Howard glanced across at Beatrice. "Trouble is, not all the

strikers are Italian. There are all sorts of nationalities, and many are Britishers."

Her father said, "We must re-employ most, but I understand their ringleaders are being monitored by your men, Howard. The ones you mark will not be re-employed, not anywhere in the industry."

Beatrice stared at her father. "But surely…"

Howard interjected again. "I have one in my sights already." He smiled at Beatrice and then spoke to her father. "He's a friend of the communist leader and one of the principals of the strike. All I need is a bit more evidence and I'll have him."

Beatrice wanted to shout a protest. She had to get away and warn Mark, but she remained silent. If they had any inkling she knew any of the strikers, let alone their leaders, she'd be packed off back to Sydney.

"Good grief. Well, he must be the first to go." Her uncle began to pace. "Howard, we cannot have communists all over the town. I am sworn to protect Australia from this menace. They should be outlawed, banned from coming into the country. Lyons must take decisive action. Howard my boy, any help you need—just ask."

Beatrice gulped the remains of her whisky and pretended an indifference that her racing pulse belied.

Aunt Emily walked into the room, looking flustered. "I'm so sorry to be late. Hello Howard, it's lovely to see you again." She sank down into a chair as if exhausted.

Beatrice peered at her face and took a step closer. "Are you all right, Aunt?"

"I'm fine, dear." But she didn't look fine. Her face was pale, and her eyes were bright and glassy. "I just had rather a fright. George dear, we really must do something about the rats. A giant whitetail just ran across the scullery floor."

Her uncle said, "Yes, yes. The council are dealing with it, but really the whitetail is a native. If we were living in India you'd have to cope with tigers, my dear. The odd rodent is hardly worth troubling about. A drink is what you need." He turned to make her one. "Can I replenish any other glasses?"

Beatrice held up her glass to no avail.

Howard sidled up to her father and said, "José Paronella is hosting a special event to celebrate opening the Park gardens and picture theatre to the public. I wonder if I might have your permission to take Beatrice for a spot of dinner?"

Beatrice shook her head, but her father took no notice, patting Howard on the shoulder and saying, "Certainly my boy. It will do her the power of good to meet some of the local leaders in the region."

17. Arrest.

From early morning until late at night, Mark threw himself into helping the strike cause, distributing leaflets, talking to the men at the unemployment camp near Mourilyan Mill, listening to their fears, suspicions, anger, and frustration, quashing rumours, persuading men not to scab.

He drove out to talk to the small farmers, many of whom had relatives cutting and were concerned for them. Their wives pressed vegetables and eggs on Mark, and one farmer gave him a whole slaughtered bullock, saying it was to support the men.

By the end of his day, Mark's head was full of suggestions and the tray of his truck was full of gifted supplies. He dropped off the supplies at the strike camp, where Bert, with the help of other gang-cooks, had organised a temporary kitchen. Then he went to Guido's where he stayed the night in the bedroom at the end of the veranda, which Aunt Zarah had made up for him.

The next morning, he got up and went in search of coffee. Uncle Guido and Jack lingered in the pergola's shade, a coffee pot between them. Mark thought he had never seen Jack look so grim as he listened to Guido talking about the local Fascista.

Jack said, "The bastards are forming scab gangs using local Blackshirts and some from further afield. A bunch of them arrived from Babinda to join the Innisfail mob this morning, and more scabs are being recruited from across the state, even as far as New South Wales."

Mark knew of the Babinda and Innisfail Fascist clubs. Who didn't? But he wouldn't have believed they would do such a thing as betray their fellow workers. He lifted the pot, poured coffee into a spare cup, and sat down. This was serious.

Jack stared at Mark as if in accusation. "Three of your gang have chucked in the towel."

Mark frowned. "Are you serious? Who? Billy will be one for sure, and I guess Lance and Keith. What about Javier?"

"No, not Javier. In fact, he was thinking of joining the Party." Jack paused, a smile smoothing the creases across his forehead. "He told me that if the union is siding with the bosses on this, what's the point in being a union man, so he signed up." Jack shook his head. "An anarchist joining the Party! Wonders never cease. Still, there is hope for you yet, Mark." His half-smile turned into a full grin and then became serious again. "But you'll need to sort out your gang first. The bosses are using their usual divide and conquer methods."

Mark gulped down his coffee and stood up. "I'll speak to them. I have to go back to the barrack anyhow, to pick up some clean clothes."

Half an hour later, Mark drove along the rutted bush track towards the barracks. When he arrived, he saw a truck parked outside. In front of it was a police van. Three police officers were wrestling with someone.

As Mark drew closer, he recognised the struggling man was Danny. He had his arms stretched out, his massive frame pushing against the van door in resistance.

Danny shouted, "This is illegal. You can't force us out."

"What the hell?" Mark stopped the truck and got out.

One of the officers brought his truncheon down on Danny's fingers, another kicked Danny behind the knees. They pushed him into the van and slammed the door.

Mark hurried over to them, his pulse rate accelerating. "What's going on?"

The constable said, "Move along there."

"Hey. I live here."

"Not anymore you don't. This barrack has been reallocated to a new gang." The constable pointed to five men standing next to the truck, suitcases at their feet.

Mark hadn't noticed them. He'd been too distracted by Danny's arrest. Some of the scabs at least looked uncomfortable but others smirked.

Mark's forehead creased. "Bull. This is our barrack."

A muffled shout came from the van. "The bastards are turfing us out, giving it to scabs and those treacherous turncoats inside."

The constable used his truncheon to bang on the side of the van. "Quiet in there."

Another police officer turned to Mark. "Clear out chum or you'll be joining your mate in a cell."

174

"What's he done?" Mark asked in as mild a voice as he could muster.

"Threatened an officer of the law." The police officer turned back to his men. "Clear the area."

The constable walked back to Mark. "You heard the sergeant, clear off."

"I need to pick up my things." Mark didn't want to antagonise armed police but if he could get inside, he might at least talk reason to his gang.

"There's nothing of yours here." The sergeant walked over with his hand on the sidearm he wore at his belt.

Mark hadn't seen the police wearing arms until this strike and they looked like they were itching to use them, so he maintained his calm exterior. "I need my stuff."

The man thrust his chin forward. "I said clear off, or you'll be my next arrest."

Half an hour later Mark found Javier with a group of men at the Goondi pub and leaned against the bar next to him.

"Ho ho, Mark, where you been?" Javier said. "You missed all the fun on the picket this morning. Some of these Mourilyan boys were almost arrested for standing in the middle of the road, trying to stop the trucks carrying the scabs."

"They've arrested Danny." Mark's voice was flat.

"What for?" Javier stood up.

"And they've kicked us out of the barracks. 'Except for some fucking traitorous leeches.'"

"Who?" Javier downed his beer.

"Mackay, Bannerman and Hewitt of course."

"You're kidding—the bums."

"I can think of better descriptions for that kind of scab," Mark said and pulled himself together. The incident with Danny had left him shaken. "Are there enough men on the pickets?"

"They're arriving in droves. Hey boys," Javier turned to the other men, "time to head back. The bastards have kicked us out of our homes. Now, we need to show 'em we mean business."

The men looked at each other and shrugged. Mark waited for the questions, but none came. Instead, they downed their beers, put on their hats, and turned to leave the pub with Javier in the lead.

"Sort out Danny, Mark. No one will get through the pickets today."

Mark left the bar and drove to each one of the pubs, speaking to the men, telling them about their evictions, recruiting for the pickets and then he drove to Tully looking for Jack. He needed the Communist Party's barrister to help get Danny out."

Jack rang Fred Paterson, who said he'd take care of it.

By the time Mark had finished for the day, the sun had already dropped behind the mountains leaving a blood red smear across the sky. On a whim, he drove to his farm. May as well keep occupied doing something useful while the world imploded around him. At least he had somewhere to live. It was more than the other men had. For some, the barracks was their only home. Where would they go?

The strike dragged on, week after week. Men lived wild in the forests and on the beaches. They built humpies from branches and leaves to keep out the rain. Mark found them living in squalor without sanitation, and in horror, he went in search of Jack and

Party funds.

The men needed organising and together they set about building a strike camp near the unemployment camp. Bert had the communal kitchens going well and Mark organised men to dig latrines, build wash areas and a camp barrack. They added a cooperative to dispense supplies for the families. To keep despair at bay, wives, daughters, grandmothers, and friends banded together to organise entertainment. Beatrice joined in despite Mark's misgivings.

One Saturday they went to an afternoon dance at the Mourilyan Italian Progressive Club. The club was a large community-built structure with a balcony overlooking the street. When they walked in the gramophone was scratching out, *You're Driving me Crazy*.

Men and women swirled clockwise around the hall, some gracefully, some with halting steps. Other men stood around the walls, waiting their turn for a dance partner.

Mark couldn't dance. His mother had tried to teach him but when dancing lessons came up, Mark had always found a way to be too busy. Now, he wished he'd paid attention as he stood, arms hanging by his side, watching Bert lead Bianca effortlessly around the floor.

Javier asked Mark if he minded if Beatrice danced with him.

"Mate, you'll have to ask her."

Javier bowed to Beatrice. "May I have the pleasure?" He held out his hand like some toff.

Beatrice smiled and took it without a glance in Mark's direction. The two of them sailed onto the dance floor.

Mark noticed the way Javier pronounced his name differently when speaking to Beatrice. They all anglicised their names for Australian consumption, but why? In an effort to be accepted but what a joke that was. It would never happen.

He leaned against the wall and folded his arms. The only men who seemed able to dance easily were the older Italian men and a few younger ones like Javier. Most of the Australians stumbled around the floor counting steps and watching their partners' feet, carefully avoiding stomping on delicate toes as women piloted them around the floor.

The men leaning against the walls, waited with a mixture of impatience and nervous humour as they commented on their comrades' technique. A young Yugoslavian mill-hand held an elderly Italian widow, in a black dress, carefully as if she might break.

Grey tendrils escaped the woman's headscarf, and her eyes sparkled like small black diamonds in a face as crumpled as petrified wood. Frowning, she pushed and pulled the mill-hand around the floor.

One of the other waiting men called out, "You're supposed to be dancing chum, not marching."

Mark heard the woman say, "Ignore them, they're jealous you dance with such a beautiful woman."

The Yugoslavian looked startled, and she threw her head back laughing then pushed him away. "Go find a young woman and show her how you can dance. I teach this one." She dragged Mark onto the dance floor. "Let's see how you march then, young Inglese."

He spoke to her in Italian. "Not British, Nonna."

"So, who is your family?"

She plied him with questions, and he tried to respond while he watched her feet. When she had enough information to place him and his family, she spoke of the righteousness of the strike. Her voice held approval and her benediction lifted his burden.

The weight of the strike, the lack of wages, the fear of not being able to feed the men, provide for the women and kids, worrying about what was to come, fury at the company and his concern over Danny, had sapped his energy.

Concentrating on dancing helped push the dread to the back of his mind. In here, the strike seemed so far away, no one appeared concerned, and everyone was included in the party mood.

A commotion at the entrance interrupted Mark's concentration. He turned his head and saw a mob from Tully, all with wives and kids in tow. Cheers went up as they came through the doors. Their Party funds and support had enabled the strike to last this long. Yet communists, anarchists, and union men, Britishers and immigrants, were in it together because they believed the fight was worthwhile.

Mark turned to the woman who was teaching him the dance steps. "I want to ask that woman to dance." He nodded towards Beatrice.

She sniffed. "I'm not beautiful enough for you?"

He gazed at her for a moment. "You are too beautiful for me. You need to find a handsome man. A rich one." He bowed and kissed her hand.

Her laugh was deep and throaty, and her black eyes shone with humour. She marched up to Beatrice and tapped her on the shoulder. Then she whisked Javier away leaving Beatrice standing alone.

Mark stepped into the void. "I can't dance," he said. "Maybe you can teach me."

She smiled. "Dancing's easy, look. Slow." She took a step backwards, and he followed. She took another step back. "Slow, now quick, quick, and ... slow."

The gramophone screeched as someone stopped the record. The dancers slowed and waited, and Mark gazed around as he held Beatrice loosely around the waist. The hall was packed with people chatting, laughing and happy.

The gramophone cranked up again this time playing the introduction to a rousing march. The communists started the singing, but one by one other voices joined in:

Stand up all victims of oppression,
For the tyrants fear your might.
Let racist ignorance be ended,
For respect makes empires fall,

Beatrice elbowed him in his ribs. "Sing,"

"You sing," he said.

"I don't know the words."

Mark joined in. "*So, comrades come rally, For this is the time and place. The international ideal, Unites the human race.*"

He slid his arm around Beatrice's shoulder, and she moved closer to his side. "*Let no one build walls to divide us, Walls of hatred nor walls of stone.*"

His shoulders straightened and buoyed by his comrades he lifted his chin. They could do this. It was right. To hell with the capitalist exploiters. They could really do this, and Beatrice would join them.

But Beatrice had another life to lead, and it was one from which Mark was excluded. After the dance, he could only stand by as she left to go home and change for the party she was to attend with Howard that night.

She said she didn't want to go, didn't have a choice, but Mark felt the weight of brooding prescience as he watched her ride her bicycle along the dusty road towards Sunrise Estate. Rainer had an entry into Beatrice's world that he would never have.

By the time Mark pulled into Guido's driveway, the sun had dropped behind the mountain range. As he got out of the truck, Jack called over the fence.

"Come over and join us."

Mark went inside to tell Zarah he would be next door and then went through the gap in the fence.

Jack sat on a wooden chair, his legs stretched out across the floor, his fingers interlaced across his chest. Uncle Guido, Javier and Bert were with him, and Mark could see they were worried.

When Mark sat down, Jack took a breath and spoke in his slow drawl. "You could lose this one, mate."

Mark shrugged. 'What do you know?"

Javier said angrily. "They've brought in more scabs and the some of the Union men are caving into pressure."

Jack interrupted. "Scabs are a curse but who can blame them for their ignorance. The bosses have honey in their voices and cash in their hands when they want to persuade, and for the unemployed, it's scab or starve. What they don't realise is the scab today is the oppressed of tomorrow, and they will come to rue the day. Our job is not to condemn those with nothing, but to bring them to our side by showing them the truth of their oppression." Jack drew a breath. "I was the same once, until the Party set me straight. Must be seven years ago now, but to my eternal shame, I voted against employing immigrants along with the rest of the union members." He glanced at Mark. "You ever hear about South Johnstone going out in protest at employing immigrants? It was in the late '20s?"

It was before Mark's time, so he shook his head.

Jack continued, "The bosses, and some union men, tell you lies and if you don't know any different you believe those lies. They said the immigrants were stealing our jobs and I foolishly believed it. I was ignorant then, just like those who believe their lies now, but the Party gave me an education. I read at night in my bunk, with a candle balanced in a saucer resting on my chest." He grinned. "Ruined my eyes but it was worth it. Reading opened my mind, but the capitalists are oblivious to the liberalist air they breathe. They are so immersed in the capitalist beliefs they can't see any other way. It's not immigrants who steal our jobs but greed for profit." He took out his handkerchief and blew his nose. Then he said, "The bosses divide us, set us up against each other, black against white, men against women, nationals against immigrants, natives against settlers, employed against unemployed, even Catholics against Protestants and that way they get to stay on top. But one day we'll be ready to stand together, which is what they fear most. When that day comes we will seize our chance and the rules will change. The workers, no matter their stripe, will make those rules."

He looked around at the men, the silence only broken by the cry of a distant nightjar. "But remember, no struggle was ever easy. Win or lose the future owes a debt to the efforts you make now. The kind of society we want for the future depends on what you fight for today. If you lose the battle, we must join together and work harder to win the hearts and minds of the workers, so we live to try another day. The system is unjust and must be changed for the good of all society, not just the rich."

Mark had never heard Jack open up like that before and he hunted for words of support. An image of Beatrice's father flashed into his mind. He pushed it away, agitated. Perhaps Jack was right.

Those bastards were only rich because of the men who worked for them.

He said, "Stop working for them, and we're all equal."

Javier said, "Buddy, that's easier said than done. Men are trickling back like starving mutts with a tail between their legs."

Mark reflected on the fate of workers. He had a farm now. He had the means to walk away once he had a cane crop to harvest, but most of these men had nothing more than what they earned from a six-month season in the cane. Good pay if you could get a job in the slack, but if not, that six months' wages had to cover 12 and you were doomed if you had a family to support.

He took a deep breath and then said the words he'd always tried to avoid. "Maybe you are right Jack. Maybe it is time to abolish the wage system and take over production for everyone's benefit, not just the few. Wages are never the true value of our work, and any profit taken by the bosses from what we have made by the sweat of our labour is theft."

The system was stacked against them, but even so, he'd always wanted to be a part of it. Now he realised he had to make a choice. At school, despite his leaning towards his dad's brand of Fabianism, the nuns had taught him to admire the British Empire's ingenuity. He saw its dominions colouring the atlas in pink and felt a sense of pride in belonging. Yet, it was capitalism that had brought that wealth, but only to some. The rest were plunged into poverty.

Then he was shown how mistaken he was to believe that he belonged. He won the senior scholarship and became a target of resentful retribution. He was the dago upstart who thought he was British, and they soon showed him he wasn't and would never be one of them. In a way, he should be thankful, for the school bullies taught him to fight for what he believed in. He learned the lessons quickly and well. But after that beating, all he could see was that Empire-pink as the gaping maw of the greatest of all bullies, gobbling up the world with a voracious hunger that consumed humanity and could never be sated.

That was when he made the decision to beat them at their own game. He had begun buying tin shares with every penny he earned. On weekends, on holidays and when he left school with his senior certificate, he worked on the dredge. His dad hadn't liked it, but Mark knew that if he was to change anything in this country, he needed power. Then the economy imploded, and his shares became useless pieces of printed paper. Land was a better bet, but even that seemed like an illusion now.

Despondency threatened his determination, and he was torn between wanting to belong and wanting to destroy. Beatrice made him want to belong. But could they ever make it in this world the way it was? Her father wouldn't allow it and anyway, a life like hers couldn't transition to a cane cutter's wife, even a cane cutter with his own crop and a bundle of useless tin shares.

How long before he could afford to keep her in comfort, if ever? She wouldn't know how to live. Her happiness would wither and die like a starved plant. Maybe it was nature. Maybe what she had told him her uncle had said was right, and the classes couldn't mix. He glanced across at Bert, and his own thoughts faded as he noticed his agitation. "What's on your mind, mate?"

Bert took a breath. "Perhaps this is my destiny." He looked at Jack. "I can teach the philosophers at the Party classes on Sundays if that is permissible. I teach Marx and Engels now, but we can broaden that to show all the other ways of seeing the world, including the liberal capitalist way. It is important for people to see and understand the ideology they breathe as if it were natural rather than made."

Jack nodded, and Mark felt a surge of exhilaration. "I'll be there."

Javier said, "Philosophy!" He shook his head and then shrugged. "Can we do it over a beer?"

Two cars pulled up on the road outside the house. Mark walked to the front door. The vehicles had police markings. "Hey Jack, are you expecting trouble?"

Jack joined Mark before turning to Bert. "Can you try and get Fred on the phone. His number's on my desk."

Howard Rainer opened the gate and walked up the pathway, followed by three police officers.

Jack's voice was overtly genial. "Evening Rainer, welcome to my humble abode. I didn't know our relationship was on a calling card basis."

"Perhaps it's not a good idea to rile him," Mark said under his breath.

Howard opened a notebook, stared at it for a minute then said, "Marchio Alessandro Anders." He paused. Then he asked, "Is this your name?"

Mark frowned. "You know it is!"

Jack said, "Alessandro! Give me a moment."

Mark shot back, "And you reckon Clyde is any better?"

Rainer glowered. "You joke, but you won't think it's funny down at the station."

"I don't imagine he'll be joining you at the station," Jack said.

"That's where you are wrong. I have a warrant for his arrest for cattle duffing." He pointed at Mark.

"Cattle duffing!" Mark pursed his mouth. That's the last thing he would imagine they'd try to pin on him.

Rainer's chest expanded. "We have the evidence at the station." He stepped aside for the police officers to handcuff Mark.

As the police officer pushed Mark into a car, Bert came out of the house. "Fred says he will deal with it, but I heard about the cattle. I think I understand the problem."

Rainer paused but he wasn't interested in staying to hear what Bert had to say and ordered the driver to move on.

18. Paronella Park

The Spanish castle at Paronella Park was lit up like a fairy tale. In the foreground, fountains played, and in the background, Mena Creek tumbled over a cliff in a silvery veil of water.

The creek lay south of Innisfail and was named for the training camp of the First Australian Imperial Force heading for Gallipoli in the Great War. Spray from the falls drifted on the mild night air and the sky above glowed with the extravagant band of hazy light from the Milky Way.

Despite her earlier misgivings, Beatrice felt a surge of pleasure and wished only that she could have been there with Mark. She walked into the northern wonderland with her gloved hand resting lightly on Howard's arm. He'd been late and was very apologetic, saying he'd been held up by the arrest of a member of a criminal gang. She wondered if she was supposed to be impressed.

On a dais in the castle gardens, a lone guitarist played *Spanish Romance,* its haunting chords filling the evening air with magic. Fireflies flitted beneath trees, whose branches held aloft glowing Chinese lanterns. People in evening dress strolled in the gardens or stood chatting on the veranda outside the new picture theatre. Waiters moved between the guests with trays of champagne and canapes.

Howard beamed. "I doubt you thought we had anything quite so sophisticated in the north."

Beatrice shook her head. "It's enchanting. I had no idea."

He patted her hand and said, "Come, I want to introduce you to some friends."

Beatrice's heels sank into the soft grass as they walked towards a group of dignitaries clustered on the veranda.

After greetings and formalities were done, Howard handed her a glass of champagne.

His eyes caught hers as he lifted his glass. "Salud!" He turned towards their host. "That's what the Spanish say, isn't it, José?"

She raised her glass and took a sip, gazing out into the bewitching gardens.

A man stepped up to her side and said quietly, "He built all this for love, you know."

Beatrice had already forgotten his name although they had just been introduced. She racked her memory. "Mr Riley?"

He smiled. "Bill, please, Miss Langham. I have the honour of knowing your good father."

She recalled her father mentioning a Riley in relation to the industrial strike and inclined her head in acknowledgement. "Who built this for love?"

"José." He nodded towards their host. "He built it for Margarita's sister, Matilda."

Beatrice frowned and glanced across at José and Margarita. "Isn't Margarita his wife?"

"Hmm, we do not often get our first choice." Riley glanced regretfully at his wife who had collared Howard. It looked like Mrs Riley was complaining about something.

Beatrice took another sip of her wine, and then said in a low voice, "Then I should have no one."

A gong reverberated through the moist evening air. "I think we are summoned for dinner." Riley held out his arm to Beatrice. "May I?"

As they walked into the dining room, Beatrice said, "Daddy mentioned you are involved in the court proceedings in the cutter's dispute."

He glanced at her sharply. "Surely that is of no interest to you?"

"On the contrary, anything that affects my father's business is of interest."

Riley's face coloured. "In my opinion, there is a great deal too much energy given to the braying of donkeys. These militants believe in the froth and bubble of their doctrine more than they do in honest work." He shook his head. "They can deny the truth but the trouble mongers who preach the gospel of this strike cannot make the worker more prosperous." His voice rose. "It's high time that sensible men paid heed to the facts." He paused as if remembering where they were. "Here we are, my dear, you may wish to sit next to my wife." And with that, the man dismissed her.

Beatrice stifled the urge to laugh as she sat down next to his wife. Was she one of the braying donkeys? The sobering truth was that these people would never accept Mark. Their bigotry would never allow them to see his goodness. Could she defy them? Did she have the courage?

A man across the table from her said, "Miss Langham, I had the honour of meeting your father."

Her shoulders slumped. Was every meeting to begin with how people knew her father? The man was dressed in the usual formal dinner jacket and bow tie. He was unremarkable except for his eyes. They seemed to flash with what seemed like anger from behind his thick horn-rimmed glasses.

He said, "Although I am sure he would not say the same thing about me. I think my words were rather heated and I might have phrased my concerns better, but I think the release of Bufo marinus as a biological control for the cane beetle is a mistake. It will be the next cacti invasion, similar to what happened with the rabbits, and it won't work."

Beatrice had no idea what he was talking about and opened her mouth to ask, but Mrs Riley interrupted.

"Really Doctor! This is not the place and Miss Langham is not the one you should approach. Your passion for your beliefs is commendable but needs to be channelled more appropriately perhaps."

The doctor scowled. "They are not beliefs, Mrs Riley. My hypothesis will bear out as evidence accumulates. But my apologies, Miss Langham, I did not mean to assault you with science."

Beatrice glanced from Mrs Riley to the doctor, but smiled at him tentatively, shrugging her shoulders in temporary defeat in the face of protocol. The story could wait, but she admired his forthrightness. Could she ever stand up for her beliefs in the face of such relentless censure? She shuddered at having to confront such judgement as she saw directed by Mrs Riley towards the doctor.

Mrs Riley leaned in closer and spoke, sotto voce behind her fan, "Scientists! Enthusiastic but impractical people with their prophecies of doom." She folded her fan and paused a moment before saying in a more normal voice, "Negativity is so damaging to the economy, don't you think?"

Beatrice said nothing, keeping her eyes firmly fixed on the table in front of her, wishing she had the courage to defy Mrs Riley and interrogate the man.

Later, Beatrice asked Howard what he knew about the release of a beetle-eating toad, but he said he hadn't heard anything about it.

The next day she confronted her father, wanting to know the truth.

But all he said was. "It's done. We will see whether it's a mistake or not. Something must be done to prevent the damage the pest does to the cane. It is costing the mills and the farmers. What would you have us do, ignore the problem, and let the beetles destroy the industry?"

She remembered the scientist's angry eyes. "What will happen if it doesn't work?"

"My word Beatrice! Haven't you something else to occupy your time?"

She lapsed again into silence, wanting to rail at her father, hating him for it, but recognising her refuge and knowing she was to blame. If only she could find an acceptable way to assert herself, without her father accusing her of sounding like a harpy or worse, threatening her with a stay in an asylum.

19. Death

Mark sat on a fixed wooden bench in a brightly lit remand cell. The light came from electric bulbs along a corridor wall opposite the cells. The place stank of vomit and stale body odour.

The constable had said he was lucky it was a quiet night, only the drunk next door to worry him. Mark couldn't see anyone next door because the cells were side by side with a solid wall between them, but he heard a man groan.

He waited until the constable left and then he called, "Are you all right in there."

"Mark, is that you mate?"

"Danny! We were worried about you. Jack rang Patto and he's going to get you out of here."

Mark waited in silence, then Danny groaned again. "Mark my eyes hurt. The light."

Mark stood up and walked to the grill in the door. "What's wrong with your eyes. Did they do something?" Silence. "Danny, speak to me."

Danny groaned again.

Mark shouted for the constable, but no one came. He looked around the cell for something to make a noise but could see nothing. He yelled and tried to shake the cell bars, but they didn't budge. He yelled louder until his voice cracked.

The constable came back. "What's all this racket about? You looking for another charge then?"

"The man in there is sick. He needs help."

"You must think I came in with the tide. He's drunk, vomited all over the place. Call me from my dinner again and you'll be charged with disorderly conduct." The constable slammed the door shut.

Mark yelled and beat the bars, but to no avail.

Danny groaned again.

Mark called out, "Danny what's up with you."

"My head." A few minutes of silence passed, and Danny shouted. "Fire! Fire!"

Mark stood up and sniffed the air but could not smell smoke. "Where's the fire, Danny?"

Danny laughed. "Heads. You bastards! I won. Look—It's fucking King George."

Mark stared at the wall between his cell and Danny's. "What the hell..."

There was a thump and then silence. Mark could get nothing more.

Time passed before Danny spoke again. "It's fucking freezing in here."

"No mate it's hot. I reckon you must have a fever. Try to get some sleep."

Again, there was silence and for a while, Mark was alone with his thoughts. Eventually, he lay down on the hard bench. What was wrong with Danny? How was he to defend against a charge of cattle duffing? What possessed Rainer to charge him with such an outlandish crime?

It was pointless worrying. Head-on confrontations with these bastards didn't work. They held all the trump cards and used their system against you, backed up by flunkies like Rainer. The whole organisation needed a cleanout. Mark's blood began thrumming in his ears, and he breathed deeply through his nose to force calm. Anger wouldn't help him or Danny. He needed to think, but his mind was like damp powder.

He just hoped Fred would figure a way out of this mess for him and Danny. "Are you awake mate?"

Danny didn't answer, so Mark rolled over and tried to sleep.

He awoke the next morning as the door to the cell block opened. A small, gnarled man with mahogany skin, white hair, and sickly-looking yellow corneas came in. The man clutched a tray with two tin mugs and two bowls. He pushed a mug through a small opening.

Mark said, "Thanks mate. Can you tell me how the bloke in there is doing?" He nodded his head towards Danny.

The man shook his head and pushed a plate of porridge through the same space. Then he stepped over to Danny's cell and crouched to place the mug and plate on the floor inside the cell, before scuttling out and locking the door.

"Hey!" Mark yelled, but he was too late. The man had gone. "Danny, Danny, Wake up."

A groan and Danny said, "What?"

"Are you all right mate?"

Danny groaned again, "My fucking legs are killing me."

"Your legs?" Mark shook his head. "Can you get up and eat breakfast? You might feel better."

"Just sleep."

"Righty-oh." Mark took a sip of the cold tea and pulled a face. Then he examined the grey mess that he assumed was porridge, wondering if he could hold out until lunch. He took a mouthful and swallowed it with the tea. The only flavour was of the burnt bottom of the pot. It was sustenance, but one mouthful was enough. Lucky Danny didn't want any.

Mark sat on the bench on which he'd slept and watched the light from a high window track across the wall opposite. Hours passed. Danny slept, and Mark fretted about his powerlessness to help. Finally, he heard a key in the lock. This time Rainer came in with a constable behind him.

Mark jumped up. "Rainer, I never thought I'd be glad to see you, but Danny's sick. You have to get him to the hospital."

Rainer glanced into Danny's cell and then turned to the duty constable. "Why hasn't anyone attended to this man?"

"Sorry, sir. I've just come on duty."

"What's wrong with him?"

The duty officer looked at the book he held. "The previous officer said he was drunk, sir."

Mark said, "He's not drunk. He's got a fever."

Rainer stood looking at Danny for a moment. "Christ, this place stinks!"

The constable looked into Danny's cell and said, "Sorry sir the prisoner seems to have vomited. I'll get someone onto it."

Rainer said, "You'd better call for an ambulance, and you can let this one out." He turned on his heel and left.

Mark didn't stop to find out why he was being released. As soon as his cell door was unlocked, he raced out and looked in at Danny. He was lying curled up on the bench, his face to the wall. Vomit was splattered across the floor, but Danny wasn't moving. He yelled at the constable, "You heard Rainer, get an ambulance."

The constable pulled in his chin and said, "Who are you ordering around. You'd better get out of here before I lock you up again."

Mark waited in the street outside until the ambulance came. Just as it pulled up, a boy walked up to stand beside Mark, his dog at his side. He was dressed in britches with a homemade flour bag shirt. His feet were bare, but his eyes were alert and shone between pale lashes.

"Orville, how are you doing?" Mark bent down and patted the dog. It licked his hand. "Dog's doing well, catch many rats?"

"Plenty. Oh, Mum said to tell you thanks. Mr Henry helped her get a job at the big See Poy's store."

Mark nodded. "The See Poy's are good people."

Just then the ambulance officers brought Danny out on a stretcher.

"What's wrong with him?" the boy asked.

Mark shook his head. "He's ill."

Danny began thrashing about and shouting that he was King George, and the heads could prove it.

Mark took a step towards the ambulance but stopped as Orville said, "My dad looked like that when they took him away. I reckon it's the rat's disease."

It was what Mark feared. He said, "Orville can you find Jack Henry or Bert Manzoni. Tell them I've gone to the hospital with Danny."

Orville nodded and raced off with his dog. The ambulance doors closed, and the van took off. Mark would have to follow on foot. His truck was still parked at Guido's Guest House.

20. All is Lost

The day was already hot. Fat biting flies hovered greedily over any small piece of bare flesh. They were worse in the sunlight and Beatrice kept to the shade as she walked around what appeared to be a deserted camp.

Eventually, she found Bert and Mark dismantling the camp kitchen. The men silently packed supplies into wooden boxes as Beatrice approached.

Mark slapped a fly on his neck before he greeted her, but his eyes told her something was wrong.

"Is everything all right?"

Mark shook his head and went back to packing pots into another box.

Bert glanced at Mark and then said, "Good morning, Beatrice. I'm afraid the strike is over." Bert shrugged and turned back to his task of loading boxes on the back of Mark's truck.

Mark said, "We lost. Tully's still holding out, but the rest are back."

Beatrice glanced from one to the other of the men. "Are you still out?" She reached out to touch Mark but flinched and dropped her hand when she saw the anger in his face.

He turned away and hammered the lid onto the box he had packed. "Sort of." His voice sounded strangled.

"What do you mean?"

"Later, all right. I just need to get this done." Mark walked towards the shed that had acted as a makeshift dining room.

Beatrice watched him go and then turned to Bert. "Is there something else?"

Bert leaned against the tailgate. He took out a tobacco pouch and rolled a cigarette. As he exhaled, he said, "They killed Danny."

Beatrice's hand flew to her mouth. She had only met Danny once, but she knew how Mark revered his ganger. "What happened?"

Bert sucked on his rollie, blew out smoke, and said, "Mark was with him in the cells, accused of stealing your uncle's cattle."

Beatrice inhaled. "But my uncle's cattle were found. No one stole them."

"Rainer raided the camp here. We were roasting a beast one of the farmers had given to Mark. Rainer jumped to conclusions, confiscated the meat, and locked Mark up for the night."

Beatrice stared at Bert in horror. While she was sipping champagne at Paronella Park, Mark was in a prison cell, and it was Howard's doing. "He's treacherous."

Bert nodded. "Mark found Danny in the cells, but he was too late to do anything. Danny died soon after they got him to the hospital. Mark blames himself." He nodded towards Mark. "He's grieving. I told him there was nothing he could have done, but he says he should have tried harder."

Beatrice followed Mark to the shed. "Mark, I'm so sorry. Sorry for Danny." She clutched her reticule to her stomach as if in pain.

His eyes were shard-hard with unshed tears. "The rat's disease got him, just like it will get us all in the end." He walked into the shed.

Beatrice's eyes smarted as she watched him walk away.

Bert called to her. "Let him be. He needs time."

She swung back to Bert. "If the strike's over, why isn't Mark back at work?"

"The company won't have him back. They say he was one of the ringleaders, so he's victimised. But it's not just that."

"What is it?" Beatrice felt the pulse in her neck thrashing, and she took a deep breath. This wasn't about her needs now, but his.

"Revenge." He shrugged. "That policeman friend of yours has Mark in his sights." Bert gazed at her blandly. "Mark said I shouldn't mention it. But you should know. He's just looking for something to charge him with, something that will stick." He took another puff of his cigarette and threw it away. Then he stood upright. "You should go. Leave Mark alone now or both of you will find trouble. You cannot be seen here, or even speaking to him."

Beatrice's eyes filled with tears. "What does Howard know; what can he do?"

Bert shrugged. "I don't know. Bianca's nursing colleague has a brother who is a policeman, and he told her that he'd heard Rainer was coming for Mark."

Beatrice shook her head. She didn't believe Howard could do anything even though she recalled him saying he had one of the strike leaders in his sights. It was bravado to impress her father. Mark hadn't committed any crime, and Howard didn't know anything about her involvement with Mark or he would have said something.

She had met Bianca's friend and could see she had competition. Beatrice shrugged off the warning, imagining Bianca's friend was just jealous, but she also realised the seriousness of the situation Bert and Mark were both in. "Now both of you have no work. What will you do?"

"Mark and I will go into business. I will bake bread, and cakes and make cheeses, hams and sausages and he will grow the food. We have a plan for a providore."

"What's that?"

"A grocery store, but we will stock Italian food."

"But I thought you wanted to teach?"

Bert pursed his lips. "No one wants an Italian academic, it seems."

She watched Bert follow Mark into the shed. They came out with more boxes.

Mark said, "Look, sorry, I'm a bit busy, but we're just about finished. We have to get this done before the police come and confiscate it." He nodded toward the little Morris Minor she had parked under the trees. "Whose car?"

"It's my aunt's. She has another car, so she lent it to me. Now I can go anywhere, anytime." She smiled tentatively.

"How was dinner with Rainer?"

Beatrice screwed up her nose. "That's not fair." She gazed at

Mark for seconds. There was something distant and remote in the way he spoke to her, like a fading apparition in a dream.

21. The Farm.

Even in summer, the stream was cold, and Mark was hot after his morning labour. The clear waters swirled around his shoulders as he swam across the small pool formed by a bend in the creek. Occasionally, his knees brushed underwater debris, but he was pretty certain crocs didn't come this far upstream. All the same, he had watched the pool every day since he had been here and seen nothing but grunter, and jungle perch, along with a few turtles, a platypus, and an eel.

His farm was mostly forested, with only 20 acres cleared by its previous owner before his accident. Mark had bought the place from the widow, who had moved back to family in Adelaide with her children. He'd got it for a good price, although he tried not to think of the other bloke's misfortune as his luck. That was the thin end of the wedge.

A further 45 acres, covered in jungle, backed into the foothills of the range west of Innisfail. The uncleared forest also made the land affordable. He would start small. That was all he could do until he made some money from a crop. But good timber would also bring in cash to pay the mortgage until his crop was ready.

In any case, a small scale would give him time to learn, and he wouldn't risk too much by starting with more than he could handle by himself. It would be a long time before he could employ help, if ever. It would take years to clear the forest by hand and it might be many more before he could afford any mechanical means to help, but it didn't matter. He had the rest of his life to worry about it.

At least the land would provide him with food and shelter if nothing else. The little shop he and Bert had set up was already doing well, so farming wasn't urgent although it would be nice to be able to supply the shop with fresh produce.

Across the stream from where he swam, thick jungle descended to the creek's water line. Occasionally he spotted a large cassowary plying its way along forest corridors. He kept his distance, wouldn't go in that scrub unless he had a compass and an axe, even a cane knife and perhaps the rifle, although in such density the rifle would be almost useless.

Once he thought he saw a man watching him. Afterwards, a rancid smell lingered so he couldn't be sure of what he'd seen. He'd found an old brolga nest near a swampy place downstream so perhaps it was a bird. Although it was said that the old tribes still walked through these forests, moving from the escarpment to the sea depending on the seasons.

How they found their way through that dense jungle amazed him. His mother had her own theories and once said they know because they are the souls of this land. Mark floated on his back staring at the sky, remembering his dad's response.

No, Gina, he'd said, they are not souls, they are men and women like us, just with less power. Anything mystical was anathema to his father.

A couple of months earlier, Mark had gone with Jack to meet some of the local tribespeople. They had a camp just north of the town, which they shared with some of the remaining South Sea Islanders, who had managed to evade deportation in 1908.

Before the White Australia policy, the Islanders had harvested the cane under a policy of indentured labour. Mark thought he and his comrades were badly off but at least they weren't abducted from their homes and brought into slavery, like those poor people. Since the deportation order, scarcely any jobs were available for the South Sea Islanders outside of serving in some white master's house or farm.

The camp's conditions were dire. Houses made from whatever they could find. But slowly, with Jack's encouragement, they too were organising, although they had less to bargain with than the cane cutters.

Yet, Australia's original people were even worse off than the Islanders. Before Mark was born they had been pushed into reserves, like exotic animals. Occasionally, one or two, on good behaviour bonds, were allowed to live outside the reserves, and this camp was where many found a place to call home, even when it might be miles from their homeland.

At the camp, he'd met an old man with snow-white hair, who said his name was Yamani after the rainbow. He told Mark his own family were gone as were most of the Waṟibara people, killed by the Guwuy; ghosts that brought opium, sickness, and bullets.

He told Mark the tale of the explorer, Christie Palmerston, who with his Kanaka servants had slaughtered his grandparents and most of Yamani's tribe when they came down the North Johnstone river from the mountains.

Mark decided he needed to learn the Dyirbal language. He figured that with language came a better understanding and he was certain the language held subtleties ungraspable in English.

He began to visit Yamani at least once a week for language lessons. Then one day Mark arrived at the camp, but Yamani had gone. No one knew where, although they speculated he had been picked up by the police and incarcerated in one of the reserves.

Mark had stomped off in search of Jack. They had to do something. But what? He remained convinced the system needed to change, but any form of power to change the system seemed more and more like a pipe dream. People like Arthur Langham would never allow things to change. It would be a fight all the way.

He might have succeeded in growing his power base if the company hadn't prohibited him from growing and selling cane to the mill. He could have made money quickly with a sugar crop in this capitalist system, and that would have been the start of power. Power to be used for good. But by refusing him a cane quota the bastards would make sure he would never be a challenge.

Perhaps it was better to focus on what he could control. He turned his mind to the plan he had devised for his house. So far, it was two rooms of iron and wood with a small veranda overlooking the creek. Nothing grand but serviceable, and it would grow.

A picture of Beatrice's uncle's house flashed into his mind. It would never be that grand. How could he ask her to share a life in a shack with no running water, no electricity, a fire out the back for cooking, a dunny secluded behind a grove of trees, no bathroom and none of the comforts she was used to?

What had he been thinking, even dreaming they could be together? He rolled onto his stomach and swam back to the bank. When he'd first met her, she'd said all she wanted was to be friends. The rest was his fantasy and he'd thought it had become hers too. Who was he fooling?

Mark collected the eggs and then fed the pigs. The sow was nearing her time and soon would have piglets. The beans and tomatoes he had planted were sprouting. They'd need trellises to climb on, if only he could keep the bush turkeys from scratching them into a heap. He'd fenced off the vegetables to keep out the goats, but he hadn't counted on forest animals. They seemed able to thwart his best defences. He would need to figure out how to solve that problem.

The house held little by way of furniture, a wooden table with two kitchen chairs, a meat-safe and a bed. Mark had made the table, meat-safe and bed frame himself, but the chairs Zarah had given him, along with a mattress and some bedding. It wasn't much, but he didn't need more at the moment.

He broke off some of Bert's ciabatta and spread it with goat cheese. Then he went out to the veranda and sat on the top step to eat. While he chewed, he gazed at the river, thinking about what jobs he should tackle after lunch.

Just as he bit into the last mouthful, he heard a car. Perhaps it was Bert, but he should be at the shop on a Friday. Although Mark wasn't entirely certain about the day as it was so easy to lose track. He got up and walked through to the back of the house.

Across a sloping paddock, where Mark had planted rows of fruit tree cuttings, Beatrice picked her way along the avenue between the lime and lemon saplings.

Mark drew in a breath and ran his hand across his chest. He hadn't expected her to find him. Instead, he'd let time elapse, thinking she would soon forget him, and he'd convinced himself that was for the best. But now as he watched her pick her way down the slope, squinting against the sunlight, red mud clinging to her beige Oxfords, a surge of hope flooded through him.

He said, "I wasn't expecting you. How did you find the place?"

She held up a piece of paper. "Bert drew me a map. I was worried." She frowned and glanced inquiringly at him, but he didn't want to get into a discussion about his weeks of silence.

"Come in," he said, jerking his head towards the house. "I'll show you around." He turned and walked back inside. Beatrice followed but stopped at the door.

Mark glanced at her. "What?"

She looked down at her muddy shoes. "I don't want to bring mud into your house."

He stared at her for a second and then laughed. "You think a bit of mud is a problem. Come in."

She bent and took off her shoes and then stepped into the room in her white ankle socks. "Oh," she gazed around at the tiny space, the rough-hewn walls, the table, and chairs. "What's through here?"

The bed was rumpled and looked as though someone had just got out of it. In one corner hung two white cotton shirts and his old moleskin trousers. Below was a shelf with a couple of pairs of fraying shorts and two work shirts. Piled on the floor were books.

She bent to examine the titles, reading each aloud: "*The Ragged-Trousered Philanthropists; Capital: A Critique of Political Economy; Ten Days That Shook the World; An Introduction to Philosophy.*

She pulled a face, then picked a pamphlet off another pile, her eyes scanning the page. "You have terrible taste in literature." She wrinkled her nose. "Is there a kitchen?"

"Outside." He realised he knew very little about her, and she him. Yet, there was so much to know.

"Where? Can I see it?" She stepped over to the window.

He waved his hand to encompass the outside. "Sure, look around, it's wherever you want it to be." He wanted her to see the unvarnished truth of his life and wasn't going to promise anything. Perhaps she would come to see how impossible it all was.

She ran her fingers across the rectangular window frames, pressing the tips against the wire mesh covering.

He couldn't afford glass yet and the wire kept the bigger bats, birds, and snakes at bay, but he didn't want to explain. It would sound like an apology, and he was not going to apologise for his life.

"There's a lot of skill here," she said as her fingers ran along the polished wood sill. "I have no useful skills. I sometimes worry that if another war came and civilisation was lost, I would not survive, but you would."

"What?" Mark peered into her face to see whether she was serious. "Of course, you would survive or as well as anyone can in war." What he didn't say was that the rich do better at surviving than the poor in any circumstances, civilised or not.

She turned to stare out the window opening. "My family are all equally incapable of doing anything for themselves. Uncle George gives instructions to his overseer and then reads the newspapers. Or he goes to the Returned Soldiers' rooms to drink whisky and read the newspapers or play billiards. He goes to the races and stud farms to look for new horses to breed, but he has never in his entire life lifted a finger to make anything or to grow food other than cash crops like sugar. If it wasn't for his money he wouldn't know how to survive. Daddy's no better."

It was as though she spoke to herself. He watched her perplexed, not knowing what to say.

She shook her head and said, "Your house is amazing. I didn't know you were so accomplished at making things."

And then with what seemed to Mark like a complete non sequitur, she said, "I spoke to Bianca about nursing ..."

He nodded. "That's a useful skill."

"Yes, but I'm not sure I have the stomach for it. I don't mind volunteering. All I do is roll bandages, but actual nursing is rather daunting. Bianca suggested it, and it's the only way I can think of to remain here. I spoke to Daddy, and he's agreed I can give it a try when we come back."

Mark frowned. "Are you leaving again?"

Beatrice pulled a face and took his hand. "We're going to Europe to bring Mummy home, but I am here now. Let's not be miserable, please."

She stepped onto the veranda and gazed toward the creek. "Oh, Mark it's beautiful."

He followed her out, still trying to get his head around all she had said and was surprised by her enthusiasm. "The house?"

She grinned at him. "Well, the house is all right. It's very well built, I think. Not that I know about things like that, but I can learn. And it's dry. It's a bit smaller than I'm used to." She wrinkled her nose. "But enough for two people I suppose although it's a bit basic. Never mind, the rest will come." She exhaled. "But the view's perfect. Can we go down to the stream? Do you swim in it? What about the farm? Can I see that also? I'll put on my shoes."

She ducked back into the house and walked to the back door where she retrieved her shoes. She carried them back to the veranda and sat on the steps to put them on, gazing at the river and the forest beyond as she tied the laces.

For several seconds he stared at her, trying to fathom her meaning, and then he started laughing. He laughed until he had to sit on the step next to her. It released all the tension from the past months and now he had started he couldn't stop.

The laughter turned in on itself and Danny's death reared up in ambush, pushing him back into a pit of anger at the company's callousness towards his ganger's death, and their refusal to allow Mark back in his gang.

He put his forehead on his crossed arms to hide the tears in his eyes and sat in silence with only the echoes of his laughter howling around his head. Beatrice would think he'd gone crazy. He lifted his head and ran his forearm across his eyes.

She took his face in her hands and kissed him. For long seconds he remained frozen, then she slid her hands from his face to his chest and around his waist. Her mouth was soft against his, her smell familiar and warm and his resolve tumbled.

To hell with it, and he gave in to the pressure of her lips. His arms surrounded her and the void in his gut closed. Then he was kissing her with a desperate ferocity, unable to bear the thought of letting her go.

She leaned back slowly until she lay on the veranda floor and her hands ran down his spine, tracing the muscles in his back, down to his shorts, her fingers slipping beneath his waistband.

He stopped kissing her and raised his head to look into her eyes. "I spoke to your father."

"What!" She sat up; her face screwed up in alarm.

"I asked him if I could call on you with Bianca. I just haven't had time to organise anything since."

"He didn't say anything."

"Perhaps he was busy. We've all been a bit busy, but he thinks I'm just a farmer." He smiled at her. "And now I am—just a farmer that is."

⊱⎯⎯⎯⊰

The next day, buoyant with enthusiasm, Beatrice drove Emily's car to Mark's farm with only the occasional jerk and shudder. She was really getting the hang of driving now. She wore her oldest clothes and a straw hat.

Mark laughed when she told him. "They'll be ruined."

"It doesn't matter, they're old."

He insisted on giving her a pair of his shorts and a shirt but had to hunt out a bit of rope to hold them up.

"I'll drown," she said, laughing up at him.

Mark showed her how to clean and size eggs for the little shop Bert ran in the town.

She helped him feed the pigs, and watched as he milked the lactating goats, and then at her insistence, he left her weeding the vegetable garden, while he began to fence the top paddock. By the time he called a halt for lunch, she wasn't sure it had been a very good idea. She was hot and sore. Her arms, thighs and back ached with the unaccustomed labour. Her hands were raw and cut from pulling weeds and her nails broken. She looked at her hands ruefully. "I should have brought gloves."

She followed Mark to a pool at the bend in the creek. He sluiced his hands and splashed water on his face. Beatrice groaned as she squatted next to him; every bit of her body hurt.

He looked at her, his face furrowed, but she merely smiled and toppled sideways into the water, stretching out her arms and legs to keep afloat in the soothing current. The water smelled like tea leaves.

Mark stood up grinning, took off his boots and shirt, and slid into the pool. He untied her laces and pulled off her shoes, chucking them to the bank, followed by her socks. "It's hard work."

She felt his hands under her back, keeping her afloat. "Not for you though and you've done five times as much as I have. Sorry, I'm not much help."

"You'll get used to it." He looked stricken and hastened to add, "I mean, that's if you want to."

She pouted. "Are you certain I'll get used to it. I didn't know I had so many muscles that could hurt in my body."

He leaned over and kissed her wet mouth and she curled towards him, wrapping her legs around his waist. They stayed in the water motionless, mouths locked together as sticks and leaves swirled and eddied around them.

Eventually, Mark broke off and said, "Come, you need to get out of those wet clothes."

At the bank, he helped her out and picked up her shoes and socks. They squelched back to the house dripping water. He gave her a small threadbare towel to dry herself and left her alone.

Beatrice stripped off and wrapped the towel around her.

Mark came back in through the door and without looking at her, picked up her wet things, and walked out to hang them on the veranda rails.

She followed, watching as he hung up the shorts and shirt and even her underwear. She was embarrassed as he hung up her knickers and brassiere, but he seemed unconcerned.

He turned to look at her. "You'll want to put on your dress," he said.

Rebellion ran through her, and she raised her arms. The towel slipped. She wriggled, and it fell to the floor.

He stared, and Beatrice felt her face growing hot. What was she thinking? He'd think her brazen. She bent to pick up the towel, wondering at the madness that possessed her.

"You're beautiful."

She looked into his face and saw the emotion she longed to see. The towel remained where she dropped it. Her eyes never left his face as his hands rested gently on her hips, palms rough and calloused, searing into her skin. She gazed into his eyes, tawny and uncertain, but beneath, something unfathomable, ephemeral.

"What?"

He shook his head, a small slight jerk sideways. "You should go inside and dress, or we might do something you will come to regret."

Was he rejecting her? She stood still.

His hands remained on her hips.

Time froze as damp breezes played across her skin making tiny goosebumps. She watched the wind ruffling through his hair, whipping it against his forehead. Behind him, clouds raced across the purpling sky, casting moving shadows across the paddocks.

He broke the spell as he glanced at the sky. "Looks like rain." The edge of his wet shorts touched her naked thigh.

She shivered. "You should take off your wet clothes."

He dropped his hands from her hips and took a step back.

The space between them grew into a vast and impassable chasm and she wished she'd said nothing.

A fat droplet of rain hit the dirt pathway next to the veranda steps. Dust spurted in a tiny volcanic eruption followed by another and another. The smell of rain and damp dust filled her senses.

"Come, you're cold." He picked up the towel and held it out to her as if she'd dropped it by accident.

"No! I want to run naked in the rain." She walked down the steps and turned to him. "Are you coming?"

He unbuckled his shorts and followed her. Rain pelted down, drumming on the tin roof, stinging Beatrice's bare flesh and she ran back up the steps onto the veranda.

He closed the gap, his hands sliding around her waist as he pulled her towards him. Her cold skin squished against his warmth.

Roaring sounded in her ears, dulling the rattling rain. The world faded, except the feel of his skin, the shape of his mouth, the smell of tea leaves from the river water dripping from his hair. Time slowed and then stopped moving to become one with the shape of their bodies; teeth so close to her lips, she touched them with her tongue and a bubbling frenzy coursed through her veins.

He murmured into her mouth, "Are you sure?"

She nodded and took his hand, leading him to the bedroom

where she lay down on his bed and smiled up at him. "Come here."

His body crushed hers, the warmth of him absorbing her chill, his mouth soft on hers, becoming more demanding as it moved down her throat.

She lay on the bed as if in a dream, feeling his mouth, his hands touching, exploring, moving, tenderly, gently until with a surge of desire she pulled him to her.

Later, Beatrice opened her eyes, seeing long shadows outside the window. The whole afternoon had disappeared. She sat up looking for her petticoat, skirt, and blouse.

Mark went out and came back with her underwear, and socks, stained red with mud.

"They're not dry." He said as he tossed her fine white lawn knickers and little pointy cupped brassiere onto the bed. "Your shoes are still wet, so I left them on the veranda."

She blushed and looked away from her underwear, muttering, "They'll be dry by the time I get home." Then a thought struck her. "We didn't get all the work done."

He grinned. "It's not going anywhere, and we have the rest of our lives." He took her in his arms. "I won't always be poor, Beatrice. One day I will have enough and then we can be married."

"Don't spoil it, Mark."

"Why? I'll speak to your father."

"No!" She softened her voice. "No, Mark he can't know about us. He'll … you don't know him …"

"He'll see reason. I have land. I have a partnership in a shop."

"It's not that."

"What is it then?" His eyes darkened. "Because my family are not British?"

She shook her head.

Mark said, "I'm a naturalised British subject. I want you to meet my parents. Your father will understand if he meets my father."

Beatrice said, "Not yet, oh God. I don't know ... Please let's just leave it for a while before you do anything. I'm scared he'll do something terrible."

Mark's face was grim. "What can he do?"

"Please, Mark."

"Beatrice, doesn't what we did mean something?"

"Yes." She could feel her eyes prickling and she sniffed. "Mark I want to, but I'm afraid."

"Of what?"

"You don't know my father." She stared at him silently remembering the woman with her children, begging at the quayside in Bombay.

Beatrice was six years old, and didn't understand what she was seeing, just that it was horrifying. Her father had explained destitution to her and how she should give thanks that she would never have to face such penury. She had nightmares for weeks afterwards.

"But we have to tell him at some point."

"Yes, if I am nursing, I will be in the nursing quarters away from him. It'll be easier. Then, so long as I am independent and earning my own money, he won't have any say in what I do, or who I see."

22. Spanish Manoeuvring.

The sky hung low over London as Charles West made his way along Pall Mall towards Bury Street in Mayfair to meet with Lady Margaret. She was his aunt by marriage to his mother's brother, but he had always found it difficult to call her that. Everyone referred to her as Lady Margaret and Charles preferred to do so too. There was an air about her that brooked no familiarity, regardless of family relationships.

He assumed he was summoned to meet her over the charity she had set up. He had run it in her absence and written an article on the good work it was doing. A difficult task given it hadn't been doing much other than begging for money. The article had helped with that, particularly with raising funds for the Quetta earthquake victims. The best thing about being involved was that she was happy for him to claim expenses. Volunteering was all very laudable, but it didn't contribute to life's costs and Charles had a penchant for the finer things in life.

Streetlights flickered a feeble glow against the dark winter evening. It was now past the hour when workers clogged the streets as they rushed for the tubes and busses home, and the quiet streets allowed a gentle amble, swinging his carved ebony-handled umbrella of which, he was rather proud.

When he arrived at the restaurant, Lady Margaret was already seated at a table with another man. Charles handed his hat, coat, and umbrella to the man at the door and sauntered over to the table. Lady Margaret introduced him to Sir Auckland Geddes.

Charles had heard of Geddes, should have recognised him immediately of course. The man had a formidable reputation, professor of medicine, a Brigadier General in the Great War, a Member of Parliament for Basingstoke, and one-time British Ambassador to the United States. He was currently the Chairman of the Rio Tinto Company and Charles wondered why he had been summoned to a meeting with the man.

Charles sat down carefully and arranged his trouser creases. A waiter hovered at the table to take their orders as Charles took the time to glance through the menu, glad he was not paying for this.

When the waiter left, Lady Margaret said, "Charles dear, I spoke to Sir Auckland about your new role with *The Times* and he was happy to grant you an interview regarding his fears for Spain."

Charles blinked. An interview with Geddes. He hadn't thought that particularly newsworthy in this era of European manoeuvring, but he'd go along for whatever ride Lady Margaret had chosen. He had nothing else on and the food in this place looked superb. He relaxed and looked at Geddes.

Geddes drew a breath and said, "What would you like to know."

"Anything you care to talk about sir. Perhaps start with what's top of mind for you at the moment."

Geddes fiddled with a knife on the table before saying, "I suppose my most pressing concerns are Rio Tinto's interests in Spain."

"Go on." Charles took a pencil and notebook from his pocket.

"Well, since the deposition of King Alfonso XIII in 1931 the Republic has faced ongoing turmoil and unrest, particularly after the last election which was disputed by both sides and resulted in an anarchist rebellion with the takeover of Asturias in 1934. You recall the bloodshed."

"That was Franco and his Moroccan troops..."

"Yes. He put an end to the uprising. Unfortunately, it was a pretty bloody affair."

"So, is there more.

Geddes nodded. "Since then, there have been constant attacks and counter attacks in the countryside, which makes doing business difficult. I fear civil war."

Charles raised his eyebrow. "That's rather extreme. I know landowners have been expelling workers from their land and there are claims of starvation, but disposed people usually don't have the means to wage war. Besides, hasn't President Alcalá-Zamora called for new elections to put an end to the disputes?"

"He has."

"But you are still worried."

"Even more so I am afraid. Manuel Azaña has put together what they are calling a *Popular Front*. It is a coalition of liberals, socialists, and anarchists and I fear they will take the election from the conservatives."

"I see..."

"I am not sure you do. We have had nothing but strikes and general unrest and I fear for the country if this *Popular Front* gets in. The socialists and anarchists are in the ascendency calling for increases in workers 'rights, social and economic reform, and land redistribution. They want to break up and redistribute land held by the aristocracy. The church is under threat. Your aunt tells me you are a good Catholic."

Charles nodded. He was a Catholic although not a very pious one, he admitted. Still, it was a club to which he belonged, and supporting one's clubs was a sacred duty.

"Convents and church buildings have been set on fire as are other places linked to the establishment, and to which the leftists take exception. Political assassinations become more frequent and there is some fear, warranted I must add, of a communist takeover. I fear the country will implode."

Charles jotted down a note. "And that will hurt your business interests..."

"Yes, but it's more than that. The British hold a lot of the foreign investment in Spain, mostly in metallurgy, but also in agriculture, manufacturing, and telephonic systems. Last year London bought one fifth of all Spanish exports and it is a similar story with France and America. Together they own upward of 70 percent of all foreign capital in Spain."

"I see." Charles again scribbled in his notebook.

Geddes looked around before saying, "Well, I must be off."

Charles covered his mouth with his hand. That was a bit abrupt. What the hell was going on? "You're not staying for dinner sir."

"Unfortunately, I have another engagement, but it has been a pleasure to meet you young man. Your Aunt mentioned you are working at *The Times*. I hope they are treating you well."

"Yes, very." Charles stood up.

"You get along with your editor?"

"We are great pals." Charles smiled wryly at the thought of Dawson even noticing he worked for the newspaper.

After Geddes had taken his leave, Charles sat down again and turned to his aunt. "That was an interesting diversion Lady Margaret."

"Darling, you may call me Aunt. At least in private. And you would never have been able to interview Geddes if it hadn't been for my introduction."

"Of course, I am grateful, although Spain is really not my bag." Charles smiled, wondering if he would find out what this meeting was all about. Lady Margaret didn't strike him as someone who would do something for nothing.

Margaret said, "I think it is time it became your... bag. Your father may have mentioned that my husband Arthur has decided he and Beatrice will come to England in the next few weeks."

Charles nodded, and she hurried on. "Your father has asked Arthur to look into some business interests we share."

"Yes Father wrote saying he wanted me to take more of an interest in the family's finances. But he didn't say more. Said Uncle Arthur would explain when he got here."

She nodded and placed her hand on his arm. "The thing is, although Arthur will be flying across from Australia to Egypt, it will be some time before he is back in London, so he has asked that I speak with you." She paused and examined his face before continuing. "It is rather urgent, which is why I asked you to come and meet with Sir Auckland, so that you would understand the position our two families are in."

Charles waited, supposing she would get to the point eventually.

The dinner arrived and while the waiter poured wine Charles glanced around at the other guests. This was a pretty posh place. Not one he could afford to eat at on his wage, not even with the allowance his father gave him.

When the waiter had gone, Lady Margaret took a sip of her wine. "Now dear. We have a proposition to put to you."

By the end of dinner, Charles understood the financial predicament his uncle was in and his father's own concerns. Hell, they were his concerns too. The family money was in jeopardy, but his uncle's financial dealings were more serious still. Uncle Arthur had found himself a little exposed, both legally and financially, for he'd borrowed heavily against Beatrice's trust to finance his shares. No wonder Lady Margaret had brought Geddes in.

Charles gazed at his aunt speculatively. 'What is Geddes role in this.'

Margaret pursed her lips. "Our financial interests align. Our two families collective investments make up a very large percentage of Rio interests in Spain. While I was over there, I made some very well connected alliances. It appears that some of the more enlightened leaders in the country are becoming increasingly concerned over the direction the Republic is going. I am not a Catholic, but I am a monarchist and the two factions of conservative Spain have aligned with a view to the overthrow of the Republican government."

"Via the forthcoming elections?"

"Certainly." Margaret dabbed at her lips with a napkin. "But if that is not possible by whatever means necessary."

"Interesting. A Spanish coup d'état."

Lady Margaret tapped his arm. "Don't be vulgar Charles. That sort of thing may be of interest to a newspaper man, but it is in nobody's financial interest."

"What are they planning then?"

"They are creating a coalition of conservatives in the hope they will win the election."

"And if they do not?"

"There will be chaos. The anarchists and socialist will slaughter the leaders of the establishment in the streets. The military will have to step in to retore order."

"Is that not a coup?"

Lady Margaret glared at Charles. "Don't be difficult."

Charles raised his eyebrows. "So, what does this have to do with me?"

"We need you to smooth the way in the British public's mind that a military takeover in Spain is the only option. An event of good, triumphing over evil. The British ambassador to Spain is a close personal friend. I could give you a letter of introduction. You may want to interview him. He also entertains many of the Grandees and so on, who are worried about Spain's future. I understand some of his diplomatic staff are calling the situation in Spain similar to that in Russia before the Bolshevik revolution."

"Oh, come now, surely not." Charles examined her face. "What does Lord Denton think of all this. Isn't he a British diplomat?"

Lady Margaret frowned. "Tread warily Charles. I only repeat what I have been told. But you are correct. My father is a British civil servant and therefore, should not be privy to our discussions." She pushed her plate away, the food barely touched, and glanced at him. "Arthur assured me that your father has guaranteed your discretion in these matters, or I would not be speaking to you. I hope you are not going to let me down. Perhaps I should rethink your role on the board of the charity, which is also now heavily invested in Sir Auckland's ventures."

Charles smiled in reassurance. "You have my word Lady Margaret."

"Good. Now I suggest you join the Anglo-German Fellowship. I am friendly with Violet Astor, your proprietor's wife, and while I am not acquainted with your editor Geffrey Dawson I understand he is a member of the Anglo-German Fellowship. If you join it will allow you to gain his ear. I will also introduce you to some of the other members who will ensure you are accepted."

Margaret smiled at him. "You see my darling, your little newspaper could do a lot to ensure the British do not intervene in any efforts by the military to reestablish law and order in a country which has certainly lost its way. If the British take the lead, others will follow." She looked around again. "Be a dear and order champagne. We have something to celebrate."

1936

23. A Letter

Christmas passed, and the New Year ushered in 1936. In January Mark saw Jack off on the tram to Mourilyan Harbour from where he took a ship to the Torres Strait without fanfare. Aside from a few of the Party men, hardly anyone knew he had gone. Then came news of the Torres Strait strike.

The Communist Party weekly newspaper headlines called the Islanders' treatment *Terrorism against Aborigines* and said that the Islanders were pressing for actual payment for their labour rather than credit in the Government-sponsored stores of the Aborigines Industries Board.

It was nothing more than slavery, and the Party's 9th District could not stand by and see their fellow workers oppressed without doing something. Mark called on the union members to donate financial support for their comrades while they were on strike, just as the communists had supported them.

King George V died, and his son succeeded to the throne as Edward VIII, but Mark was more concerned with the weather than the lives of kings. The rains arrived in torrents, gushing off Mark's roof, filling the dam to overflowing, eroding, and overflowing the creek's banks. The farm was on relatively high ground, so the run-off was rapid, but the creek swelled and swallowed up the slope of land below his house.

For a while, he expected it to swamp him, but the flood stopped yards below where the new house stood. Water inundated his vegetable garden, but the animals were safe. It rained so hard that he had little to do other than to look after their welfare.

While the rain fell, Mark sanded back a large slab of rainforest timber he had selected to make a writing desk for Beatrice. Sweat ran down his sides and he took off his shirt. He checked the sketch he'd made from a magazine picture she'd shown him, and the measurements he'd chosen to suit her frame. It must be perfect for her when she came back, whenever that might be.

She had been gone for four weeks, leaving by train for Brisbane, from where she told him they were to take an Imperial Airways flight to Cairo. It was the modern thing to do, she had said, but he wasn't so sure.

He had never travelled in an aeroplane, and they didn't look safe. She insisted it was so much better than taking a ship. The aeroplane would only take 11 days, all going well, and they would stop at so many exotic places. She had listed them but Mark either had never heard of them or couldn't remember the names, except for Singapore and Cairo. Her eyes had glistened with the adventure of seeing the great pyramids as well as seeing her mother again.

Then Mussolini invaded Abyssinia as a means to extend Italy's colonial holdings. It was a grandiose attempt at returning Italy to Rome's past imperial glory. Egypt was just next door and Mark fretted about Beatrice stopping in Cairo.

Then Jack came back from the Torres Strait and threw a party to celebrate the Spanish election of a popular front government. But by March a growing cloud had appeared on Europe's horizon as Germany marched unchecked into the Rhineland, and the British and French did nothing.

Beatrice was now in danger anywhere in Europe and still, he had not heard from her. If he didn't receive a letter soon... Well, he didn't know what to think. He wasn't even sure how long a letter would take to arrive.

He ran his hand over the wood grain of the desk. It was almost finished. The weeks of rain had given him more time to work on it, and it now looked almost like the finished product in the magazine A surge of longing swept through him, and all the while he feared for her safety. He left the desk along with his thoughts and roused himself to attend to the animals.

The rain persisted and more weeks went by with Innisfail cut off by floodwaters. Trains became marooned in the station and the mail didn't arrive. Then the rain cleared. The earth baked, and fat flies tormented the dairy cows, the goats, and the pigs.

Easter came and went, but Mark spent most of his time on the farm, only going into town once a week for the mail and supplies and to the occasional business meeting with Bert.

Then towards the end of May, a letter arrived. Mark waited until he was home before he read it. He sat on his veranda in the amber glow of late afternoon and ripped open the bulging envelope.

Excelsior Hotel
Askanischen Platz
Berlin
Germany.

My Dearest,

I miss you so much although every day has been terribly busy, with sightseeing and travel, I feel quite worn out. I have taken so long to write to you because I am barely left on my own for a minute. Tonight, I begged off with a headache as Daddy and Mummy have gone to a celebration. It's Herr Hitler's birthday, and everywhere we travel through Berlin we see great red banners and flags flown in his honour. Berlin also gets ready for the Olympic Games and no expense is spared.

Oh, and tell Bert that when we were in Rome, I saw Mr Mussolini in a parade celebrating his success against poor King Selassie of Abyssinia. The man is really very excitable (Mussolini that is) and quite ridiculous as he stood in his car all puffed up. He reminded me of your rooster crowing on the fence post, but Grandfather says the League of Nations are not happy and will institute sanctions against Italy.

We were supposed to go to Spain in March but as you will have heard, a Popular Front government was elected, and rumblings of trouble have created headlines in the newspapers ever since.

Daddy says he will go by himself to Madrid for he has some business interests to sort out, but he says it is not safe for me and Mummy. Although I think he exaggerates because I heard that Barcelona will hold an alternative to the Berlin Olympic games, as a protest against Herr Hitler's new Germany.

We go to Paris next, and I will get to see the famous Eiffel Tower. I thought Jack might like to hear that the Soviet Union had signed a treaty with France promising mutual assistance in case of invasion, although when Germany crossed into the Rhineland nothing happened.

Daddy says the left leanings of the Soviets and the French are making them unnecessarily paranoid about Germany. You would have been proud of me because I told him leftists weren't any more paranoid than rightists, and we had a silly argument, so he's not speaking to me.

Anyway, he's off to Madrid and Mummy thinks we must go home, so it's back to London and then to Sydney. Mummy refuses to fly so we must take a ship home through the Suez Canal, which she says glows at night like multitudes of phosphorescent fairies. I looked it up in the library and the glow comes from minute plankton-like creatures disturbed by the ship's wake, like King Neptune's fireflies.

I didn't tell you that in Cairo, I rode on a camel when we went to see the pyramids. It was ever so scary, and the beast smelled worse than your goats. My camel had a great fat lolling tongue that seemed to turn upside down in his mouth. But the pyramids are amazing, rising up in pagan worship of the sun, which reflects off the surface leaving mysterious shadows to soften and disguise the edges of their massive flanks.

The trip along the Nile was lovely although a little tedious with so many English people on board. They ignored the sights to play bridge, drink gallons of gin, and were terrific snobs. They called Daddy a colonial behind his back as if this was somehow disparaging.

I did like the Cairo bazaars and the children who clutch your hand and drag you into their grandfather's shops, trying to persuade you to buy, buy, buy, so much stuff and all so exotic. I can't begin to describe it: the smells, spices, and dare I say, the sewers. Dear me, I have so much to tell you, but it will have to wait until I see you in November. I can hardly wait. It seems so far away.

Yours forever B.

Mark stared at the letter trying to see the world through her eyes. She had seen and done so much it was overwhelming. How could she want to come back here with his smelly goats? He smiled at the thought of her riding on a camel, but he was torn between fear and longing. He needed to make more money so he could give her that kind of life. It was impossible. She should just forget him, but he didn't want that either. He was ready to do anything but not lose her. His life wouldn't be worth living without her.

Could the farm make enough? He had no idea. The bakery and providore were doing well. At a business meeting back in March, Bert had suggested they buy one of the new espresso machines for making coffee. They would sell a cup of coffee and a slice of cake to the office workers and civil servants.

They can sit outside at café tables on the pavement, Bert had said.

Zarah had interrupted the discussion with her usual scornful expression. Boh! They won't sit outside, not them. Anyway, they all drink tea or that filtered cows' piss they call coffee.

But Bert had argued, saying more and more Britishers had

developed a taste for coffee taken in the European way.

To prevent an argument from Zarah, Uncle Guido sent Mark next door to bring Jack over for his opinion about whether Britishers would drink espresso.

Jack had settled the argument saying, well, you know how much I like the stuff, and I heard espresso is all the rage in Melbourne and Sydney, why not Innisfail?

So, it was agreed, and the machine was ordered. By May the little shop had become too small for the crush of people who frequented the place and Bert was now looking for larger premises.

Mark refocused on the letter in his hand. At least the business side of his life was panning out, thanks to Bert's baking skills and his good business sense. He went inside to the writing bureau. It gleamed with beeswax, and he ran his palm over the smooth brown and golden grain of the Queensland maple. He pushed a panel back and opened the secret drawer he had hidden inside the bureau where he now laid the letter. Then he went outside to milk the dairy herd.

24. A Christmas Party

The late November evening breeze was damp after an earlier rainstorm, and Beatrice pulled her silk shawl around her shoulders as she walked among the guests. Vehicles filled Sunrise's long circular driveway, and tiny bats flittered in and out from under the house eaves.

Groups of people stood around in their finest. Men sweated in dinner jackets as women preened in silk or chiffon georgette, their perfumes merging with the scent of garden flowers. Politicians strolled along pathways; their heads bent as they listened to barons of industry complain about the economy. Beatrice inhaled the tropical air, glad to be back once more. She found her father and mother with Aunt Emily and Howard.

Her mother's face had the startled look of an indignant rooster as she said, "Did you know that our own government is planning to provide some form of Christmas cheer to the jobless this year? When did it become the government's role to interfere in charity? It's that kind of lackadaisical attitude that encourages brazen behaviour." She paused and then added, "just like that dreadful American woman."

The non sequitur caused her Aunt to frown, but Beatrice knew her mother was back on her favourite topic bemoaning the King's adoration of Mrs Wallis Simpson.

Beatrice felt an affinity with the poor woman, who was forbidden love. She stared thoughtfully across the garden, wondering why people were expected to pair only with those like themselves. Surely that wasn't necessary or even good for the world.

The sun slipped behind the range casting long shadows across the land. Chinese lanterns flickered in the trees, linked by long loops of red and green crepe paper. A large Christmas tree stood in pride of place in the centre of the lawn and glittered with silvery baubles and pretend snow. It was all so jolly.

Beatrice's cheeks still glowed with memories of her reunion with Mark two days before. She longed to go back to the farm instead of listening to her mother going on about Cousin Charles and his work with *The London Times*. She supposed Aunt Emily would want to hear about her son although anyone listening would think Charles was Margaret's child.

Her mother called her, "Beatrice dear, run along and see where your uncle might have got to with my martini." She turned back to Aunt Emily. "One should really keep champagne for dinner, don't you think?"

Beatrice felt sorry for her aunt under the onslaught of her mother's snobbery.

Her aunt's cheeks grew pink as she looked into her glass of champagne. "What's wrong with champagne before dinner?"

Her mother rolled her eyes at Beatrice's father who was standing next to Howard.

Her father frowned. "Apparently, champagne with dinner is de rigueur with Her Majesty, Queen Mary," he said to his sister.

Beatrice turned away, wishing her mother wasn't so mean and that her father would stand up for Aunt Emily occasionally. She walked up the steps to the veranda as her Uncle George came out of the house with a martini in hand. She followed him back to the group.

Her father and Howard had moved a few paces away and were deep in conversation. After her uncle handed the martini to her mother, he stepped over to join them and said, "Gentlemen, raise your glasses to a quick Carlist victory."

The men raised their glasses and her father said, "I've heard word that Germany and Italy have recognised the Spanish Nationalist government under General Franco, and his troops have Madrid under siege."

Her uncle pressed his lips together. "Thank the good Lord. Our investments are saved. It won't be long now before the antichrist heathen are chased into the sea. May they rot in hell for their treatment of the church and her servants!" He paused, then raised his glass once again. "To the annihilation of communism and the continuing prosperity of Rio Tinto."

The men raised their glasses. "Annihilation of communism," they murmured.

Howard said, "There's still the small matter of Russia."

Her father rubbed his chin. "In my opinion, Spain is just the beginning. Germany will see to Russia; you mark my words."

Her uncle waved his cigar in the air. "Said the same thing myself. The scourge must be wiped out everywhere. Australia can no longer tolerate it. Something must be done to outlaw all communist sympathies."

"Hear, hear." Howard raised his glass.

Her father clinked his glass against Howard's glass. "I must say I was impressed with Germany when we visited."

Two other women joined her mother and aunt, and Beatrice took a step back into the shadows. She wanted to hear more of the men's conversation.

Just then Howard said, "I do like the idea of a corporate state."

Beatrice took a step towards them. How could they think Mussolini's corporate state or Nazi Germany were good things? Didn't they know what was happening in Italy and Germany?

Before she could say anything Howard said, "Excuse me, gentlemen," and stepped towards her. "Can I refresh your drink, Beatrice?" He took her empty glass.

Beatrice walked with him toward the house. "What were you and Daddy discussing?"

"Oh, nothing to bother your pretty head over."

She bit back fury and looked down at her feet.

Howard said, "Some friends are having a small soiree tomorrow night. Would you do me the honour of accompanying me?"

Beatrice shook her head, glad to have an excuse. "I have arranged to go along to a fundraising event and lecture tomorrow."

"Ah well, another evening perhaps. It's so good to see you back, my dear. I have missed you. Your father says you have enrolled to begin nursing training at the hospital in Innisfail."

Beatrice nodded.

"I admit I was a little surprised, although of course delighted. I take it there is something keeping you here, rather than going back to Sydney?"

He looked sly and Beatrice sighed. It was her Uncle George who had hit on the idea that she wanted to stay here because of Howard and Beatrice hadn't corrected him. But the omission had turned into a lie, from which she could find no escape.

25. A Film Night

Mark sat on the top step of the veranda of Innisfail's Communist Party headquarters. Bert sat next to him, smoking a thin cheroot. Music drifted from somewhere across the neighbourhood.

The smell of tobacco made Mark think of his dad, and the twinge of nostalgia took him by surprise. He should go home for a visit. The last time he'd seen his family was when he took Finn home. He would take Beatrice to meet his mum and dad and let them know this was the woman he was going to marry.

On the veranda and in the garden, men and women chatted, some leaning against tree trunks, others perched on whatever seating they found. The night was cool after the rain, but it brought out a dusk raid of mosquitoes from the creek nearby.

Mark slapped the back of his neck as Jack came out of the house and sat on the step next to him.

"Mate, I need a favour," Jack said. "Can you take around the hat after the film, for the Spanish Relief. I don't want people thinking we are collecting for the Party..."

Mark nodded.

Bert said, "Bad business, this war in Spain,"

Jack nodded. "It's only the beginning unless we can do something to stop it. The fascists are gaining the upper hand and Australia is no help. They remain in lockstep with Britain again."

"I heard Ernesto's volunteered to join the Spanish Republican Army." Mark didn't know what to think about that. War! Someone he knew was going to fight in a war. It seemed so far removed from anything real, something belonging only to Dad and Bert's generation, a distant irrational thing that old people talked about.

Jack nodded. "He's determined. Can't dissuade him."

Mark said, "Do you think we should go, Jack? The people ..."

Bert interrupted. "War's no good." He turned to face Mark. "You are too young to remember." He paused, then he said slowly, "I too was once idealistic although much younger than you—only 17 years old, but I believed fervently in the rational man. I saw how reason had brought the machine, epitomising an optimism for a future never before seen by the world." He paused and frowned. "It was the most exciting time, but I found man is not rational. Instead of hope, his greed brought war. The machine turned to beast of slaughter, striking life from humanity like a plague." He took a breath and waggled his finger from side to side. "Now, we must retrieve the social man, focus on the collective endeavour of humanity. Not as a return to the superstitions of the past, nor in a quest for the purely rational, but to make the future a better place for all humankind, a future without killing, poverty and injustice." He stopped speaking and stared into the night.

Mark was surprised at Bert's impassioned speech. He knew Bert had driven ambulances during the war, somewhere up near Italy's Austrian border. He participated in the Battle of Caporetto, which alone saw 11,000 Italians killed. Bert might be vehemently opposed to any form of war, regardless of what it was about, but Mark wasn't satisfied. The Spanish war was different.

He said, "But this is about democracy, isn't it? The Spanish people voted for Azaña. Then a bunch of generals come along with an army and say the people are wrong. We should kill them. Imagine if that happened here. We'd want help, but no one seems to give a shit about that."

Bert glanced at Mark as if he hadn't understood. "No one wins except the capitalists, especially those who make the armaments. It's not Australia's war. You should stay right here, Mark. You have a business and Beatrice to care about."

Jack intervened. "I think each man can do only what he thinks is right. And it's a fight against fascism so it's a good fight. But I reckon if Spain can persuade Stalin to step in, they'll be all right."

Mark wasn't ready to concede. "Defending a democracy of the people against the designs of imperialism is always a good fight. The position of governments like Australia is bull. That bastard in Canberra secretly supports the imperialist insurgents."

Bert glanced at Jack, and in a modified tone he said, "This makes you angry, Mark, but you must think with your brain, not with your heart."

"Hell! It makes me angry with both." A rush of energy ran up Mark's spine, but he could see he was causing Bert some concern.

He composed his face into blandness as he stared into the shadowy yard, but inside the anger grew.

Jack said with his usual mild calm, "A few blokes are thinking of going along with Ernesto, but we need money and passports. It's not easy. The government won't sanction Australians taking part in the war. *The Movement against War and Fascism* has raised money to send nurses and an ambulance, but we need more. You can contribute just as well by fundraising." He hesitated then asked, "What about your friend Beatrice, will she help?"

"No! Leave her out of it." Mark stood up. He was agitated by the whole notion of the war. It was senseless but if under attack by their own army, what could the Spanish do but defend themselves? The aggressors were fighting for power to prop up what to him seemed like a feudal system of another age, against workers who just wanted the freedom everyone expects, along with a bit of peace and prosperity. He ran his hand through his hair. "Why can't people just live and let live?"

Jack laughed and gave an exaggerated eye roll. "There he goes again with his liberal slogans. Poor bloke has no idea how deeply indoctrinated he is."

"What the hell are you talking about? I'm as committed as any of you to..."

A car pulled up in front of the building. Mark recognised the Morris Minor and his throat tightened. The argument with Jack and Bert was forgotten. Beatrice had made it after all. He had seen her only once since she had got back from the trip to Europe. He strode down the stairs and out the gate to the roadside as she opened the car door.

Mark took her hands and pulled her into his embrace, kissing her and ignoring the whistles and comments from the garden. "I didn't think you would come." His voice was gruff with emotion. "Are you sure you should be here?"

A vehicle driving along the road shone its headlights on them, and Mark stepped away although he held onto Beatrice's hand.

The high beam made her squint and she turn her face away. "My family think I am at the hospital for a lecture." She sighed. "In a few months I'll be independent, then I can do what I like."

"What will that be, then?" he asked.

She looked up and saw Jack, tall and silhouetted among the crowd on the veranda. "Oh, I don't know. I might run away with a handsome communist."

Mark followed her gaze and said, "Well, I wouldn't blame you."

She screwed up her eyes at him, and he laughed. "Come on, let's get inside."

She said, "I can't stay too long. She leaned in to kiss him again.

The car drove past, leaving the pathway to the house dimly lit as they walked hand in hand towards the steps leading up to the crowded veranda.

A little while later Jack called everyone inside. He was screening a film, and in the reception room a film projector commanded centre stage. Men and women crowded in and sat around on the floor.

Jack fiddled with the projector. "Lights out, please."

He set the film in motion, his large and capable cane-cutter hands winding the film methodically from reel to spool. Black-and-white images of a city shuddered across the screen, followed by what looked like a city park.

"The Casa de Campo," Jack said, "where our brave comrades routed the fascist. This is Madrid under siege. Just three weeks ago

20,000 rebel troops supported by Mussolini and Hitler's thugs attacked the people of Madrid."

The film panned out to focus on a white-grey sky with small black dots that grew larger. "The planes you see are the Nationalist insurgents, supported by the German Condor Legion and Mussolini's so-called Corpo Truppe Volontarie, except they're not volunteers at all, but regulars."

The erratic pictures showed bombs falling like lazy slugs through the grainy air. Then a woman, terror etched in her eyes as she clutched a screaming child, ran down a cobbled street fragmented by bomb craters. The building behind her was in flames; a building beside her, crushed. Walls had splintered into what appeared like stacked matchsticks, exposing the gaping wounds of family living rooms.

Jack said, "Never in the history of the world has such an atrocity been perpetrated. Air bombing of civilians. It's unconscionable. Twelve thousand badly equipped civilian men with little or no experience, defending a legitimately elected government against the onslaught of their own rebel army. And the world turns a blind eye."

From the back of the room, Javier Cruz stood up. Tears wet his cheeks. He raised his fist and shouted, "No pasarán!" Then he collapsed back to his seat on the floor.

Jack looked at Javier with compassion and said, "No indeed comrade, they shall not pass for hope arrives. Look!"

The film showed men marching in formation along a boulevard, crowds on either side cheering them on.

Jack said, "The International Brigade arrives. The city lives to fight another day as together our brave comrades from across all nations arrive to drive off the invaders."

The room rang with relief as men and women cheered.

The film reel fluttered to an end, and Jack said, "Lights, please." The lights were switched on and for a moment silence settled on the group as they digested what they had seen.

Mark gazed around at the sombre people in the room, seeing horror echo in their faces. He squeezed Beatrice's arm as she wiped her eyes. But all he could think of was the person behind the camera lens.

The thought of taking pictures like that filled him with an excitement that both embarrassed and confused him. The people were real and suffering, but the film conveyed that to the world. How could he get to do that? What did it take other than the right camera?

Jack surveyed the members and said, "The International Brigades are our comrades, volunteers from Germany, France, Britain, Russia, America and many other places, and soon they will have Australians joining them."

Two men at the back of the room stood up and bowed and the group clapped, their faces sombre.

Javier stood up again and said, "I will go too. I am Spanish American and have obligations. My mother's family, my cousins, my grandparents all live in the Basque country."

Jack nodded but his face was grim. "Good for you, mate, but you don't need to go and fight. There are other ways to support the Spanish people. Besides, if you want to go over there, we'll need Party approval now you're a member. It's not a problem... Just a formality, but the Spanish need more. While the rebels have all the support they need from Hitler and Mussolini, the Spanish government is cut off by British sanctions. The Spanish Republic is unable to buy supplies or weapons to fight off the rebels. They need provisions, arms, ambulances, nurses, and drivers, just as much as the International Brigade needs fighters."

He nodded to Mark, who stood up and moved around the room with a collection box.

Jack said, "The hat will be coming around. Dig deep. This is a tragedy, a terrible forerunner for the next world war if the fascists are not stopped. Spain is Hitler's testing ground, and the capitalist world will not lift a finger. It is down to us, comrades. We must do all we can to help our brothers and sisters in Spain."

The next morning Beatrice entered the breakfast room, her mind still hazy with the imagery from her nightmare. The vision of the woman's terrorised face as she ran from the falling bombs clutching her baby had plagued her sleep.

She wanted to help, but how? She had no money of her own. At least, not until she inherited her grandmother's legacy, but that wouldn't happen until she was 25 or was married. Either way, she would not have control over the money for years yet, which was why she wanted to earn her own money.

Arthur sat in the dining room, reading the paper. He folded the broadsheet as she sat at the table. "How are you feeling today, my dear? You look a bit peaky. You were very late home from the hospital last night."

"The lecture went on a bit, I'm afraid, and I stayed on to talk to some of the nursing sisters afterwards." Her face flushed pink with the lie but her father didn't seem to notice.

He nodded. "All set for the nurses' quarters today, then? Your mother and I will miss you. But your commitment to a worthy career is a credit to any young woman."

Beatrice glanced at him in surprise. He'd never before said anything good about women having careers and positively frothed at the mouth when she said she wanted to be a journalist.

He looked nostalgic for a moment. "I recall the wonderful Red Cross nurses during the war. They were an inspiration to the nation."

Oh, now she saw it. He imagined his daughter a heroine of national pride, feminine and respected, something about which he could boast. She wasn't sure she even wanted to be a nurse. It was a means to an end that was all. "When do you and Mummy leave, Daddy?"

"We'll travel up to Cairns today and board ship this evening." He sighed. "I do wish I could persuade your mother to fly. It would be so much quicker to take a flight from the new service out of Mundoo aerodrome. Now is there anything you need, my dear?"

Beatrice cringed. "Well, Daddy I will need a bit more money."

He frowned. "What's happened to your allowance?"

"I spent it all. Things are so expensive here." She hoped he wouldn't correct her. She had no idea whether things in Innisfail were any more expensive than anywhere else, but last night she had tipped the whole contents of her purse into Mark's collection.

"I suppose I could raise your allowance a little. You will have more expenses throughout your training and certainly, the wage you will earn is trifling."

She covered her resentment by leaning over to take a slice of toast from the rack. As Beatrice spread marmalade on her toast,

Arthur Langham went back to reading his newspaper.

The crunch of gravel on the driveway signalled the arrival of a vehicle. A few minutes later, Ida came into the breakfast room with a fresh pot of tea. She placed the pot in front of Beatrice and bobbed her usual curtsey.

Then she said, "Sir, Mr Howard is here to see you."

"See me?" Her father looked surprised. Then he relaxed, and a broad smile lit up his face. "Ah ha. Here to pop the question before I leave, I suppose." He winked at Beatrice.

Beatrice had a mouth full of toast but shook her head. It was too late. Arthur was already walking out the door.

She chewed the mouthful, gulping tea to wash it down. Then she stared out the window, absently using the butter knife to repeatedly stab the table. What if her father was right and Howard was really going to ask permission to marry her?

His timing was appalling, just as her parents were about to leave. How could she put him off, without creating a scene that would have her father and mother change their minds about letting her stay?

She threw down the knife, and raced upstairs to her bedroom, wanting to flee but having no idea where to go. She began pulling clothes from her wardrobe and piling them on the bed. She pulled the bell cord to call Ida to bring up her trunk. How packing for the nurses' quarters would help her escape Howard, she didn't know, but she had to do something.

Half an hour later, Beatrice heard Howard's car start up and she edged over to the window to peer out at the departing vehicle. A pulse in her neck thudded. Thank goodness she hadn't been summoned down to meet him or even have him confront her with a proposal.

A knock on her door brought her back to the task at hand. That would be Ida with her trunk.

Beatrice called, "Come in."

Ida opened the door and bobbed. "Miss Beatrice. Mr Langham would like you to go down to Mr George's study."

Beatrice frowned. "Is my trunk coming, Ida?"

"Yes, Miss Beatrice. I asked Immanuel to collect it from the storeroom in the stables. He will bring it."

Beatrice went down to her uncle's study expecting to hear that Howard had formally declared his interest. She had already made up her mind to use the nursing training as her priority for the moment.

When she entered the study, her father stood by the tabletop humidor looking grim. Her mother sat nonchalantly in a leather armchair. A shaft of sunlight fell through the tall double-sash window, lighting the air above her mother's head, but she seemed oblivious to her surroundings. Instead, she examined the backs of her hands.

A chill rushed across Beatrice's shoulders. It was a bad sign. Mother always inspected her hands when she wanted to pretend Beatrice was all Arthur's responsibility.

"Good morning Mummy. You wanted to see me, Father?"

Arthur cleared his throat. "You are to pack this instant..."

"Yes, I have asked Ida for my trunk to be brought..."

"You are not staying. You will leave with your mother and me today."

Beatrice opened her mouth to speak but he held up his hand.

"No more excuses. You have betrayed the family's trust in you."

The pulse in Beatrice's throat started up again and her breathing became erratic. "What have I done?"

"Do not pretend ignorance. The subject is closed, and we will not discuss it further. You can thank providence for Howard's discretion. He brought this disgrace to our attention before the scandal involved your uncle and aunt. He is a good man, and I am sorry he will be a loss to our family, but I understand we cannot expect him to pursue any further contact with you. I am just indebted to him for preventing public gossip about your wilful, indecorous, and perhaps treasonous, behaviour."

This must be to do with Mark but how could Howard know anything? They had been so careful not to be seen together in public. "But Daddy..."

He held up his hand. "I will not hear excuses. Ida will pack. You must change for travel and be ready to leave within the hour."

She had never seen her father this cold and determined. It was like she had become the enemy. Then it hit Beatrice. The car lights blinding her outside Jack's place. Her aunt's car parked outside. Oh, how foolish she had been. Of course, Howard would know where the Communist Party headquarters were. It never occurred to her that anyone she knew would be in that part of town. She was in more trouble than she had realised.

Beatrice didn't have much time. She ran upstairs and scrawled a letter to Mark then called Ida to post it as soon as they had left.

26. Non-Intervention.

Alfred Denton walked to work, slowly and methodically, as he had done every morning for seventeen years. He could have driven for he had a chauffeured vehicle at his beck and call, but he liked to use this time to think and besides he needed the exercise, although this morning he had a headache.

He was sixty-three years of age. His hair was almost complete grey although he still had a lot of it which pleased him. He should retire to the country to shoot clay pigeons or take up fly fishing or whatever people did when they retired.

He'd never had a hobby although his wife, before she had succumbed to the Spanish flu, had accused him of paying too much attention to politics. It was true. He couldn't see a life ahead without being in the thick of it, especially now another war was brewing.

That might be a young man's game, but maturity and experience counted when it came to planning ahead. If he had a hobby it was trying to decipher the writing on fate's wall and developing ways of tackling what the future might throw at his beloved England.

He contemplated Margaret's telegram that she was returning to London for the season with Beatrice. She treated the journey between the two countries as if they were next door to each other. The last time he had been to Australia, he had been recalled because of the Great War. At the time the young Lady Margaret had thrown the mother of all tantrums because she had not wanted to leave. She had met Arthur.

Lillian, Denton's wife and Margaret's mother, was adamant that Arthur wasn't a suitable catch, and at sixteen Margaret was far too young. Yet in the end his daughter had got her way as she always did by eroding her parents' resolve.

She had married Arthur although she was soon back in England after her husband was posted to London in an Australian liaison role. Beatice had been born at Banville Hall where Margaret had stayed with her mother for the duration, while Denton was at sea and Arthur saw out the war in a London office.

Denton's eyes became shiny, and he pulled out his handkerchief. When he'd finally come home from war, Lillian had caught influenza. Margaret had already taken Beatrice back to Australia, so she was not there when her mother died.

Even after all this time the memories still caught Denton unawares. It was such a waste. If only he'd refused to answer his duty and stayed in Australia, but that had been impossible. His country was at war and everything else played second fiddle, even those he loved.

At that time, like now, no one had believed war would come even though is dark shape loomed large on the horizon. This time he was ready. Britain couldn't be taken by surprise again. There were plenty of warning notes and he had to convince the Cabinet that British rearmament needed prioritising. This cautious appeasement policy was popular with the British public, but it would not stop Hitler and Mussolini's plans for domination. It was only a matter of time.

Still, he looked forward to his daughter coming home, and he had missed his granddaughter since her last visit. At least all the servants Margaret had hired the last time she was here, would have something to occupy them once she returned.

He sighed and turned into his office block on Broadway. Once he was seated at his desk he focussed his mind on work. The Italian ambassador, Dino Grandi had promised to reassure the very paranoid Mussolini that the British weren't plotting against him.

Denton didn't really blame the man. Even here in Britian it was increasingly difficult to really trust anyone in the ministry. There were leaks. The information he'd received from recent defections showed at least two spies were skulking in the diplomatic service. One Soviet and one German. So, the only information he trusted at the moment was what he gleaned himself.

It really wasn't a surprise. Many in the service were admirers of fascism, as were several of his colleagues in the House. Some of the intelligence brough in by diplomatic channels, was that neither Italy nor Germany really wanted war. Information he doubted given their involvement in Spain.

There seemed little he could do but argue his position. Both the P.M. Baldwin and the Chancellor of the Exchequer, Chamberlain believed British interests were not at risk from Franco's armies, and some of his Cabinet colleagues argued that if the British could get on terms with the Germans no one would care a rap for old Musso.

Chamberlain insisted it was better to bring Italy into the fold, and with that opening, Mussolini was demanding recognition of his right to Abyssinia. While Baldwin wavered, Eden refused to countenance any recognition on principle. Whitehall politics was becoming increasingly divisive.

Denton tended to side with Eden on this one. Baldwin had some wishful thinking going on because both Hitler and Mussolini were playing games to achieve their own personal aims. They'd shown they weren't averse to waging war.

Now, as far as he was concerned, the only thing for Britain to do was to prepare its defences, become militarily strong, ready for war and find as many allies as possible to gang up against both Italy, Germany and for that matter Japan's growing imperialism. Keep them in check, as Churchill had suggested.

Many of his colleagues had argued for sanctions against Italy's belligerence in Spain, but Denton was dubious about their benefit. After the Abyssinian invasion, The League of Nations had tried to use sanctions to bring Mussolini into line, but all sanctions had achieved was to convince Mussolini that the British were hypocrites, and their objections to the extension of Italian colonial holdings in Africa were borne out of fear that Italy might have its eye on Egypt. And well they might.

Italy was certainly playing a double game. They'd entered a gentleman's agreement with the Stresa Front when Britain feared Germany would take Austria from Italy. Now Mussolini was cosying up to Germany using the civil war in Spain as an opportunity to control the Mediterranean. This would be disastrous for British shipping interests and its colonial holdings if it hindered access to the Suez Canal.

Denton suspected Mussolini's motives in providing support to General Franco was to allow a Spanish takeover of Gibraltar, which in turn would scupper British domination of the Mediterranean. If he was right, the last thing Britain could afford was a Francoist Spain to come out in support of Italy's designs in the Mediterranean, yet nor could Britain afford an alliance to form between Italy and Germany.

Britain was ideologically torn between agora, (the marketplace), and agon, (the battlefield). It was causing divisions in the government with Eden challenging Chamberlain's view of friendship with Italy. In his assessment, Mussolini was behaving outrageously. Eden suggested they signal British sea strength in the Mediterranean to intimidate, but Chamberlain argued that to antagonise Italy would upset the balance of power in Europe.

As if that balance wasn't already upset with Hitler playing each off against the other. Yet Hitler had a weakness in as much as he couldn't have either Italy or Spain gaining too much strength. He gave just enough support and reassurance to keep both as allies. That weakness just might provide leverage for Britain.

Britain needed a wedge between Germany and Italy, and Denton needed to find an acceptable way to get Spain on Britain's side. Regardless of what Italy and Spain did, Denton was certain Germany was the looming threat. If Spain continued to supply Germany with raw materials and food they would be ready for war before Britain was ready.

Although he also agreed with Chamberlain they needed to get Italy on-side and away from Hitler's influence. What about Franco? If he won, would he be beholden to Italy or Germany? What if they were on different sides? The last thing Britain needed was to have hostile Italian submarine bases on Spanish territory.

The whole thing was a mess, and Denton would like to see Mussolini with a bloody nose to put him back in his box. The question was who would give it to him. Maybe Chamberlain was right, and Britian should cosy up to Italy. Denton sighed. What he needed was someone he could trust implicitly to provide an assessment through British diplomatic channels, or at least ones that weren't coloured by sympathy towards the fascist causes.

Denton needed an inside but unofficial agent to learn Mussolini's views on continuing support for Austria, but if he was to recruit one, he wanted to do it himself. It was a sad day when one didn't know who to trust in one's own service.

Furthermore, Austria was key to Hitler's plans for territorial expansion, which was the real danger. Further dithering by the PM would only strengthen Hitler's hand, and if he could gain Austria in exchange for supporting Italy in the Mediterranean, Britain was faced with significant trouble. Even Grandi was becoming anxious over Austria.

That wasn't all that was giving Denton a headache. Trying to formulate foreign policy at the moment was a nightmare. Cabinet was at loggerheads over the right course to follow, with many seeing the Soviets as the greater threat. Denton argued they should befriend Russia. Yet, it seems Russia was not in need of their friendship. The Russians were being fed a continuous stream of information through a mole.

Denton also knew Britain couldn't continue to avoid Japan's Asian expansionist plans. Russia and China might be a bulwark against Japan, for he knew the Empire of the Rising Sun was a greater threat than they gave it credit. They needed global allies and a proper rearmament program. If they could get the Soviet Union on side to keep Germany under control, Britain and France could deal with Italy, and if the Japanese became a problem they would need America's involvement.

He had a communique from Henry Chiltern, British ambassador to Spain, complaining that Claude Bowers was overtly siding with the Spanish Republic, but Denton thought the American ambassador to Spain was right. Britain and America should be helping Republican Spain to maintain their democracy. It was a forlorn hope.

Thanks to the British media, the British establishment was more fearful of the socialists than they were of any of the various fascist brands. The fear lay in the socialist's traditional struggle to overthrow the elite classes. No matter the sovereignty, the wealthy tended to support each other. The only thing that might stop the fascists was a show of unity and strength by the liberal democracies, but that required America's help and the American citizens were as anti-war as the British public.

His secretary handed him a letter. It was on Rio Tinto letterhead and signed by Auckland Geddes. Denton sighed. The situation was impossible. What Auckland seemed unable to understand was that the British were damned if they recognised Franco's belligerency rights because that would run counter to the non-intervention agreement. Yet he knew Auckland was right. If they didn't, Franco could continue to flout the 1922 trade treaty Britain had with Spain because the Republican government could do nothing about Franco's piracy.

He would have to talk to Cabinet. If they let Franco continue, the situation was equivalent to meddling through neglect. In the end, what mattered was British security. All else should be set aside. Yet, allowing Franco to send Rio Tinto's coal, copper, and pyrites to Germany, was tantamount to encouraging support for the German rearmament. Britain couldn't continue to sit on the fence. They would have to intervene. The question was, how.

His secretary knocked and popped her head around the door. "Alfred dear, are you here?"

He raised his head and smiled at her.

"Who is it?"

"Plymouth and Cranbourne want a word."

Denton groaned. "What do they want now?"

"I think they want to discuss the non-intervention committee's ban on armament supplies and foreign volunteers. It seems the ban is not working. More and more British men are travelling to Spain to fight for the Republicans."

He put his head in his hands. Plymouth, now he'd taken the chair of the non-intervention committee, definitely seemed to favour Franco's military rebels. He and Cranbourne both loathed the Soviets and would prefer anything to a red Spain.

But the non-intervention pact was a farce. Germany and Italy were almost brazen with their supplies of men and armaments, boldly coming out in favour of Franco's Nationalists. Yet Plymouth never contradicted the outright lies that came out of the mouths of Grandi and Ribbentrop in the meetings. Now the fox was being placed in charge of the chicken house with this daft control plan to monitor the Spanish borders. In this instance, non-intervention with regards to the Spanish civil war was an oxymoron of epic duplicity.

27. The Fire

Mark tied the wire to the last post and stood back to survey the fence line. Then he picked up his tools and walked back to the house. Dusk sent long shadows across months of hard work. Fenced paddocks, animal sheds, and shelters, an orchard, vine trellises, rows of corn, beans, tomatoes and other vegetables, changes created incrementally day-by-day through constant 14-hour days and careful planning. He saw none of it. Instead, he shredded and teased out his worries about Beatrice. He hadn't heard from her for days. Could he call for her at the house?

At the back door, Mark saw Bert walking down the slope toward him. "Mate, I didn't expect to see you today."

"A letter came for you at the shop. I thought it might be urgent."

Mark frowned and took the letter from Bert's outstretched hand. It was from Beatrice.

He walked into the house and slit open the envelope with a kitchen knife.

Bert sat at the table. "Is she all right?"

Mark scanned the few lines quickly. Then he scanned them again. He laid the letter on the table. "She's gone." He felt his shoulders sag as if all his strength had deserted him. "They sailed on the Manunda two days ago. Rainer saw us together at Jack's and told her father."

Bert shrugged. "You really love her?"

Mark nodded.

"Then, go and get her back."

Mark stared at him. Of course, why hadn't he understood that immediately? "I don't know where she's gone."

"You ask her Aunty. Wait until the husband is out and go to the house."

"I'm not going near the place, Bert. I'll be arrested."

"For what reason can they arrest you?

Mark sighed and said, "Having a good reason has never stopped them before."

He'd have to take the chance and go to the house if he wanted to find out where Beatrice was. So, on the following Wednesday, he drove out to Sunrise Estate and parked in a grove of trees. He waited and watched for a good 20 minutes before he built up the courage to walk up the driveway.

As he strode towards the house, he felt as though a large target was painted on his back, or perhaps eyes watched him from the trees. He was being fanciful. This was the end of the road and unless traffic was destined for Sunrise or the cane paddocks beyond, no one would come, but still, the hair on his neck prickled.

Clouds scurried in from the coast, drowning the coastal world in shadows as Mark paused at the front veranda, waiting in case someone challenged his right to be there, but the place seemed deserted.

He walked up the steps. Two enormous, studded doors confronted him, but he boldly approached and knocked hard. Then he noticed a bell, pulled the cord, and waited.

The sawing of cicadas filled the air, and a dog, over at the stables, set up a frenzy of barking. He hoped it was tied up. He banged on the door, but no one answered. It was as if the house was unoccupied.

Finally, the door opened and a Melanesian woman in a starched white uniform stood in the opening.

Mark said, "I'm looking for Mrs West. Is she in?"

The maid shook her head. "Missus is in Townsville."

Mark's heart sank. "Is Mr West here?"

Ida shook her head.

"In Townsville?" Mark asked.

Ida nodded.

"Do you know when they'll be back?"

"They are home tonight."

"All right. I'll come back tomorrow." He turned away and then swung back as the maid was closing the door.

"Wait, please."

The maid peered out.

"Do you know where the Langham's have gone?"

The maid nodded. "Sydney."

Of course, they had gone home. "Thank you." He held out his hand. "I'm Mark Anders, a friend of Miss Langham."

The maid looked astonished but touched his hand briefly with limp fingers as if he was somehow untouchable. Then she stepped inside and closed the door.

⊳⊏⊐⊲

Later that same day, Emily West walked up the steps to her front door where Ida was waiting. She was tired after the journey and all she wanted was a cup of tea and a sandwich and then early to bed. Of course, George had other ideas, merely dropping her off before saying he would be at the returned soldiers club until late and not to wait up for him.

Perhaps she was foolish punishing herself. George was the adulterer. Sometimes she fantasised about telling all their friends, but she knew she never would. He wasn't the only one who needed to maintain their position in society, and anyway she suspected his colleagues were doing the same thing. But to let out such a well-known secret as George's affairs would create a dreadful scandal and her brother wouldn't support her. He'd told her as much before he left to go back to Sydney.

It's what men do Emily, get used to it, Arthur had said when she confided in him. He added that disgracing her family in this neck of the woods would affect his business dealings and his career and he warned her against telling anyone. His tone had been threatening when he asked if she was quite clear about her duty.

Abundantly! Gloss over the cracks. Make as if everything is perfect. Forget happiness. It's not the lot of women. She remembered her own mother telling her that romantic love was an illusion. It was wonderful when her niece had arrived. She had never really got along with Arthur, but Beatrice brought a new joy into the house and George behaved himself when Arthur was around. She sighed and took off her hat, tidying her hair in the hall mirror.

Ida took the hat from her and said, "A man, Mr Anders, came looking for Miss Beatrice."

Emily sighed. She was too tired to deal with this. "Tell Mr West tomorrow, Ida. I'll take tea in the drawing-room now."

Perhaps she would have been happier if she tried to ignore George's infidelity, involved herself with the community, the dances, shows and fetes, the morning teas and country women's groups. She had so loved the gaiety. Perhaps she should taper off the pills a little but not tonight. She was just too exhausted. She reached out for her Bayer's heroin bottle. Just a small one with a cup of tea to relax a little.

Night had fallen by the time Emily roused herself to go to bed. She took her embroidery off her lap, abandoned when she had dozed off, and placed it on the occasional table. Ida had switched on the lights and left Emily's dinner and a glass of milk in the warmer, but Emily didn't want food. She would have the warm milk and then bed.

In her bedroom she took another two pills, just to help her sleep, and stood at the window sipping her milk, watching Ida walk away, the Tilley lantern swinging in her hand.

Emily's mind was clouded, and her hands shook as she raised the glass to her mouth. Her gaze fixed on the small point of light made by the swinging lantern in the dark shadows outside.

Ida Littlewood had finished work for the day, her last duty to leave the Missus's supper and a glass of warmed milk. Now, she walked along the path away from the big house, head down and singing quietly to herself as she approached the Little Wood. The stand of trees called the Little Wood was a name given to a remanent patch of forest separating the West's home from the servants' quarters, the name adopted by Ida's family a generation ago.

As Ida walked home, she reflected on her job. She'd told her parents it was like the Missus had Kuru, the brain disease. Initially, Ida had shied away from looking after Mrs West when she took her pills and Mr George was away, but the boss said the sickness wasn't catchy, just made her crazy. In the end, Ida did as she was told.

The family all worked for the Wests. Her mother cooked and rarely left the kitchen, so she saw little, but when Ida complained of Mrs West's crazy behaviour when she took the pills, her mother said it was better not to question the ways of white people. Her mother and father sometimes discussed what they should do about the pills with the pastor but in the end, their livelihood, their home, and everything else was the boss's grace to give or take away.

They all remembered it was boss George's father who had allowed them to stay on the farm when the others were sent away in 1908. When they were sent back to islands they had never known, to live with people they had never met, even though it was their ancestral homelands. Now, they knew to whom they must give allegiance, and boss George was the biggest of the Big Men in the region.

Ida hurried towards the path that led through the forest. She was already late for church. This was an important decision for the family to make as it meant the marriage of her oldest brother. The pastor was waiting for the conference.

Ahead of her something moved. Ida caught her breath as she approached the bend in the path. She tried to slow her pounding heart. This wood was still a testament to what the West's were capable of doing.

She walked on with caution, for there was the unknown with which to contend. Despite her self-talk, apprehension increased as she approached the bend where her grandfather remained, unreconciled with his life's abrupt end.

Her uncle told her that even the dead remembered, and Grandfather would still feel the choking fury of his final betrayal by boss George's father, boss William, who had accused him of the young girl's murder. Her uncle said, boss William had killed the girl to cover rape and then blamed Grandfather. Those white men had strung him up, legs kicking and face purpling until his breath was gone.

She stood at the entrance to the wood and fear flooded through her. She whispered those words of protection from malevolent spirits that her mother had taught her as a child. She would not be afraid. She passed the tree every day and knew no ghost inhabited it, but today she had a bad feeling.

Scarcely breathing, she walked into the wood's shadow. The pastor had told her it wasn't her grandfather but other demons that lurked to pray on the godless. She didn't know what to believe and thought maybe only live ghosts existed, like the Missus who had a sickness of the head. She hurried around the bend and the Kauri pine loomed before her, shadowed in the dim light. She held the lantern high and stared at the branch that still bore the rigid scars from 50-year-old rope chaff.

A flash of light rippled across the trunk of the tree, and a whoosh of wind lifted Ida's skirt as it rushed along the path towards the great house. Ida screamed and dropped the Tilley lamp, smashing the glass. The flame went out, casting the wood in darkness. She fled back the way she had come. When she reached the backyard of the house she paused, unsure of what she had seen. Then she saw the flames licking at the eaves of the big house.

Ida ran to the scullery door screaming for Mrs West.

The following morning broke, with the sun's misty yellow orb carving through a blood-red sky. Lazy air currents created a grey pall over the old plantation home, while a breeze from the river split off smoke tendrils to float like silver-grey souls away from the smouldering ruins.

Firemen rolled up their hoses and stashed them on the fire wagon, weary now the inferno was out and only the cold relics of tragedy remained. George West sat slumped on the cupid seat next to the pond, Emily next to him, still in her nightgown, weeping into her hands.

George had rolled up his shirtsleeves to his elbows, collar askew, a jacket folded across his lap, grime along his jawline. Sweat stained his shirt, spreading out from his armpits and down his spine. He had arrived home from the club to find the house ablaze and his wife in the garden in a heroin-induced confusion.

He suspected her of setting the place alight but could get no sense from her. At least the stables were spared. Now, he placed his arm around her and squeezed a warning as he saw Howard Rainer pull up behind the line of police cars.

George watched Howard pause for a moment to survey the scene before him. He looked to be a tall man, but it was an illusion along with his air of studied authority. Behind him, vehicles filled the long circular driveway. Mock-orange blossoms scented the air, creating a sickly-sweet cocktail as their perfume merged with the aftermath of the fire.

A light breeze blew across the water falling from the stone maiden's vase into the pond. It sent up a fine mist that fused with residual smoke. In nearby branches, butcher birds warbled to each other and cocked their heads to eye the activity below. As Howard approached, cockatoos screeched and flew away.

"How did this happen?" he asked.

George lurched towards him and grabbed his arm. "It was them... Communists. I told you they would create insurrection. This is the start."

Howard raised a sceptical eyebrow and smoothed his moustache with a forefinger.

George insisted. "Ida said someone by the name of Mark Anders was here. Said he wanted Beatrice's address in Sydney. Find him and you'll have the culprit."

Ida fidgeted, her hands in her apron pockets fingering the now useless house keys. Her dark eyes rolled away from George's gaze, and it dawned on him: no one ever paid any attention to the servants. Perhaps that was the problem. If Anders was here talking to Ida, perhaps all the servants were communists, and no one had known. They had to go. The lot of them.

George sat down on the cupid seat and for a moment teetered on the brink, but he held himself back. This was not the time to give in.

The 9th District.

No one should know his wife had started the fire.

28. Escape

Bert drove Mark to the railway station. By the time they arrived the sun was already high. The day was muggy and tropical, one of those days before the summer storms arrive when everything struggles to breathe.

Potted begonias hung limp in their hanging baskets as Mark bought his ticket and turned away, eyes cast down, his breathing shallow as if the heat closed his throat. Steam billowed from the train's boilers, enveloping him in its sulphury folds. He scanned the platform. His narrowed gaze sweeping north to south across the crowd, looking for a sign of the distinctive khaki uniform of the Queensland police among the throng of dark-suited men and their pastel wives.

Mark had on one of Bert's hats, which were in better condition that his, but it was a band of steel crushing his head. He pulled it lower on his forehead, and moved unobtrusively through the crowds, his breathing easing as he made his way toward where Bert waited with his kitbag.

He took the battered kitbag from Bert's grasp and threw it into the carriage vestibule just as the train's boilers wheezed their intention to be on their way. Then he turned back and held out his hand.

Bert's eyes creased with worry. He was jacketless, also having given it to Mark along with his new hat, and he said, "Buona fortuna e buon viaggio, amico mio – Good luck and safe journey, my friend."

It was Bianca's friend who had warned Mark to leave. At first, he hadn't believed her, but he'd made plans to go to Sydney, anyway. Now he hoped he could get away before they arrested him. He ran his palm across the back of his neck, still not believing such injustice was possible.

Thunder rumbled in the distance and from habit he looked towards the western horizon. The distant rain-mountain usually dominated the range, but from the platform only towering cumulus cloud above the shrouded summit were visible, indicating an imminent downpour. Mark hoped his animals would be all right.

"You'll take care of the farm?"

Bert nodded.

Mark realised he was running away. Unless he could clear his name, he might never again gaze upon that mountain massive. Suddenly it seemed precious, something of beauty to which he had never paid attention other than to forecast weather. This was home. This was where he had thought he belonged, but he was being evicted as surely as if they had bodily thrown him out.

He tried to fix the image in his mind, recalling the view from his farm. The clear depth of sky beyond the gathering storm clouds, the rust-red volcanic soil, the undulating landscape of cane, broken by the dark gullies of remnant jungle, all fading away into the distant blue mountain shadows. Perhaps he should stay and tough it out, but he knew that wasn't an option. He crossed his arms, running damp calloused palms down his jacket sleeves as he tried to soothe the prickling fear rising under his skin.

The train huffed and wheezed as it built up steam. A metallic tang of grease leaking from the steaming bogies mingled with a faint whiff of rotten eggs drifting in from a nearby creek. To the north, sweet steam billowed from the Goondi Mill, sending white clouds rolling across the town. Everything was as it should be, except it wasn't.

He placed his foot on the rung, grabbed the rail, and swung onto the train, shouldering his kitbag to walk into the half-full carriage. He placed his bag on a luggage rack just as the train jolted, pistons protesting. The whistle shrieked on a shunt of steam and Mark dropped onto an empty bench next to the window and stared at the movement on the platform as if a last-minute reprieve might appear.

Mark watched Bert walk towards the platform exit, shoulders hunched, head bowed. He had on his old Fedora, having given Mark his good one. Now he pulled the brim down low on his forehead. He didn't want to be recognised either.

Mark hoped he'd be all right, but it was him they were after. Arson was an unforgivable crime and there would be no quarter. In the distance lightning sheeted across the slate sky, and he imagined the void yawning before him. He forced down panic, reminding himself he was innocent, although that didn't matter to some.

The guard, standing on the steps of the luggage van, blew his whistle. Wheels sighed and carriages clanked, jerking against their couplings. Tardy passengers scrambled aboard to find their seats as the train lurched forward.

The engine gathered speed, revealing countryside dominated by the great hulk of Bartle Frère. East of the town, the river waters raced towards the Coral Sea at Flying Fish Point. That was where he had first kissed Beatrice, lying back on that small towel to keep the sand from her hair. But already the train was rattling over the bridge crossing the Johnstone River, away from everything he had built just for her.

Mark needed advice or a miracle. Bert thought Fred Paterson might provide one but at least Mark could be sure he would help, so long as he reached Townsville before the police got to him. He leaned his head against the window frame as the train rushed through newly ploughed cane paddocks. He had been deluded by the idea that life was somehow his to control.

While he was in Townsville, he stayed at the Party office in Flinders Street where he saw Fred and told him the whole sorry tale. Fred made some enquiries and advised Mark of an impending inquest, but the coppers didn't want to see Mark Anders back in the region, ever. At least an arrest warrant hadn't been issued, not yet, but Fred warned him against going home for a while. If he returned, he could expect no fair dealings, not with enemies like Rainer. Mark was certain it was Rainer's revenge after seeing him with Beatrice.

Fred's advice was to get to Brisbane and keep low until the results of the inquest were known. Mark would be better off in a city where no one knew him, although Mark did know people. Javier and Jack were both in Brisbane. So, after he'd seen Fred he travelled on to Brisbane.

As the train entered the city of Brisbane, the bustle of the place surprised him: cars and lorries, horses and carts, motorbikes and trams, busses, bicycles and so many people. The train pulled into Roma Street station and throngs moved back and forth along the platform, reminding him of the currawongs wheeling above the forest at home.

The train slowed to a clanking rest and passengers waved out windows or stood up and pulled luggage off racks in readiness, but Mark remained slumped in his seat. He was in no hurry to get off the train and move into the unknown.

An hour later, he entered a house in Skew Street. He found Javier on the back veranda reading a paper.

Without looking up Javier said, "Sixty thousand of those fascist bastards are helping Mola, boots on the ground, tanks and planes and what else ..."

Mark dropped his kitbag onto the floor. "You'll need to be a bit more specific, mate?"

Javier looked up. "Mark, it's you? Thought it was Jack. How the hell are you?" He looked at Mark's bag and jutted his chin at a rusted iron bed frame with a lumpy mattress at the end of the veranda. "That's free and not as comfortable as it looks."

"Thanks." Mark took his kitbag over to the bed and sat down. The springs sagged and squealed in protest. "Sixty thousand what?"

Javier looked puzzled and then his face cleared. "Oh yeah. Nazis." He paused. "The war in Spain, you know. My cousin has come over here to raise money." He drew a deep breath and blurted. "No one helps the poor beggars except Stalin. I never thought I'd say it, but that bastard's come good for once." He hit his open palm with his fist. "He's not sending troops though, just some guns and advisors." Then he cocked his head. "Although France sent weapons too."

"Javier, mate, I don't know what you're talking about."

Javier took a breath. "Which bit?"

"All of it."

Javier frowned and spoke more carefully. "Germany and Italy are sending troops, weapons, tanks, ships, and planes, helping General Mola. Bombing cities... civilians, Mark!" He glared, and his voice became excited again, racing over the words. "Civilians, and against an elected government, no less! And no one lifts a bloody finger... says, no proof. All just horseshit! I'm going back to Spain with my cousin?" He said the last bit with a rush, staring at Mark as if in challenge.

"I know mate. I was there when you told us."

Javier said. "Are you coming? This is not just a Spanish problem. This is an international problem. We have to stop these fascists. This war is just the beginning and if we don't stop it now, we're all doomed. Here," he chucked a pamphlet at Mark, "read about it. There's a fundraising rally tonight."

That night, the house filled with people who had come to hear from the *Movement against War and Fascism* and to support the Spanish Relief Fund. When the meeting began Javier stood up. "Comrades." He held up his hands and the crowded room became silent. "My cousin, Carmen Rodoreda from my mother's side of the family, has come here tonight to speak about Spain. She's from Bilbao and is here in Australia to raise awareness about Spain's terrorist invaders. She wants to share her experiences with you."

A woman with short bobbed black hair stood up and bowed. She wore trousers and a workman's shirt tucked into a belt too large for her tiny waist. The heavy work boots on her feet clomped on the floorboards as she crossed the room. The outfit looked strange on such a tiny person, like a child dressed in her father's clothes. Mark had a flashback to Beatrice dressed in his clothes on the farm and felt a pain in his chest. He took a breath and focused.

Carmen said, "Please excuse a minute." She unrolled a poster-sized photograph from a tube and pinned it to a board propped up against the wall. The large grainy black-and-white photo showed dead women and children lying in a rubble-strewn street, bombed by planes flying overhead. Mark could see the Nationalist crosses on the wings in the photo.

She turned to her audience and in heavily accented English said, "This is Madrid. I took this photo myself. Look hard. If you accept this can happen in Spain, you will accept it here in Australia." She pointed at the photograph. "Here are innocent women and children who lie dead in the streets of Madrid and other places, killed just a few weeks ago by the Nationalist killing machine. They drop bombs indiscriminately, on the defenceless citizens of democratic España, invaded by our own traitors led by Generalissimo Mola and Generalissimo Franco. The Nazis, and Mussolini's Fascists, support them."

Mark thought she was going to spit on the floor, but she placed her hands on her hips, arms akimbo and stared down the room. He was mesmerised.

She took a breath. "If we do not stop this atrocity, the next world war has already begun, and Spain is the starter gun." She was silent again. Then her voice changed and became desperate. "Please, please, I beg, help the Spanish people. All over España, people are dying from bombs, they are dying from bullets, they are tortured and many also die from starvation. Please, I know your government and your bishops say this is not your war. Australians must stay to defend Australia. But if this is not stopped in Spain, it will be your war next. Please do not believe this is not your fight, for it is every working man and woman's fight. It is my fight, and I will take up a gun again when I get home. Papa already fights for the people's democracy with the Basque army, as do my brothers, uncles, and cousins. It is a fight against great evil."

She stopped speaking and looked around the room. It was silent, not a movement, not a sound, as people stared at the black-and-white photograph. No one looked at her except Mark. Then his gaze went from person to person, willing someone to say something. The silence stretched out until he could stand it no longer.

"What do you want from us?" he asked.

For a moment, she didn't look at him, but then she turned, and he felt skewered by some mysterious dark power. "We need money, guns, supplies, men, and women to fight, drivers to run blockades, medicine, doctors, nurses. We need support from your government and the British." She paused. Then with a shrug, she said simply, "We need what you can give."

She stared at him, unblinking black eyes, fathomless. Mark couldn't drag his eyes away.

Javier broke the spell. "Okay, you good people. I have a collection coming around." He pointed to a man leaning against the wall who stood up and walked around the room with a tin can.

The photo remained, day after day. No one took it down. Mark walked past it every morning and stopped to stare. The child in the middle of the picture looked like a rag doll, flung down, broken, and abandoned.

It was her who got to him most. The other dead in the street seemed unreal somehow but that one small body got to him, making him angrier and angrier at the atrocity, done in the name of what? Some bastards who thought they knew better, who thought they should run the country in preference to the elected government. Why? What was the point of all this killing? He didn't get it. But that one photograph told it all.

He shook his head and left the house, going to the station to buy his ticket for Sydney.

29. Defeat

Beatrice paced back and forth in her cabin, rage at her parents incandescent to the point she could scarcely breathe. First her father, now her mother. It was more than she could tolerate and there were still days, perhaps weeks, before she could get another letter in the post.

She pulled her cardigan closer. Since leaving the Suez, the weather had become dull and was getting colder as the ship approached the Gibraltar Straits. Mark wouldn't know what had happened to her. She couldn't imagine what he thought, but it wasn't as though she had left of her own free will.

Her father wasn't speaking to her but still managed to keep a tight rein on her movements. In Sydney, Beatrice had asked the housekeeper to post a letter but instead, she had delivered it into the hands of Beatrice's father. When he had confronted her, she at first felt guilty, then it hit her that she had nothing to feel guilt over. For the first time in her life, she defied him, shouting that he had broken the law by intercepting her mail.

But all her rage succeeded in doing was having him decide she and her mother would go back to England immediately. Her father was to leave on a business trip to America before he went on to the inaugural sugar conference in London. He would meet them in London when he had finished his business. He had booked their passages, ensuring Beatrice hadn't a moment of privacy before she boarded the ship.

Now, she had discovered her mother had intercepted the letter she had left with the ship's purser to post onward when they docked at Perth. Beatrice came across the seized letter when her mother asked her to fetch her shawl. The resulting argument must have been heard across all the first-class cabins on their deck. Beatrice had completely lost her temper and now felt quite embarrassed about it, but she wasn't sorry. As soon as they were in London, she'd get away somehow and send a telegram. Her mother couldn't watch her every second of the day.

A sick child was on board and Beatrice had been visiting her. It was a means of keeping out of her mother's way, knowing Margaret wouldn't be seen dead on the lower deck. Beatrice hunted out the book she'd promised to read to the child and then collected a packet of biscuits and an apple to take to her.

Vomit rose unexpectedly in her throat, and she ran to the basin, retching. When her stomach settled, she drank a glass of water and stared at her reflection in the mirror. This was her first bout of seasickness ever. She splashed her face with water, straightened her blouse, buttoned her cardigan, and went off to visit the girl.

Across the other side of the world, George West sat in the hotel lounge. Emily sat on one side of him staring vacantly out the window towards the river.

George refused to believe the verdict and demanded an explanation from the coroner. Then, when the verdict was confirmed, he called Howard and demanded the Investigation Branch do their job, or if it wasn't their job, then the police must investigate properly.

To add to the insult, Howard told him he had applied for a transfer to Canberra, the new Capital of Australia. After all George had done for the man, he was leaving, and the inquest verdict remained.

At the inquest the fire brigade chief gave testimony that it was an electrical fire, evidence of rats in the ceiling. To George, it made little sense. How could the two things connect to make a fire?

Rats! He acknowledged he should have done something sooner to get rid of the blighters, but who on earth thought rats would eat electrical cable, and then that it would cause a fire. That was the trouble with all this modern fandangle stuff: it was unpredictable.

He was so sure his wife had started it. As if any of this was an accident, but if it was rats, then it was not her fault, and perhaps it was his. He almost wished it was the start of a communist insurrection and was surprised at his disappointment that it wasn't. The desire to fight someone grew with every new setback.

George pondered whether he should leave the region. Negotiations would take place in London for the first International Sugar Conference, which Arthur was to attend. One of the aims of the conference was to find an agreement on a solution to the worldwide sugar glut, either by creating more demand or further restricting growers' quotas.

The latter was unlikely, so they would need to increase demand. George had a good idea for doing just that. He'd even come up with a slogan: *Sugar: Sunshine for Health!* He thought it had a positive ring.

Perhaps he should go to the conference and volunteer his services. The farm would be safe enough. More trouble in the region was unlikely now that the communist leader had moved to Brisbane, so he doubted any further industrial strife would cause a problem for his current sugar crop. He could leave that in the hands of the mill. He ran his finger under his collar.

They had taken rooms in the hotel, but it wasn't comfortable, not like his home. Perhaps, instead of rebuilding they should retire to England and buy a little house in the countryside. His land would fetch a good amount, although he didn't need the money, not unless the Rio Tinto mines in Spain were compromised by the socialists. That might cause him some hardship.

He hesitated. This was all he really knew. It was his family home. He had expected to be buried on the farm in the family cemetery. What would he do without his position in society?

An alderman walked towards him hat in hand, along with two politicians, one of whom was a candidate in the next state election, the other, a federal politician whose term was nearly up. They approached his table, and he stood up as they commiserated with his tragedy. He wondered whether they would be here if this was midterm in the electoral cycle.

Emily was clearly charmed by them. Something about her had

changed. She looked younger, smarter, and altogether more aware... Animated, as he hadn't seen her for years. She seemed to know everyone in the hotel. Even walking along the street, people greeted her.

He shook hands with the dignitaries, thanking them for their concern but he knew why they were here. He gave a lot of money to their campaign coffers, but he remained circumspect. He had worked too hard to throw it all away on a sharp word. He wouldn't yet decide, not until his mind was clear.

30. A Fateful Decision

Grey clouds hung low over the city made festive with Christmas decorations. Mark bought a ticket to Sydney for the following day, before catching a tram back to the shared house. When he arrived at the tram stop, he saw Javier walking across the road and hailed him.

It began to rain. Not the relentless deluge of the north, but cold soaking rain. The wind whipped around their legs and Mark stepped onto the pavement to shelter under a shop awning, pulling his jacket closed against the sudden chill.

A newspaper page wrapped around his leg, and he pulled it off. The headline caught his eye and he laughed.

Javier followed him under the shelter. "What's funny?"

"Nothing, mate." He hesitated, then held out the sheet of newspaper. "Look at this." The headlines said, *South American cartels return tin to pre-depression values.* "Here I am driving myself into the ground farming, and the tin price is going through the roof. I'm making money doing nothing."

Javier grinned. "You're becoming a fucking capitalist."

Mark shook his head perplexed by the randomness of his situation. "All I need now is for my name to be cleared so I can take Beatrice back home."

Javier said, "You know Mark, I do know what it's like. Having the police after me was how I ended up in Australia."

"What happened?"

Javier shrugged. "Distributed anarchist literature."

Mark stared. "For literature! Hell, I thought I was hard-done-by."

"The New York cops had me pegged as a subversive and once they get you in their sights, they don't let go." He drew a breath. "Anyway, I got in with a crew on a ship, thought I was heading for my mother's family in Spain, but I ended up here. So, going to Spain now, well it's by way of a small detour. You should come with me."

Mark was surprised at Javier's persistence, but Spain held a compelling appeal. He asked, "What do I know about fighting?"

Javier tilted his head. "I've seen you with a rifle; you can take the eyes out of a rat in a tree branch at three hundred paces."

Mark laughed. "That's a bit of a stretch, mate."

"Ha! Is it though? I saw you hit a wild boar bolting across the other side of the paddock. Besides, you know how to set explosives from your mining days with your dad. You can drive. The rest, they'll teach us."

A muscle jumped in Mark's jaw. "I'm going to find Beatrice and when this whole inquest mess is sorted, I'll take her home. Fred said he'll represent me, and once my name is cleared, I can take Beatrice back with me to the farm."

"Well, think about Spain, will you? The Queensland coppers can't get you outside Australia."

"Don't fool yourself."

Javier grinned. "They have to find you first! But anyway, I told Carmen I won't be fighting. Told her I didn't think I could kill someone. She said she'd arrange for me to get involved with a blockade runner to run supplies. They need people who know how to drive." He looked at Mark hopefully.

An image of the little girl in the photograph filled Mark's mind but he pushed it away. He had to find Beatrice, then build her a proper home, with a kitchen and a bathroom. With the shares in tin going up, and his and Bert's business doing so well, he could afford that now, so long as the police left him alone.

It had stopped raining by the time they arrived at the shared house, and Jack was waiting for them at the top of the stairs. He had a telegram in his hand.

"Look what the postie just delivered." He grinned at Mark and Javier. "Good news, mate." He held out the telegram.

Mark read, *All clear. Accidental misadventure. Telephone soonest. Bert.*

He was no longer a wanted man. The world seemed to lighten. He placed both hands on his head and had an overwhelming urge to caper down the street, but he remained motionless, trying to sort through colliding emotions. Today must be the luckiest of his entire life.

Jack glanced at Javier. "Come on, I'll shout the beers. I reckon a celebration is in order."

"Hang on, Bert says to phone. What's that about?"

"You can call into the post office on the way." Jack grinned.

They walked down the street to the pub a few blocks away, Jack and Javier talking, Mark between them, silent but jubilant. He could go home. Tomorrow he would go to Sydney and then, he didn't know how, but he would take Beatrice home.

As they waited for the barman to pull three beers, Mark went across the road to the post office to phone Bert at the shop.

Bert answered immediately. "I'm glad I caught you before you went to Sydney," he said.

A feeling of dread lurched in Mark's chest. "What's up, mate? Is everything all right? Is it the farm?"

"Everything's right here. I have offered the old farm shed to Immanuel and his family now they're homeless."

"Who?" Mark didn't recognise the name.

"Beatrice's uncle's overseer. He and his family are without work since the house burnt down. That bloody, heartless bastard George West kicked them out. Now they have no job and nowhere to live. Immanuel says he will run the farm and send in the shop supplies in your absence, if they can live in the shed."

"Sure, but the shed is not in a liveable state."

"They will fix it up. He wants to build traditional houses like the ones they had before, and it will be good to have some help."

"Right oh. That's a relief. It'll be good to have someone looking after things, but they will have to take a fair share of the produce, or you can pay them from my share of the profits. Tell them they can use my house until they build their own. Oh, and tell them they're welcome, but hey, I thought you wanted me to call for something urgent." Mark waited, but all Bert did was clear his throat and Mark could hear paper rattling. "What's up Bert? Speak man."

"You know how the newspapers list travellers and shipping news?"

"What about it?"

"There's an announcement."

"Come on Bert. What does it say?"

"Mark my friend, it is very bad news. Beatrice has left for London. Wait, I read it." Bert cleared his throat, then read aloud.

> *The only daughter of Lord Alfred Denton, the Lady Margaret, and her daughter the Hon. Beatrice Langham, heiress to her grandmother's cotton fortune, boarded the RMS Otranto for London. They will arrive in plenty of time for the start of the next social season when Miss Langham will be presented at Court. They will also attend King George VI's coronation in May.*

Mark said quietly. "Bullshit!"

His mind was reeling as he hung up and wondered back to the pub. When he walked into the bar, Jack placed a hand on his shoulder.

"Are you all right, mate?"

The firm pressure and warmth of the touch helped but his mind seethed in confusion. The paper wouldn't lie, surely. His eyes smarted and his throat burned. He looked at the untouched beer on the counter in front of him and said to Jack in a strangled voice, "Sorry mate, I have to go."

Mark walked out of the bar not knowing where he was going, his mind in turmoil. He walked all night, at times lost in unfamiliar streets, at times just sitting on benches staring into the night. He'd known the story before, saw it in the newspaper, but Beatrice had said that *The Johnstone River Advocate* had exaggerated the whole thing.

She had explained that her grandfather had been born into an aristocratic family, but they'd lost everything during the Baring Bank crisis in 1890. She'd told him that her grandfather now worked in some civil service ministry and lived in London just around the corner from his office.

Clearly, that was not the whole truth. Mark had been deluding himself, wanting to believe they could be married and be happy together on the farm. He put his face in his hands and began laughing. He was such a mug.

The next morning, he walked into the shared house and found Jack and Javier. Jack was leaning against the veranda rail with his arms folded. Javier sat on the bed, his head in his hands.

"Mark?" Jack's voice reflected his relief as he pushed away from the rail. "You're back."

Javier stood up. His face was creased, and his eyes were red as if he hadn't slept. "You okay?"

Mark nodded. "I had a long think. I'm going to Spain."

Jack leaned back against the rail and refolded his arms. "What's brought this on? I thought you were going to Sydney today?"

Mark relayed the story.

Jack said, "I can't believe she'd lie about something like that."

Javier said. "Maybe she didn't lie, just left bits out of the story. I do that all the time."

"Really? I'll remember that." Jack said.

Doubt plagued Mark. "It was a Sydney newspaper. Why would they print it if it wasn't true?"

Jack stepped closer and laid his hand on Mark's shoulder. "Don't know mate, but you don't need to volunteer for Spain. If you want to help the cause, you can do the work in Australia. The SRC needs volunteers to raise awareness and money. Spain is dangerous and things aren't looking good, from what I hear."

"No. You don't understand. I want to go and take photos. If I sell my shares I will have the money to buy a good camera with a flash, without impacting on the business or the farm, and I can report what is really going on there. The papers here don't show the human cost of the war. I can show the truth. I'm not going to fight."

Jack shook his head. "Everyone has to fight." He paused, and his brow cleared. "Although you are right. Not journalists. We need stories and photos to raise money and awareness. Maybe you can do that for *The Movement against War and Fascism* while you're over there. If we organise a press pass you can get into Spain and get some real information, not just capitalist propaganda."

"Mate, I'm no reporter."

"But you're an artist. You can go as a photojournalist. We'll get you a camera."

"Hang on, I'm not working for the Party," Mark shook his head, "that'll get me into all sorts of strife."

"You can work for *The Movement against War and Fascism*. It's not a Party organisation. Not officially anyway. Just let us have some good fundraising photos. You understand how things work and you're pretty articulate and can write well. I'm really warming to the idea. What do you reckon, Mark? We can make your life easier. We have contacts everywhere, and I personally know the editor of *L'Humanité*, a daily newspaper in Paris. I know you won't join the Party, but you have been a good friend... I am sure we can get you the right press credentials. Besides, a Party member would not be able to infiltrate some of the places you might get to go, especially if you find Beatrice again."

Mark frowned. "Two things. You are asking me to spy on your behalf and you imagine I will see Beatrice again. You are way off mate, but hey if you want to give me a camera I'll send you some pictures, no problems." A feeling of destiny had settled on his shoulders as if this were inevitable and he couldn't change it now anyway.

Jack said, "I'm serious. Real pictures and stories from the heart will raise more money, and it gets the truth out there. You'll be more help to the cause than one extra member."

Mark said, "What about you Javier? Do you think it's possible?"

"Mate, anything is possible. You just have to act like you believe it. I reckon it will still be dangerous though. Can you speak Spanish."

Mark laughed. "No, other than the swear words I learned from you."

"I'll teach you on the boat going over. You can speak Italian so it should be easy to pick it up. Practice introducing yourself as a journalist on board while you learn the language. And Jack's right, it all helps the same cause. Look at the impact Carmen's photo had on you. What could photos like that do for the people of Australia?"

Mark remained silent for a moment and then said, "Bert will take care of the farm. All right then. I'll go to Spain and get some good photo stories."

Jack frowned. "Getting passports might be tricky but so long as you don't tell them you're going to Spain it might be all right. Can't guarantee anything, but we have a comrade on the inside, maybe he'll have some advice. I'll arrange your press credentials and see what I can find out about passports."

Mark leaned on the ship's rail as the RMS Orcades left Melbourne in its wake. He could no longer see the dock and felt a mixture of relief and sadness as he stared at Australia receding into the grey drizzle.

Earlier, fog had slumped stubbornly across Port Phillip Bay and delayed their departure. Now it lifted, leaving a cold damp shroud obliterating the sky, but with enough visibility to see the smudge of land receding.

He pictured his farm bathed in sunlight and shivered. He'd never been this cold in his life. His fingers were frozen, and this was summer. Would he see his farm again? He didn't know, but he'd left all the necessary official documents with Bert to manage the farm and business, and to take it over if something should happen to him.

He turned away and went down to join Javier and a couple of other Australian volunteers in the tourist-class saloon where they were playing euchre. Now, he just needed to concentrate on what was in front of him, nothing more.

1937

31. A Telegram

The telegram gave no information at all, just said, *Your letter forwarded 16 King Street, Covent Garden, London. Telephone soonest, Innisfail 209. B.*

Beatrice sucked in her bottom lip, frowning at the slip of paper in her hand. She recognised the telephone number. It was Bert's café, but what did it mean and why had Bert sent a telegram saying he'd forwarded her letter to London. And most importantly, why hadn't Mark sent a telegram or a letter?

The postman, or rather the boy for he looked no older than seventeen, was still standing on the doorstep. Was one supposed to tip in England? Her glance travelled past him to his motorcycle on the pavement, and then across the road to the park and back to the row of respectable houses with their classical proportions, porticoed entrances, and first-floor balconies. Blind-eyed windows stared out of white stucco faces, into the middle distance, as if she and the boy were nobody's business but their own. A tip might be insulting, and she didn't want to give offence. After all, they paid posties a proper wage in Britain so it couldn't be too different from home.

"Thank you." She turned indoors. It was lucky that she had been passing or the telegram might have fallen into her mother's hands. She shut the black lacquered front door, folding the telegram, and slipping it beneath her waistband, just as her mother swept down the stairs.

"My dear, what are you doing out of bed. You know the doctor said complete rest."

"Oh Mother, he said that weeks ago. I'm fine now and sick of being cooped up. I think what I need is a walk in the fresh air."

"Absolutely not. You know very well how ill you've been and if you do not heed the doctor, you may have a relapse."

Beatrice sighed. "I'll just sit in the morning room for a little while then."

She did feel a bit shaky. It had been almost a month since they'd arrived in London, and she had been ill ever since. It had started with the German measles that she'd caught from the child on the ship. Then she'd miscarried. Until then she hadn't even known she was pregnant, but then she got pneumonia. She was as thin as a scarecrow and even walking down the stairs left her exhausted.

She made her way to the morning room where the late winter daylight pooled palely through the wide windows that overlooked the street, almost deserted at this time of mid-morning. It always surprised her how, just blocks away from the main thoroughfare, London streets could exude such quiet. Yet, she hadn't remembered it being so cold the last time she had visited. Her grandfather said it was because she was unwell that she felt the cold so bitterly.

She flopped onto the little sofa hauled under the window for her use and thought of the golden tropical light she'd left behind. Her eyes filled and she swore she would get back just as soon as she was well and had accumulated a sufficient amount of her allowance to buy a ticket.

The doctor had told her to bare her skin to the sun every day, but what sun? It was such a spineless thing. Her mother came back into the room and began to fuss about, placing a blanket over Beatrice's knees. Beatrice touched the back of her hand gently. She hadn't fully forgiven her, but it was unusual for her mother to be so solicitous.

Beatrice ran her hands over her flat belly and choked back desolation. The miscarriage was her secret and one she had only shared with Gladys Fuller, the nursing sister who had first attended her when she was admitted to hospital. She couldn't have hidden the miscarriage from Gladys or from Doctor Goodall. Gladys and Dr Goodall were the only friends she had in London and now she was home, she missed them.

Her mother's voice penetrated her reverie. "Now my dear, Your presentation. It was such a pity you were so ill and weren't able to participate in the finishing school practice sessions. Still, there is time. We can hire a private tutor. We want you perfect by May."

"Oh Mummy, I'm too old to come out. The others will be sixteen or seventeen-year-olds." Beatrice hated that sort of thing, and she never quite knew how to behave. She was sure she would make some horrible social gaffe. She might be born British, but her upbringing in Australia made her seem something other. Sometimes their ways left her flummoxed. It exhausted her just thinking about it.

Nonsense lots of older girls are presented. Besides no one will ask your age. Now, you will need to learn to brush up your French, perfect your dancing and deportment, and of course learn the royal curtsey. That is of utmost importance.

"Mummy, I don't think I am well enough yet." Beatrice lay back on the sofa attempting to look wan.

"You won't need to lift a finger. I shall arrange everything. A new wardrobe will be essential. I have ordered the white for the Queen Charlotte's Ball, but you will also need other formal and informal gowns as well as day dresses, silk I think. Then there are the hats gloves and shoes. Oh, and handbags. My dear it is a wonderful experience. You will attend Ascot, Henley, Eton for the Fourth of June celebrations, and so many of the great houses will host parties. You are sure to be invited. We may even open Banville Hall and host a ball ourselves. What do you think?"

"What will you do with the tenants, lock them in a cupboard?"

"Don't be sarcastic dear. It is so unbecoming for a young lady. I've asked Grandfather to use his influence to ensure you are on the Palace list, so we don't need to worry on that score."

Beatrice pulled down the corners of her mouth knowing she should just keep quiet and do the expected thing, but she was sick of it. Sick of her mother and father deciding what she could do and couldn't do. They couldn't chuck her out on the street here. She shuddered.

When she was thirteen they had locked her outside one night because she had refused something or other. She didn't even remember what it was, just that the woman and her children on the quay at Bombay grew large in her imagination. It had been summer, but it was cold and dark outside. She wasn't going to apologise and had crept into the gardening shed to make a bed with hessian sacks, until an animal ran over her legs. She had run screaming to the house, sobbing to be let in, promising she would behave.

But this was England, and her grandfather would never allow anything bad to happen to her. If she had to work in a shop to earn some money, she would do it, although she wasn't sure a shop would employ her. As her mother was fond of telling her, she was useless outside of being an ornament on a husband's arm.

Mark had said that wasn't true, but he didn't know what it was like, and for men it was always different. Yet, he was so brave standing up for his principles, and even though her father had kicked him out he had gained a new freedom with his farm.

She took a deep breath. "I am not going to be presented at Court, Mummy. I'm sorry. I know your heart is set on it, but the whole Deb thing is an anachronism."

It was as though her mother hadn't heard her. Margaret clutched her pearls and gazed out the window. "I remember when I was presented. Oh my dear, it was so wonderful."

Beatrice sighed and blocked out her mother's rambling. Mark would hate it. It was the kind of thing he said turned human beings into commodities.

Her mother's brow creased. "The whole issue with King Edward's abdication and King George VI forthcoming coronation makes the timing for a presentation at court fraught. If you won't be presented, and I haven't made up my mind about that yet, you will have to have some sort of coming out do. I will speak to your father when he gets in... But I do think it's high time we found you a husband. One of good English stock. Although," her mother gave her a coy look, "your father says Lawrence Anderson is doing very well in Sydney. Perhaps we could invite him over. You'd like to see a familiar face I'm sure." She hesitated. "He might take an aeroplane to be here on time. What do you think?"

Beatrice sighed again and closed her eyes to defend herself from her mother's persistence. "I'm very tired Mummy. Can we discuss this later?" She wasn't ungrateful and didn't want to show anger, but she wished her mother would just behave with her usual lack of concern and leave her alone.

"We'll have to discuss it soon, my dear. I shall ask the doctor when he visits this afternoon when he thinks you'll be well enough."

"I am quite well now Mother, just a little tired." Beatrice picked up the book she had been reading and opened it, hoping her mother would take the hint.

The new maid, Annie entered the room with the laden tea tray and just as she did the telephone jangled in the room next door. The alarm on Annie's face made Beatrice want to laugh. Poor girl, she was still terrified of the thing.

Beatrice levered herself up. "I'll get it."

"No, stay where you are my dear. Symons will get it. Put the tray over here next to the sofa Annie. We'll pour our own tea."

But Symons was running errands for grandfather, so Beatrice ignored her mother. She walked out to the hall to pick up the phone.

When she hung up she returned to the morning room. "There's an emergency at the hospital and Dr Goodall is unable to call, but he thinks I am quite well now and will send Sister Fuller to check on me. You remember Gladys Fuller, Mummy?"

Her mother pulled in her chin. "That is just not good enough. You need a doctor attending to you."

"I would prefer Sister Fuller, she's my friend and anyway Doctor

Goodall says I am out of danger. I just need fresh air and some exercise to build back my strength." She stopped as an idea flickered into life. She took a breath as she launched her lie, colour creeping up her neck. "Doctor Goodall thinks a walk with Gladys every afternoon might be just the thing to help my recovery, and she will know when I have had enough."

Once her mother left the room, Beatrice lay back. Innisfail was on the other side of the world. What time would it be? She had no idea. Why on earth had Bert forwarded her letter to Mark to a London address? It didn't make sense. She needed to get out of the house so she could call Bert and she was certain Gladys Fuller would help.

32. Independence

Denton sat at a desk in his home study. The room was cosily old fashioned, decorated by Lillian when they were first married before she bought back Banville Hall in Surrey. He had never changed this room, nor would he let Margaret rearrange anything.

She'd done that with the rest of the house, and that was enough! His study remained exclusively his and Lillian's room, with his desk to one side, and a small sitting area with table lamps shedding soft light. It was where Lillian had sat to read. Sometimes he imagined her there still, curled up with her feet beneath her, a shawl around her shoulders, engrossed in a novel.

Bookshelves lined three walls. On the fourth wall, two tall narrow windows brought light slanting into the room. The windows overlooked a square of garden, now shrouded in snow. On the wall between the windows was a small Queen Anne fireplace. A fire glowed in the grate, for it was chilly. A cold front had brought a sharp drop in temperature and there had been heavy snow across England.

Denton ignored the weather and concentrated on composing a reply to Winston. There was a knock on his door. He was glad of the distraction. "Enter."

Symonds came in with a tray. "Tea, my Lord."

"Thank you, Symons. Tell me, do you think the world should be run by power, the rule of law, or by pragmatic considerations."

Symonds laid the tray on the table and turned to face Denton, his face a study in seriousness. "You don't really expect an answer, my Lord."

Denton laughed. "No, I don't even have the answer myself."

Symonds remained opposite him, clasping, and unclasping his hands.

"Is something bothering you Symonds?"

"Yes my Lord. It's a difficult thing to say and it's only a possible problem, one which may be of no concern."

"Spit it out, Symonds."

"My Lord... You know I have a cousin serving in the 1st Queens Battalion and he has just come back from India."

"Yes, you mentioned it."

"He asked me to tell Lady Margaret how grateful they were for her donation to the Quetta disaster."

"Very appropriate. But you don't need me to pass that message on. Tell Lady Margaret yourself."

"Yes my Lord, but the thing is they thought it was a personal donation. Very little by way of donations reached the people of Quetta."

"What are you saying?" Denton leaned forward in his chair.

"My cousin didn't know of any charity, sir."

"Good God! Are you telling me the Lady Margaret has given the charity's money to Quetta as if it was from her own pocket?"

Denton glared at Symonds, who remained erect, shoulders back, hands clenched against his thighs, looking straight ahead as if on parade. He said, "Yes my lord although it was a small sum."

Denton took a breath, his mind reeling with the consequences. "Just to be clear, what you are saying is tantamount to accusing my daughter of embezzling the charity's money. Does your cousin know about the charity?"

"No, my Lord, at least not from me."

Denton sat back in his chair. This was a disaster. He needed to think. "Thank you, Symonds, I am most grateful you have brought this to my attention. It may be nothing, but I will certainly look into it."

"Yes my Lord." Symonds shifted his feet but remained in front of Denton.

"What is it Symonds; please don't tell me there's more?"

"Sorry my Lord. It's just that I overheard a conversation between Mr Charles West and the Lady Margaret, shortly after she returned from San Sebastian last year. It was about the instability in Spain since the election and how a socialist government was creating volatility in Rio Tinto's share price. They were concerned that a socialist government would leave the Langham and West families financially exposed. I didn't think much about it at the time, but it made more sense to me in the context of my cousin's expression of gratitude for the Lady Margaret's small gift."

Denton jumped up and walked over to the window. "You know

what you are implying Symonds?"

"Yes, my Lord, which is why I brought the matter to your attention. I have said nothing to anyone else."

"Please ask the Lady Margaret to see me the moment she returns."

An hour later Margaret knocked on Denton's door. "You wanted to see me, Father?"

"Yes." He got up and walked towards his daughter. "Sit down my dear. I need to clear up an issue." He paused to examine her face.

"Well," she demanded, "What is it? I must change for dinner. It's getting late."

"The subject is rather distressing, and I apologise in advance if I have got the story all wrong."

"Goodness that does sound dire." She smoothed the pearls at her neck and sat on the chair indicated. Denton walked over to shut his study door.

"Now Margaret. It's about your charity…"

When Denton finished explaining his concerns Margaret remained silent for a minute, a frown on her face.

"I am not sure what you are getting at Father, but my charity was set up as a general charity, not just in relation to Quetta. There are many worthy projects of which Quetta was just one.

"I wasn't aware of that. But the money you raised for the Quetta victims, what has happened to that?"

"I gave it to them."

"It seems you have given the money as a small personal gift from yourself, not the charity."

"That's true. I know it was strictly speaking the wrong thing to do, but at the time we didn't have the right systems in place, and really after all the expenses, particularly Charles and my honorarium, there wasn't much money left from the fund-raising efforts."

"You and Charles took a payment from the funds you raised?"

"Naturally, and for our expenses."

"Good grief, why? You are not short of money, are you? Does Arthur know?"

"It was his idea."

Denton stiffened. His voice became cold. "What do you mean—why?"

Margaret gave out a theatrical sigh and shifted in her chair. "He was really very foolish and borrowed heavily against the Surrey house to invest in Rio Tinto. When the Spanish war broke out, well you know what happened…"

Denton's face took on a look of horror and for a minute he was speechless. Eventually, he said, "Just a minute. Are you saying that Arthur, as a trustee, borrowed against Beatrice's trust assets for his own personal purposes? Is that what you are telling me?"

"Yes of course."

"Margaret! You do realise that besides being morally repugnant to interfere in your mother's bequest, it is illegal."

She clutched her pearls. "Surely not. The trust is for his own daughter, and it was my mother's money. Rightfully she should have left it to me! I never knew why she didn't."

Denton ignored her welling tears. They had been through this so many times over the years although Denton had never told her the real reason behind setting up the trust for Beatrice. Lillian had bought back Denton's ancestral home after his own father had lost it and she didn't want it lost again. Beatrice had been born in that house as had he, and Lillian had never fully trusted Arthur's financial acumen or his ability to hang on to the old place, regardless of his claims. It seemed his astute wife had been right.

He said, "Nevertheless, it's against the law. I do wish you would have come to me before getting into this mess."

"Would you have given Arthur the money?"

Would he? He didn't know if he would easily pass over money to Arthur to gamble on the stock market, but he would never have let any of this happen. So, he supposed he would have if it prevented his daughter from committing fraud. What was he thinking earlier about women being better at compromise for the good of humanity? He revised his statement to women of reason, who didn't blindly think their men knew best. Perhaps he meant women of reason who had a developed a moral disposition, a quality it sadly seemed his daughter was lacking.

"In the circumstances, yes. I would have loaned Arthur the money. Loaned not given, mind. I would have been unhappy about his placing your security in jeopardy, but rather than what you have both done, I would have ensured you had ongoing financial security under conditions, which would prevent him from doing it again. In any case, couldn't you have waited? Everything I have will be yours when I am gone. You are just lucky the information is confined to the family alone. You are also lucky that Beatrice is unaware of your perfidy. I take it she is in the dark about this. I will need to speak with Arthur. The sooner he repays his 'borrowings' and relinquishes his trusteeship the better. I will not have Lillian's wishes thwarted or endanger Beatrice's inheritance."

"Who will run the trust?"

"Beatrice will manage her own affairs."

Margaret looked triumphant. "That's impossible. The terms state that Beatrice cannot have access to the trust's management until she is twenty-five years old."

"That is easily changed. I will speak to Arthur about arranging the legal transfer."

Margaret leapt up. "You cannot give the management of the trust to Beatrice. You have no idea who she is or what she has done. I won't have it."

Denton paused. "What do you mean? "He had thought there was something up when his daughter had arrived back in England with her daughter but as no one confided in him, he had assumed it was really about Margaret's desire to have Beatrice presented at court.

Margaret pursed her lips. "You always take her side, but you don't know..." She shook her head.

"Well, are you going to tell me?"

Margaret inhaled before she said, "She was seen kissing a Bolshevik in the street."

Denton paused and contemplated his daughter. Parents never think a prospective suitor is good enough for their offspring His own parents didn't want him to marry Lillian. Her father was in cotton and had inherited money made from growing tobacco. Denton's mother couldn't countenance an association with new money or trade. It was ridiculous actually, as his father had lost everything he'd inherited, and they were as poor as the proverbial church mice.

Lillian's money got the family out of an awful pickle, but that wasn't why he married her. He loved her. Then when it came to Margaret wanting to marry Arthur, Lillian was opposed. Now it seemed it was Margaret's turn to disapprove of her daughter's choice.

All he said was, "We never think our children's lovers are good enough."

"Gracious, that's not it at all. She knew that sneaking around behind our backs with a... A... I don't know what... Well, it was a betrayal. The man is a unionist. He led a strike against Arthur's company. Now he has corrupted her mind to the extent she is refusing to be presented at Court."

Denton blinked. Then after a minute or two said, "What's your objection to the man, Margaret?"

"Isn't that enough? He's completely unsuitable in every way. Where can I begin... He's a field labourer, a foreign immigrant, as well as being a Bolshevik?"

"An immigrant!" He looked bewildered for a moment but continued. "But labouring is honest work although not one that brings in much money granted, but we can protect Beatrice's inheritance from any nefarious designs."

"Didn't you hear what I said. He's a Bolshevik!"

Beatrice's grandfather cocked his head and examined his daughter. Then he said, "Have you met the man? Is he a decent sort? I've met a few Bolsheviks in my time, and they seem quite normal: no horns or tales. Granted they seek to rid the world of capitalism, but if its Beatrice's money that concerns you we can tie it up so that he has no claim on it."

"They're a threat to national security!"

"At the moment, I very much doubt that. I wonder if the Soviets really want world domination. I met Joseph Stalin before the finalisation of the Montreux Convention. My assessment is that he's more afraid of being attacked at home than of setting out to conquer others, despite the Third International. The communist ideal is global, but Stalin has subverted it and made it national. Now I think he uses the Comintern rhetoric of world revolution as a distraction. When countries are focussed on internal divisions they have little time to look farther afield. I suspect all he wants is recognition from world leaders and protection from his own people. He's terrified Leon Trotsky will overthrow him, or that the western powers will sneak up through the Bosporus and Dardanelles and attack him through his country's soft underbelly. It's making him quite paranoid and erratic for which, unfortunately, his own people are suffering." He shook his head. "I'm quite sure he's not in a position to plan world domination, not just yet at any rate."

"What about the Bolshevik uprising in Cable Street last year? We might have been murdered in our beds." Margaret screwed her long strand of pearls into a knot.

Denton compressed his lips. "I think that little fracas must be laid at the feet of one of our own. Sir Oswald Mosley is probably more of a threat to Britain with his allegiance to the German National Socialist's Party. But enough of that. We are discussing a young Australian man. Do you remember meeting Arthur, Margaret?"

"Of course."

"And do you remember your mother trying to prevent you from marrying him because she thought he was too old for you?"

"No. She was afraid I would live on the other side of the world, and she'd never see me or my children."

"That too." Denton nodded. "But you did marry Arthur. You insisted, and we didn't stop you. Do you regret it now?"

Margaret said, "But Arthur is British. It's different."

Denton raised his eyebrows. "Is Beatrice's young man not an

Australian. If he is, he is a British subject. Is it ethnicity, class, or creed that bothers you, Margaret?"

Margaret curled her lip. "You just don't understand what these people are like."

"I think I do, and really if Beatrice wants to see this man, I don't see what say any of us have."

"Over my dead body!"

He sighed. "She's an adult, so perhaps rather than jumping to conclusions we should make an effort to get to know him before we judge. Beatrice is a sensible young woman. Besides, this conversation about Beatrice's love life is a mere distraction. You have no choice. Either Arthur relinquishes his trusteeship, or I report his activity."

Denton felt a sudden weariness and got up again to walk over to the window. He took a deep breath. "Ask Arthur to join me when he's available will you, and on your way out, tell Symonds to bring in the whisky decanter and some ice."

Margaret flounced from the room and Denton gazed out the window wishing the global mess was as easily sorted out as his daughter's indiscretions. Perhaps he should retire. Really, he was fighting an uphill battle to encourage the government to take a firmer stand. He wiped his palm over his mouth and went back to his desk to continue writing his letter. He agreed with Winston. Britain must rearm.

33. Leaving

Mark looked around the dormitory he shared with several other men, then went over to the window, and gazed down into narrow Litchfield Street. So, this damp, dull, grey place was London, the capital of the British Empire, the economic bastion of the capitalist world.

The sun barely lifted its watery blotch above the smog before it plummeted back into what Mark imagined was a swamp. It was supposed to be spring, but it was like the artic. He'd bought a coat in Melbourne, but it just wasn't warm enough, and his shoes syphoned in water and froze his feet. His fingers and ears had turned a permanent shade of blue.

Jack had given Javier and the others a letter of recommendation for Robbie at the London Party office. The letter included Mark although he wasn't a member. That wasn't so unusual as many of the volunteers heading to Spain weren't. It was through Robbie that they had found this dormitory to stay at while they waited to head to Spain.

Xavier had already left but as Mark was planning to pass himself off as a journalist he needed clothing suitable for the climate and his new career. Besides he was freezing.

Robbie, between chuckles, had promised to take Mark to the market. Of course, that meant braving the outside world once more. He couldn't believe anywhere on earth was this cold.

He watched the bustling street below. So many people, horses, carts, motor cars, noise, commotion, and accents he didn't understand. Mark spoke English, Italian, and passable French and Latin he'd learned at school. He'd picked up some Norwegian from his father and a few phrases of Dyirbal from Yamani, before he disappeared. He also spoke workable Spanish that Javier had taught him on the ship, but the people here spoke a language outside of his experience.

He thought longingly of his brilliant sunlit paddocks, the gentle sea breeze fluttering the forest leaves, the sorrowful cry of the currawongs, the silent flowing waters of the creek with its inhabitants, the platypus, the jungle perch, and the turtle. He closed his eyes and for a moment he imagined he felt the sun caressing his cheek. He sighed and steeled his resolve. Then he went downstairs and opened the door, plunging into the bitter flurry outside.

At the market, Robbie looked him up and down. "What'll it be then, lad? We can get you proper kitted out for a cockle."

Mark shook his head. "Sorry mate, I don't understand."

Robbie said, "I thought you Aussies spoke English. How much money do you have?"

Mark fished in his pocket and pulled out some notes.

"Aye lad, that'll set you up, all right. Come along then."

An hour later, Mark had on a warm fleece-lined leather jacket, a greatcoat, gloves, a muffler, and a tweed cap to replace Bert's Fedora."

Robbie said, "The hat tells a man who he is and what he stands for. You'll be right in the cap in these parts."

Mark also carried several brown-paper parcels with warm long-johns, long-sleeved undershirts, socks and a stout pair of boots, some warm woollen shirts, two jumpers, and two pairs of thick woollen trousers. He'd never thought clothes so important, nor bought or owned so many at one time. He dropped his parcels off at the dormitory and walked outside, muffled up, and warm against the biting wind. Now he could think of something other than the cold.

He went back with Robbie to the King Street office, where a fat envelope awaited him. He examined the multiple thruppenny King George stamps lined up to the right of the royal airmail wings. Airmail was relatively new, and Mark had never seen a letter that had flown so far before. It had come all the way from Australia, addressed to Mark in Bert's handwriting.

He took the letter through to the kitchen and sighed with pleasure as he felt the warmth radiating from a coal stove. He poured a cup of tea and sat down to read the letter, anticipating the momentarily joy of losing himself in details of life and business in Innisfail. He would never have believed a person could feel so homesick. Inside the envelope he found a single sheet wrapped around another envelope and his pulse raced. The letter encased was from Beatrice.

He read Bert's note,

Mark, this letter arrived for you on Monday, and I sent Beatrice a telegram to say you were in London. Her address is on the back of the envelope. Good luck. All well here. Bert.

He carefully opened the envelope from Beatrice, so he wouldn't tear the address on the back and smoothed the pages.

Robbie walked into the kitchen and said, "Any tea left?"

Mark nodded toward the stove where he had replaced the pot. "I think it's a bit stewed." He looked into his half-full mug distastefully.

"Just the way it should be," Robbie said.

"Do you know a place called Pimlico?"

"Certainly." Robbie took out his pipe from his jacket pocket. "It's two-mile sou-west from here." He filled the pipe and lit it.

The smell of pipe tobacco reminded Mark of his dad and another stab of homesickness engulfed him. He took another swig of the awful tea.

"What do you want with the likes of Pimlico, then lad?"

"The woman I plan to marry lives there."

"Ah, in service, is she?"

"No, she's here on holiday, staying with her grandfather."

Robbie looked at Mark sharply. "You, with the likes of them over there. A Pimlico lass?"

"No, an Australian woman."

Robbie said, "You bloody colonials! You think it's colour, not class that's a problem. Let me tell you, it's the capitalist class that created the idea of colour to keep the locals in servitude."

A woman rushed in. "They bombed Durango."

Mark asked, "What's Durango?"

Robbie introduced Mark to the woman. "Katie, this is our Australian comrade. He's heading for Spain."

She pushed the round-rimmed glasses up her nose and a red curl sprang out from a hair comb and tumbled down her face. She pushed it back into its confines and wiped a hand down her freckled upturned nose. "You men are such fools. You don't even know the place names in the country you are going to fight for!"

Robbie laughed. "That's our Katie, always the cheerful one, but he's not going over there to fight but as a photojournalist."

"That's even worse. But fight or write you'll still be killed. That's what war's for—to kill people."

The war suddenly seemed real and very close and the woman, despite her acerbic assessment of him, had a point, Mark needed to know the country better than he did. He asked. "Do you have a map of Spain?"

Katie nodded and went out to get an atlas.

Mark examined the map and Durango was not so far from Bilbao where Javier was heading, hoping to join the Basque army.

Robbie and Katie exchanged looks and Katie said, "You don't have to go, nobody will think less of you."

Mark shook his head and got up. "How do I get to Pimlico?"

Katie looked baffled at the non sequitur, but Robbie said, "You'd better put on the Fedora again lad if you want to go courting a lass from Pimlico."

An hour later Mark stood on the pavement, staring at a tall white stucco façade. It sat in the middle of a long line of houses all exactly the same, all joined, like one long building. Huge pillars stood sentry on either side of a large portico that gave entry into the house. A little way along the house, stairs descended behind iron palings, into what appeared to be a basement entry. Above, windows ran in marshalled rows, gazing down at him blankly. He glanced along the houses and saw a curtain twitch. He couldn't just loiter in the street hoping she would come out.

He squinted at the sky but didn't know how to tell the time when the sun was not visible. Maybe he should get a watch although the good thing about London was the clocks. They were everywhere, chiming the hours. Should he just march up and knock on the door?

He took a step forward and then saw two women turn the corner and walk towards him. One was Beatrice, her arm linked with another woman in nursing uniform. Mark dithered, suddenly unsure of his welcome.

The women came closer, curiosity registering in Beatrice's tilted head. Then her hand flew to her mouth, and she let go of her companion to run along the street towards him.

He remained stock-still until she stopped in front of him.

"Mark, you're here."

He lifted his hat as the nurse arrived.

She looked askance. "Beatrice?" But she stared at Mark.

"Oh Gladys. Its Mark. The man I told you about from home. Mark this is my friend, Sister Gladys Fuller." She held out her hand to touch his. "I'm so glad you're here."

He looked around. "Can we go somewhere?"

Beatrice glanced at the house. "Mummy's indoors." She turned to appeal to Gladys.

Gladys pressed her lips together, then sighed. "There's a Lyon's tearoom near the station where you can have a spot of tea in relative peace."

Ten minutes later, they left Gladys at the station and walked into the tearoom. Mark ached to hold Beatrice close. Her face was so pale, and she was thin as a cane stalk, like she'd been starved.

When they sat down, he said, "What's happened to you?"

Beatrice put her finger against her lips as a waitress took their order. Then she explained she'd caught an illness from a passenger during the crossing, which was how she had met Gladys. "But never mind that. How are Jack, and Bert?"

"They're fine. Jack was elected State secretary, and he's moved to Brisbane, so they've merged the 9th District into the State branch under his leadership."

Beatrice reached across the table for Mark's hand. "I missed you so much."

He withdrew his hands to his lap. but said nothing.

"I was just about to buy an aeroplane ticket back to Innisfail when I got Bert's telegram last week. Who's looking after the farm?"

Mark cleared his throat. "Immanuel."

"Who?"

"Your uncle's overseer." This was the nature of her class. They had no insight into the people who worked for them.

Beatrice shook her head in bewilderment as an uncertain smile hovered around her mouth.

Mark stared at her. "Did you know your uncle's house burnt down?"

Beatrice stopped smiling. "Yes, Mummy told me. It was lucky no one was hurt."

"Rainer blamed me." He glanced at the table knowing that he was being unfair and forced the anger down, back into the pit of his stomach where it seemed to have skulked for so long.

Her hands flew to her mouth. "Oh, how awful, because of me.

Mark, I'm so sorry. I've brought you nothing but trouble."

He shook his head, ashamed of his accusation. "It's not your fault. Anyway, it's all right now. The inquest cleared me."

"I heard about the inquest: rats in the ceiling. But I didn't know about them blaming you. That's so terrible. My family is treacherous."

"There's more." His eyes scanned her face. "Your uncle kicked all the staff out of their homes."

Tears spilled down Beatrice's cheeks and Mark took a breath. "Look sorry. But it's all worked out well for me because now they're looking after my farm." He forced a smile.

She responded through glistening eyes, but her smile remained tentative. "I couldn't believe it when Bert told me you were coming to London. I would have come back earlier, but my illness you see..."

Her eyes filled again, shining like the early morning sun on the rain-drenched grass at the farm. He wanted to reach across the table for her, but he stopped himself. "I need you to tell me the truth about your family Beatrice."

She crinkled her nose and plucked at the tablecloth. "Maybe you should just come and meet them."

"I would have liked that, but it's not going to happen, is it? Your grandfather's an aristocrat." He paused, then said, "When were you going to tell me, Beatrice?"

She remained silent.

"Why did you lie?"

"You wouldn't have carried on seeing me if you knew." She didn't look at him.

Was that true? Perhaps in the early days, he might have turned away. He nearly had when he found out she was the daughter of a

CSR executive.

She continued. "I didn't really lie. I just didn't tell you everything because I thought you wouldn't like me if you knew I was one of the people you despise." A tear ran down her cheek and she brushed it away.

"It's not the people, it's what they stand for. I always knew who you were, just not the extent. Tell me the truth now."

She took a deep breath. "All right." She picked up a teaspoon and dug it into the table, and then still without looking at him she explained. "My father is as you know him. He grew up in Sydney and is just an ordinary Australian. His father was a banker. It's my grandfather on my mother's side who is the aristocrat. Grandfather, Alfred Denton, is the Earl of Banville, but what I said is the truth. His father lost all his money in the crash of 1890. They had to sell their home, Banville Hall, and Grandfather went into the Navy. He met my grandmother, Lillian, when he was in America, and it was her money that bought back Banville Hall. Her father made his money from tobacco and cotton." She laid down the teaspoon, frowned, and took another deep breath. "I suppose that's even more of a capital sin."

"What?"

"Never mind." She shook her head. "A few years before the Great War my grandfather was sent out to Australia with Governor-General Munro-Ferguson to advise on the setup of the Royal Australian Navy. That's when my mother met my father and they got married. Then during the war, my father was in the Australian army and Mummy came home to Banville. It's where I was born. After the Great War, my grandmother died from the Spanish flu, but she left all her money and the Hall in trust to me. I don't think my mother has ever forgiven her for that. She has always blamed me although I was only three when my grandmother died. The Hall is now rented out to some American family, and we never mention it or talk about my inheritance. I think my mother and father would prefer to forget it exists. My father manages my inheritance as it remains in his trust until I'm twenty-five, but my grandfather insists that will soon change. I will become completely independent." She grinned. "No one will be able to tell me what I can or cannot do."

Mark stared at her. It was like seeing someone so familiar, they were part of you—the very breath in your body and the blood in your veins, and yet he didn't know her at all. How could he have ever thought he might marry her. It wasn't where she came from but who she was now.

It was simply impossible, and no one would allow it to go ahead. He could see himself behind bars again. They were bound to have another version of Howard Rainer in London doing their bidding. Besides he couldn't expect her to be happy living in such basic conditions as those at the farm. He rubbed his forehead. Or was it that he really wanted to go to Spain, and he couldn't take her with him.

She said, "Say something."

"You said your grandfather worked for the civil service and lived around the corner from his work."

"That bit's true. Grandfather didn't like living at the Hall, said it was too countryfied. He prefers the city, and he has lived in the Pimlico house for years."

"Where does he work? In the House of Lords, I suppose."

She paused and then said, "I suppose he does, but that wasn't what I meant. He works for the Foreign Ministry. In what capacity

I don't know. He never talks about it and whenever I have asked him, he just makes jokes about making tea and doing the filing."

She fell silent and he didn't know what to say. So, they drank their tea quietly in the middle of the noisy tearoom. A sense of futility weighed on Mark's shoulders.

Eventually, she said, "I'll have to go home; my mother will be worrying, but will you come and meet them? I think you'll like my grandfather. He's not like my parents."

Mark shook his head. "I don't know Beatrice. I came to tell you I'm going to Spain."

She frowned. "Of course. I should have guessed you'd volunteer."

He hesitated, feeling the press pass burning against his left breast. "I'm not really volunteering."

She waited.

He felt obligated to explain and told her about taking up photojournalism. While he spoke, he felt hot blood rising up his neck. She must realise what a fraud he was, pretending to be a journalist. "I'll be taking photos more than reporting, so I'm not really going as a reporter so much as a sort of journeyman. Tomorrow, I leave for Paris, where I have a contact at a newspaper. He's going to show me how to operate the camera and explain the ropes." He changed tack. "Do you remember Javier?" She nodded. "He volunteered. I guess he'll be there already."

When he finished, she said, "But you're still going."

He nodded.

"Where are you staying now?'

"It's a dormitory, in Litchfield Street, Covent Gardens."

She got up. "Will you come home with me now?"

"I'll walk you home, of course."

When they arrived, Mark stopped at the entrance to her house. He took off his hat.

She just stood staring up at him.

He waited for her to say something that would tell him what to do next, but she didn't. So, he said, "Goodbye Beatrice," and turned to walk away.

"Wait!" She called out.

He stopped and turned back.

"When you come back will you come and visit me?"

"Will you still be here?"

"Yes."

"All right. I will if you want me to." He put on his hat and smiled. "Until then, goodbye Beatrice."

About the Author

Gillian Long has a PhD in literature and creative writing, and a background in publishing, psychology, politics, and executive leadership in both civil service and the not-for-profit sector. She has lived and worked in Africa, and Europe and now lives on a farm in the Australian Wet Tropics of Far North Queensland. Her previous novels, short stories, forthcoming titles, and other writing can be seen at https://gillianlong.wordpress.com

Greenwash

Gillian Long

ISBN 978-0-6455760-5-4

Set in Queensland this global conspiracy acts out through a local crime, and an environmental disaster as Dr Jack Fallon races against time to expose the truth before catastrophe destroys all he loves.

Jack is often accused of being a loner, but that suits his role as a mining engineer, who spends most of his time in the outback. His mother disappeared under strange circumstances when he was a child, and he took solace in the riches of the earth. But its geological structures are notoriously unstable and may yet take everything he now holds dear including Sophia, the woman he loves.

While Australia is recovering from a pandemic, fires, flooding, and shortages due to Putin's war, the Australian government is touting an economic recovery led by green gas. Green Synergy, the Australian agent of a global cabal, is the firm of choice leading the way. Increasing gas and oil exploration and extraction gives Jack the opening he needs to return to his home in Queensland, but he soon begins to doubt the wisdom of his choice.

Becoming Helen
Gillian Long

ISBN 978-0-6455760-0-9

Becoming Helen is a 1930s tale of deceit, disillusionment, and retribution after a British Intelligence Officer compromises a young German girl into spying on her own country, expecting her to lie, cheat and bed chosen German military targets for the Allied cause.

Magdalena von Herff barely knows what name to use before men begin to exploit her beauty, intelligence, and talents, but she soon realises that none are there to help her, except perhaps one— her enemy. Set in Europe, Britain, and America.

Dying Days

Gillian Long

ISBN 978-0-9942671-1-5

Matt Reid, an ex-British Special Forces soldier, arrives in Australia in search of his biological father.

He meets Alan Fletcher, a retired war correspondent, whose story about the disappearance of a Rhodesian SAS soldier in 1980, sends Matt off to Zimbabwe on a mission to find the truth.

What he doesn't plan is to become a person of interest to a paranoid secret police or to uncover plots of treachery and revenge and a half century old family feud.

This is a story about discovering family, falling in love, and finding redemption.

The Trouble with Maggie
Gillian Long

ISBN 978-0-9942671-8-4

This is a modern tale of morality, longing, lust, and lies.

Maggie had everything she wanted; a wonderful husband and two gorgeous kids. Her life was perfect, until the fateful moment she ignored her dead grandmother's warning and her life changed forever.

Set in rural Australia, this story is about the trials of marriage; secrets, guilt, love, and temptation, but most of all, it is a story about Maggie's journey to redemption, while filled with heroism, hedonism, hankie-panki, and hocus-pocus.

Watershed

Gillian Long

ISBN 978-0-9942671-4-6

It's the end of the 2020s and Australia struggles under tyranny. The economy has collapsed as terrorism escalates.

Conscript Blake Lincoln returns from an endless Middle East war, wounded and a national hero. When he meets Charlotte, all he wants is to have his old life back.

Instead, he uncovers secrets that will blow the government apart.

Watershed is set in Brisbane, Sydney, and Canberra, and takes in the vast wilderness of Cape York, and the raw beauty of the Kimberly region.

It is a story about the insidiousness of political corruption, the dangers of social injustice, the fragility of democracy and the power of family, as one man prepares to abandon all he believes in to save the woman he loves.

www.ingramcontent.com/pod-product-compliance
Lightning Source LLC
Chambersburg PA
CBHW020943030726
47496CB00005B/1335